NOT
A BRAVE NEW WORLD

DIANA

FOR JG

NOT
A BRAVE NEW WORLD

PAUL K LYONS

A TRILOGY IN THREE WIVES

BOOK TWO

DIANA

PIKLE
PUBLISHING

NOT
A BRAVE NEW WORLD

DIANA

PROLOGUE

Here I am, comfortably settled in Willow Calm Lodge, writing, or rather dictating to the wallscreen in front of me. My mind remains sharp, thanks to Dr Lipson's pill menu, but it won't for long, so I hope to finish this second volume of my reflections, and a third, well in advance of my planned deathday. Jay, my youngest son and most regular visitor, helps me by listening to memories as I try to put them in order. Increasingly, too, I find myself embellishing a story or two for Chintz.

Having reflected in some detail now on my parents – that wasn't straightforward – and on my childhood, I can see the best of my young days were at school, thanks to the influence of a history teacher, Flip, and my friendships with Alfred Ajose, a Nigerian volleyball player, and Horace Merriweather, who went on to enter politics about the same time I did the civil service. And it was at school that I met my first girlfriend, Melissa. Unfortunately, as it was painful to recount in the first volume, she suffered a terrible accident and then lay in a coma for years.

I had good times at the London School of Economics, especially with Pete and Peter organising a debating club, and in the early days with Gillian. Thanks to my father Tom – there's not much I have to thank him for otherwise – I landed a summer job in Brussels working for an oil company. This led onto to a gap year assisting a Member of the European Parliament involved in important negotiations on internet regulation. I witnessed Ojoru, then a little-known Nigerian politician, before the Parliament deliver his famous mantra on Africa. I didn't know it at the time, but Ojoru would have a significant influence over my own career, indirectly because of his standing in global politics, and far more directly – as I will explain – because he personally set me a mission of major significance.

After graduating and after a colourful trip to Brazil – ah Gabriella! – I settled down in London, working for the civil service helping to develop internet regulation policy. Gillian and I married, as if we were in business together, and produced two children, as you do – poor souls, Crystal and Bronze, both destined for tragedy. I cannot think of either of them without floods of remorse, sadness, guilt, despair. . .

And if my own impoverished family life did not of itself cause enough woe, then that unscrupulous media baron, William Caxton, certainly did, exploiting a personal weakness, to cause me much strife. Ironically, it was Gillian – like a general whose qualities only shine in war – who guided me through the worst of it, only for our own relationship to break down irredeemably.

And then Diana blazed into my life ...

PART ONE
Diana, the IFSD and the FTM

Duke: In my world, we respect the law. You are part of my world. You will respect the law.

Iridia: I'm going.

Duke: You are not. It is not legal, it is not safe.

Iridia: I don't care.

Duke: I care. I am your father. You are only 14. It is my job to care.

Iridia: Then come with me, keep me safe.

Duke: That is a stupid idea.

Iridia: Why?

Duke: Why what?

Iridia: Why's it a stupid idea for you to come with me?

Duke: You are not going.

Iridia: I am. You can't stop me.

Duke: I can. I will.

Iridia: Come with me. I'm serious.

[DUKE LOOKS AT IRIDIA WITH ASTONISHMENT.]

Duke: Why?

Iridia: Why what?

Duke: Why should I come with you?

[IRIDIA TURNS SLOWLY TO THE WALLSCREEN WHICH IS NOW SHOWING THE FAMOUS CAMCLIP OF OJORU'S MANTRA. THE SOUND VOLUME STEADILY INCREASES.]

Iridia: To change the world.

[DUKE BURSTS OUT LAUGHING.]

I'll Change the World by Finbar Oakley (2030)

I SHOW JAY SOME OLD PHOTOGRAPHS

Jay, my youngest son, is a stable, affable fellow. The Jay co-op did a fair job, I'm pleased to say, not that I personally can claim much credit. Yesterday, he came to see me as he does at least once or twice a week. It's not so far for him to come to this hospice, this place where I'm spending the last few months of my life, stoked up on a tailor-made drug regime so as to give me lucid time to write these Reflections.

He was later than usual, glossy from an afternoon session in a tavern with friends and some Australians they had met. He was rather taken, he said, by a young blond man who had made eyes at him, and then asked for a liaison. But the boy was nearly 20 years his junior, Jay confided, and would be heading back to Perth in a week's time. Besides, he added trying to convince himself, 'It was not sex I wanted but companionship.' I could sense, though, that Jay had been flattered by the attention and – still hurting after the separation from his long-term partner Vince – wished to puff himself up a tad. I too felt flattered that my son, in his mid-40s, was able to confide in me about such a matter.

Before he left I showed him a few 19th century photographs from my personal memory store, which, incidentally, I call Neil in homage to the name my parents gave me.

Eduard Isaac Asser is not my favourite of the early Dutch photographers, since I definitely prefer Pieter Oosterhuis and his glass stereographs, but Asser may have been the first to photograph the canals of Amsterdam. His still lifes, family portraits and views of Amsterdam, all demonstrate a tight, formal sense of composition, constrained perhaps by the traditions of Dutch painting. I do admire this one on the screen now – *Still life with dead chicken, grapevine shoots and pumpkin* – because of the way Asser composed the picture: the arc-like outline of the pumpkin is mirrored in the shape of one of the vine stalks, and in the curve of the breast of the chicken hanging down by one leg below the pumpkin and in front of the intertwined stalks and leaves; and the finger-like pattern of the bird's wings is similar to that on some of the vine leaves. Most of the photograph is dark grey, but for the chicken in the middle which is a bright white and the pumpkin and grapevine stalks which are light grey. All three elements also share a mottled tone. Evidently, for it was to be another 50 years before early in the 20th century colour photography was to achieve its initial success, this is a black and white photograph. Yet the bright orange of the pumpkin and the fresh green of the vine leaves ache to be recognised. Best of all, though, is the knife, barely perceived at first, which is stuck in the pumpkin, perhaps deliberately, perhaps care-lessly, resting there, waiting for something – for someone to cook fowl and pumpkin pie.

Chintz – my favourite of the nurses here – came by a few moments ago with a copy of my latest medical report. When I asked her what she thought of this photograph, I had to explain that a pumpkin was not an American fruit but a tasty vegetable, from the same family as a marrow.

'A what?'

'A big courgette.'

'It doesn't look like a courgette, it looks like a melon.'

I am more fond, though, of this photograph by Asser of Keizersgracht. Jay said it lacks soul. I agree partly, but to my mind it is another deliberate still life. There are no people any-where along the Keizersgracht, so the photograph may have been taken early on a summer morning. The water in the canal looks lifeless, and if there are any barges they are barely discernible under the distant bridge or beyond. Yet Asser takes me, the viewer, on the right of the photograph, down one side of the canal, past the church (Onze Lieve Vrouwek-erk), past a dozen or so tall and handsome four storey houses, each with their windows at slightly different levels, to the bridge in the distance. The bridge itself cuts off the view of the street beyond, so I choose to walk across the three arches of the bridge hoping to reach the other side of the canal. But then, abruptly, before concluding my stroll across the bridge, I reach the edge of the photograph, and the end of my journey.

Or do I? Although the water of the canal fills the left-hand side of the photo, Asser has not left me stranded. The dark mass of a treetop leans over into the top left corner, above the bridge, but much nearer the foreground. With the knowledge that the tree's trunk must be firmly planted on the left bank, marginally out of view, I can take that slight leap of faith at the end of the bridge and enjoy the walk back up the left-hand bank of the canal. Jay was not convinced. He did point out, though, that if all the people, scooters, bicycles and moored barges could be removed from the scene today, the very same picture taken, 250 years on, might not be much different. Yes, but only thanks to advanced, extensive and very costly dyke engineering.

What Jay did not know, until I told him, was that my tentative relationship with Asser (visiting an exhibition in Rotterdam and culling these photos from the net) started because of this very photograph of Keizersgracht, and not because of some expert appreciation of the artist. After moving to Holland in early 2033, I had neglected my interest in antique photographs and it was only with a spring in my step wound up, if I can put it that way, because of a walk with Diana along the canal, that I set about trying to find the earliest photographs of it.

There is a more soul-full and interesting picture (two photos, a stereograph) by Oosterhuis but it was taken at a different spot on Keizersgracht, and captures a scene across the water rather than along the canal. Jay preferred it to the one by Asser. He noticed the reflections in the canal and the way the real light and the reflected light formed a cross with the line of the street. I showed it to Chintz too. She spotted the difference between the two parts of the stereograph, as if it were a quiz in a journey book: 'Oh look, that cute Dickens street lamp has moved.'

I could lie here until my deathday revisiting my own collection of photographs or browsing through Portia, re-appreciating hundreds, thousands of these images. The importance of the photographic record was not so widely acknowledged when I was a boy as it is today, although it was by the 30s, I suppose. I believe this was partly because digital photos did not entirely replace film photographs until the 10s and it took another decade for any sweeping cultural nostalgia for the old form to emerge. And when the nostalgia did emerge, it encompassed the whole 200 years since the origins of photography in the 1830s and 1840s.

To my mind, though, it is only the photographs of the first 80 years that are so special. Before them, the only visual snapshots of time past were art works, whether paintings, drawings and the like. And from the early 20th century, moving pictures eclipsed ordinary still photos, and all other art forms, in their power to record and preserve the state of the world. But for that period of seven or eight decades, say 1840 to 1920, still photographs (such as those safely stored by the great Daguerreotype Museum in Boston, the National Media Museum and The Josephine Collection in England, the Rijksmuseum-Rotterdam extension, and Japan's Nikon Gallery and Archive) are the most important and significant records we have of what life was actually like at the time.

CHAPTER 2

IN WHICH MY LIFE BEGINS TO MOVE ON

I had separated from Gillian, my first wife, in the spring of 2031, and taken a second floor flat in Randolph Avenue, Maida Vale. Mostly I saw my children, Crystal and Bronze, together every other Saturday, and I made an effort to vary our schedule. About once a month we would drive to Godalming and spend the day with my mother, Julie, exploring the open heath land or the North Downs. If Alan Hapgood, her brother and my only uncle, was around he would usually find time to join us.

Much less often we met up with the man I called my father, Tom, at the zoo or an adventure park, but, if cold or wet, at the cinema. He brought my children gifts, and made them laugh. Once only did we make the trip across town to his home in Epsom, not the horrible semi-detached house he had lived in after Julie divorced him, but another larger property he had bought with his new wife, Fragrance. Tom had retired in 2026, and had taken Fragrance to the Bahamas for a holiday, and once there they had decided, spontaneously, to marry. I could not stand the woman, but they seemed to make each other happy.

Other Saturdays, I would impose myself on one friend or another for a few hours. In particular, though, I grew to rely on Miriam and Doug Turnbull who had two girls the same ages as Crystal and Bronze. Doug also worked at the Department of the Environment in Shropshire House, though in a different section. Since we didn't share any interests, I'm not sure why we became friends. Perhaps we thought and talked and operated at a similar intensity which led us naturally to seek each other out in the canteen at lunch-time, knowing it would be a simple uncomplicated encounter, free from innuendo and one-upmanship. His wife, Miriam, took a while to warm to me, and, I suspect, accepted my visits with Crystal and Bronze, who were not the easiest of kids, out of kindness.

At times I missed the long debates I used to have with Gillian (who was only ever cold and distant towards me by this time), but there were plenty of colleagues in Shropshire House (or in Brussels when I was there) willing to discuss, over a zini or pizza, the underlying purpose of bizarre drafting changes put forward by the Estonians, Serbians or Greeks.

Unfettered by the need to hide my activities at home from anyone, my internet relationship with Lola flourished, as did my monthly bill for her services. Then one day she net-vanished leaving me stranded, as it were. My determined efforts to find connections as satisfying as those she had brought me failed miserably. Instead, I had to make do with a new net madam. I did this reluctantly. She sent me, business-like, a copy of a standard Solar (the open Euronet) services form, complete with a summary of guidelines on Unacceptable Content, and required my e-sign. Within a month or two of Lola's disappearance, I decided I should make an effort to find non-virtual female company. I contacted old friends, joined a well-run singles dance and dinner group, and signed up anonymously to a few net dating agencies. I did get out and about more, but the more I did so, the more I realised how difficult it would be to find someone to be close to again.

I see, though, that I have not yet explained my move to the Department of the Environment. After William Caxton's petty attack on me through the *Daily Truth*, I'd taken a sideways shift out of the Department of Communications to the Department of Industry and Technology. But it didn't suit me, not at all.

The European Union's R&D budget was massive at the time, and I was one of many officials employed in various technical and bureaucratic positions, all aimed at ensuring the UK got the best value it could from the European projects. I found my tasks and responsibilities tedious, to be honest, and longed to be in a department which was important because of the issues it was tackling not because of the size of the budget. My less-than-glorious shift from the Department of Communications meant it would not have been wise to seek a further move in less than two years. Thus, it was only in the spring of 2030 – Gillian, Crystal, Bronze and I had moved into Lacey's

Lane, Willesden, some nine months earlier – that I began actively looking for another position.

After six months of increasing frustration, Horace Merriweather, my old school friend and an MP by then, rang to suggest I contact Judith Singleton informally at the Department of the Environment. It transpired, as far as I could work out, that Horace had, on my behalf, been asking around among his colleagues in the House, and a junior minister had recalled that Singleton, head of the climate change section, was in dire need of someone with EU experience and confidence, and with a head for complex policy issues.

I fell for Jude the moment I walked into her office: there were two Eugène Atget prints of Paris in the early 1900s, carefully framed and hung on one wall. Her desk was busy but not untidy (unlike many I'd observed which were examples either of unstable disorder or ostentatious emptiness), and she rose to greet me with a gracious smile and handshake. Her short-cut light hair and elegant simple trouser suit gave her a Scandinavian appearance. In time, I discovered she was ruthlessly efficient when necessary, in a very British way, an attribute which made her an excellent chair at meetings. At her prompt, I explained why I was anxious for a change. She outlined the job available.

When her secretary rang through with a pre-arranged signal in case she wanted to close the interview quickly, she chose instead to order tea and biscuits, which allowed us another 40 minutes, five of which were spent talking about Atget. Subsequently, it took three months to move through the required civil service job opening and application procedures. By late October, when I was installed in a bright airy office on the third floor of the Department's home in Shropshire House overlooking one of the University College buildings, I had briefed myself intensively on the background and the job in hand.

CHAPTER 3

IN WHICH **I** NEED TO EXPLAIN IMPORTANT ISSUES

Global warming, caused largely by a rapid growth in the emissions of carbon dioxide and other greenhouse gases, became an international political issue in the 1990s. It is generally accepted today that the world's efforts to prevent the consequences of climate change were, at best, marginally successful, and, at worst, without any effect whatsoever. Later, of course, the climate catastrophe of the Grey Years made any concerns over global warming utterly redundant. Many commentators, however, point out that the world's efforts in trying to deal with climate change led to alternative benefits, and that, in any case, nations often wasted resources through far less constructive activities, notably war. Personally, I believe the global warming problem concentrated the collective mind of mankind in a way that had never happened before, and thus helped it take a small step towards maturity – not that there haven't been several steps back.

Again I need to fill in some background which is readily available elsewhere, so I'll be brief. The UN Framework Convention on Climate Change was signed at the famous Rio conference in 1992 (the first World Summit on the environment) and set in motion a process that led to national and international commitments to control and reduce greenhouse gas emissions. First came the Kyoto Protocol by which most developed countries (but not the US) agreed to stabilise their emissions of greenhouse gases by 2010-12. Although the efforts were nation based there were limited mechanisms designed to allow a flow of funds for investments into less-developed countries.

Next came the Copenhagen Accord, the Cancun Agreements, and the Kyoto Protocol – second stage. The most important of these was the latter, yet it was fraught with problems and did not come into force until 2019. Basically, it set the developed countries and some of the largest developing countries stricter emission reduction targets for the year 2025. Furthermore, it put in motion better procedures for inter-governmental emissions trading, thus providing a realistic mechanism by which the developed countries could buy progress towards their targets, and by which the developing countries could attract major investment. Although this had the distinct benefit of directing investment to where it could most efficiently be employed in reducing emissions, it also allowed the US, which had rejoined the process by this time, to continue prevaricating over any significant national measures.

My uncle, Alan Hapgood, pointed out to me on more than one occasion that the US's position from Kyoto on set such a bad example to the rest of the world that the whole process was fatally undermined. He put it this way once: how could a rich and powerful ringleader who smoked like a chimney persuade the rest of his gang to give up cigarettes? The gang members tried, but, with the leader puffing away, many of them failed to put in as much effort as they might have done.

By 2014, the long-standing scientific International Panel on Climate Change (IPCC) had confirmed that the weather chaos across the globe and the related increase in human suffering (death, injury, loss of property and crops) was directly due to global warming, and that this was, as had been known for some time, partly caused by man-made emissions of greenhouse gases. Disturbingly, moreover, it had begun to suggest that, even if global warming was not progressing any faster than had been predicted 20 years previously, the impact of that warming on the climate system was becoming more chaotic than had been forecast by all but environmental scaremongers. It was one thing to have the media tell citizens each time there was a flood, famine or hurricane that it was caused by global warming, it was another to have scientists tell them that such events were going to become ever more frequent and more intense.

The Hague Protocol, signed in 2019, aimed at achieving certain objectives by 2035, was a last ditch attempt by the world to save itself from further expected havoc. As with the Delhi Annex, the negotiations were largely a battle between what the richer countries would do themselves and how much they would help the poorer countries to control their growing emissions.

So much of my life has been devoted to the International Fund for Sustainable Development (IFSD), its efforts to persuade rich countries to provide aid to poorer one, and the administering of that aid, that I feel it is important to provide a little background to the international politics of the time, however dry (and like a committee report!) the forthcoming paragraphs may seem in comparison to the more personal parts of these biographical reflections.

Theodore Roosevelt convened a world conference on natural resource conservation two centuries ago in 1909. An international conference in Stockholm in 1972, however, was the key moment in history when the environment became not only an international issue but one linked with the development of less privileged countries (i.e. those variously labelled developing or undeveloped). That same conference led to the formation of the United Nations Environment Programme (UNEP), and to the promotion of a concept called 'sustainable development'.

The UNEP-organised first World Summit in Rio in 1992 not only agreed the Climate Change Convention but a global plan of action for sustainable development known as Agenda 21. Over the next 20 years, at Johannesburg (2002) and Rio again (2012), the international community toyed and tinkered with how best to promote sustainable development, linking it sometimes less and sometimes more with environmental concerns. At The Hague in 2019, the group of developing countries, forever known as G77 despite its actual number of members, launched a major campaign calling for a new fund for sustainable development. Opposition came from the US and Japan, and Europe was divided about the idea, so the G77 proposal stalled. It was not until 2022 at the fourth World Summit in Lagos that an informal agreement was taken to launch, under the auspices of the United Nations, a major new organisation, to be known as the International Fund for Sustainable Development (IFSD).

Although the visionary Ojoru was not yet Nigeria's leader by the time of the Lagos World Summit, he played a crucial role in forging the IFSD agreement. His extraordinary non-speech to the European Parliament a few years earlier (for which I was present) and the ongoing drought and famine in parts of West Africa had reminded the world it should not be turning its back on the region. And, in time for the Lagos meeting, Ojoru had miraculously persuaded the African Union, comprising nearly all African countries, to present a unified front, and to allow himself to be its chief negotiator. With the UN agreement in principle signed, Ojoru continued to lobby furiously throughout the 20s to ensure the IFSD would become operational as quickly as possible. He also pressed for it to be provided with sufficient funds to make a real difference and to be organised in such a way as to benefit the African continent in particular.

The IFSD, with an office in Abuja and a much larger operation in The Hague, was launched in 2028. It was not as grand or as well-funded as Ojoru and many others had hoped, and there were critics a-plenty proclaiming it would make no more difference than other UN agencies had over the years. Yet, even as the IFSD was making its first grants, Europe was already forging a plan to propose a substantial expansion.

European leaders, meeting in Riga in June 2030 (not long before my move to the Department of the Environment), agreed on the outlines of an ambitious plan to divert an additional 0.3% of the developed world's gross domestic product (GDP) to the IFSD to deal with, among other needs, the consequences of climate-related disasters, and the development and strengthening of infrastructure required to withstand future climatic disturbances.

It was a small figure – 0.3% – but it packed a huge punch. This was to be over and above the 0.7-1.0% of GDP already granted by most Western nations in overseas development aid (ODA) through multifarious channels. Yet there was an even bigger punch in the European plan. The EU proposed FOUR further incremental raises of 0.2%! It announced it would be seeking rapid approval for the plan and agreement at the fifth World Summit in Beijing in 2032. However, it warned that its own commitment to raise ODA by such a huge amount would depend on other developed nations making similar commitments. The EU gave itself less than two years before the Beijing World Summit to persuade the US and Japan and its own public as to why such global philanthropy was so urgent.

And I should explain – for this is so important to my story – why Europe was intent on proposing a near-overnight 30-40% increase in foreign aid, and then a further 60-80% increase, a policy which would certainly hurt its citizens' pockets and thus make life extremely difficult for democratically elected governments.

Firstly, the Bengal Bay tragedy in 2028 and other major climate-related tragedies had demonstrated, in the most horrific way, the truth of the IPCC findings. Accepting this truth led to the inevitable conclusion that the developed world needed to make a more definite, reliable and sizeable contribution to deal with such disasters.

Secondly, because of a steady acceleration in outbursts of terrorism supported overtly and covertly by Arab and other Muslim-influenced governments, there was serious concern, in Europe more than the Americas, that the global relationship between the fairly static Christian world and the fast-expanding Muslim world was becoming unstable, and that the wealth gap between the two was at the root of this instability.

Thirdly, by the late 20s, the First Tuesday Movement had begun to scare the public and governments alike. On Tuesday 4 May 2027, the United Nations published a statistical report called *The State of Nations: a 50 year assessment*. With help from eagle-eyed non-governmental organisations, the media soon latched on to the headline message: between 1975 and 2025 the rich had got much richer and the poor had stayed relatively poor. This proved to be a most terrible indictment of the efforts made by the privileged developed nations, not least through the UN itself, to help the under-developed nations. Various demonstrations started up sporadically in cities around the world but soon coalesced, thanks to the net and the media, into the First Tuesday Movement (FTM).

Within a year, there was no major capital city which did not see marches and demonstrations on the first Tuesday of the month. The FTM acted as a magnet attracting all kinds of disaffected and disadvantaged people as well as those well-off but with a conscience. In London, Gillian and I were already burdened down with children and our own problems to be much affected by the FTM. Moreover, both of us were too straight, as they used to say, to join a demo.

In the early 30s, the FTM gatherings in hundreds of cities became characterised by rioting and purposeful anti-capitalist looting. For many, the writing had been on the wall for decades: escalating climate disasters were a direct consequence of far too little action to control emissions; and escalating political and social disorder around the world, exacerbated by ever more severe floods and famines in the regions least able to cope with them, were a direct consequence of the rich nations having failed to share their wealth over the previous decades, centuries.

And this is where, after a lengthy introduction, I finally re-emerge into the story.

My main task in Jude Singleton's section at the Department of the Environment was to facilitate UK input into the EU's plan for the IFSD. This involved liaising with other government departments (often through Jude but increasingly not) to crystallise the UK position; communicating this position to the policy group in Brussels which was negotiating and preparing the EU's position in advance of the Beijing World Summit (through a UK official in Brussels, or by attending the meetings myself); and reporting back to my masters on the outcome of relevant EU and international meetings.

Despite having to liaise with a man called Rike Thomas (not Rik or Rick or Rikky but Rike as in Mike or tyke!) my opposite number in the overseas aid section of the Department of External Affairs and the frustrations of being engaged in complicated long-term international negotiations, I felt far more comfortable in the Department of the Environment than I had done in the Department of Industry and Technology.

CHAPTER 4

IN WHICH I GO TO MALTA WITH TOM

Of the two years or so I lived in Randolph Avenue, I particularly recall the autumn of 32 because of several colourful trips I made all within the space of two months.

Tom called me one Thursday morning to tell me his father, Barry, who had lived in Malta since before I was born, had died, at the age of 91. He asked me to go with him to the funeral. I hesitated for a moment, thinking about the need to make arrangements for Crystal and Bronze and a meeting on Monday morning which I would have to miss (Tom having proposed to stay an extra day). But I had not gone anywhere with my father in nearly 15 years, not since the Bangkok trip; nor had we spent more than a day together in all that time.

On the aeroplane Tom reminded me that we had been to Malta when I was about four. Barry had invited us, and, reluctantly, my mother, Julie, had agreed. I had no recollections of this at all. Julie had never talked about the holiday, nor shown me any snaps.

'What an effing week that was. We took one of those cheap flights from Gatwick. This was long before the air traffic reforms. Delayed five hours we were. You were suffering from fidgetitis and flu at the same time. Your mother was premenstrual. I was no less short-tempered than usual, and that was before we got there. We're not one hour at the villa when Barry starts laying into me about never visiting Evvie enough when she was alive. He calls me 'son' all the time which doesn't help. I try to stay calm, but when his Maltese wife – fuck knows what her name was – takes Julie and you to the bedroom, I start on about him never looking after her well enough. Maybe not then, but sometime during the week, I probably accused him of killing her by neglect. It was fun when we went out on our own, although I expect I gave Julie a hard time. I can't remember what we did.'

I paraphrase, but Tom's voice and some of our conversations remain remarkably fresh in my memory.

'Now the old bugger's died.'

'Where's he been living? And what happened to the name-less wife?'

'She left him when his money ran out. He caught lucky in the early 1990s with a specialised computer sales outfit. Made a cool three million selling it to one of the national retailers, and then retired to Malta. Spent it all ages ago. Been in a nursing home on the outskirts of Valletta for nearly ten years. A dull place. I've been twice, both times when he thought he was dying. He was bitter about the wife not visiting him.'

He stopped, and turned his head. I was left contemplating what he had said as well as the side of his face. Being middle-aged might have suited him, but old age was not treating him well; he could have been in his 80s not his early 70s. I felt sad to realise how ancient he had become.

'I don't want to go through that, I'll drink myself to heaven rather than spend one night in a home.'

And he did too.

Barry's nursing home, a modernish construction with 20 or 30 rooms, was located in Zejtun, not one of the island's prettiest places. The staff had arranged all the funeral details. Tom and I and the proprietor, a solemn charmless middle-aged matron, were driven in a shiny black hearse to a modest crematorium, part-owned, the proprietor was proud to tell us, by herself. Three others were present at the very brief service. We took a taxi back to the nursing home, where the matron had arranged for Barry's will to be read by her son, who was training to be a lawyer. Apparently, the will had been passed on from a high-class solicitor in central Valletta, when Barry stopped paying the annual charges, to the home itself. Tom hoped there might be instructions concerning Barry's ashes, but there were none. All of Barry's estate – precisely nothing – was left to the Maltese wife (she who had not bothered to turn up for the funeral). Tom needed a short time with the proprie-tor alone, so I sat on a wall outside in the sun battling with a horsefly.

Tom came out snorting with rage at the size of the final bill. Apparently, he had been financing Barry's stay in the home and his medical bills for many years.

'Nearly 4,000 fucking euros. Charges for undertaking duties, charges for the crematorium, charges for the solicitor – can you believe that? – and for various debts. That woman's a bloody crook.' Then, after a short pause in which I said nothing, there followed a routine we had developed over the years since the fateful New Year's Eve we'd spent together. Whether he said the opening line, or I did, it made no difference, because we both knew they were his words, and that, whereas once they had been used on me with alarming gravitas, they now served as a means for us to lighten our mood, to switch almost instantly from anything too serious to laughter and good humour.

'Well, fucking say something.'

'Put it down to experience, Dad.' On this occasion, it sounded funnier than usual for being so utterly inappropriate. 'And we still don't know what to do with his ashes.'

'Anything, so long as it doesn't cost.'

Tom realised he had forgotten to ask for a taxi. Having made a nuisance of himself with the proprietor he didn't want to go back in and beg a favour. So, in our dark suits, we walked through dusty streets towards the centre of Zejtun until we found a ride back to the hotel in Valletta.

The following morning we returned to the crematorium to collect Barry's ashes, contained in a cheap casket. At Tom's insistence, we then went on a boat tour around the island. As the launch lulled in a pretty sea cave with colourful underwater flora, Tom leaned over the side, opened the casket and sprinkled Barry's ashes as ceremoniously as he could manage without drawing attention to himself.

'Goodbye you old codger,' he whispered with only a hint of regret. When we emerged into the dazzling midday sun again, I asked Tom what he would want done with his own ashes. I could have guessed his answer.

In the afternoon, as we sat in a small public garden sheltered by bougainvillaea-covered walkways, he revisited a few memories of his childhood. Later, over dinner we talked about Julie, and a moment came – I remember this distinctly – when I could have told him what I'd discovered about my real father. Having listened to Tom's drunken confession on 31 December 2019 – that he couldn't be my father since he was sterile – I'd investigated the matter as best I could and now believed, with very little actual evidence, that I was probably conceived when a doctor hypnotised and then seduced, or more probably raped, my mother. But I'd never talked further with Tom about the matter. I asked myself in that moment whether I wanted him to know, and whether he would want to know, and the answer was a resounding 'no' in both cases. If Julie had died first and Tom himself had grown old and maudlin and asked the question, 'Did you ever find out, son, who your father was?', I might have answered him.

The following weekend I spent in Manchester. Alfred, my old school friend and volleyball captain, or that African chappy as Tom had called him many years previously, had returned to Britain a year earlier to do research and a post-graduate degree on 'New techniques in the analysis of the costs and benefits of international aid: application in two sectors (health and agriculture) and three countries (Nigeria, Tanzania and Sudan)'. We had met three or four times, mostly in London where he came often to see other friends. By that autumn, he had made excellent progress on the thesis. He had also persuaded his professor to let him teach a trial unit on bio-politics in sub-Saharan Africa.

On this particular occasion, though, I was invited to join him to watch England play Belarus in a European Volleyball Championship qualifying match. The game itself proved lifeless as Belarus, decimated by recent injuries, failed to offer England much of a challenge. The result put England top of the mini-league, and almost guaranteed it a place at the championship finals the following May in Ukraine. Alfred and I discussed plans to make the trip to Kiev, but they never materialised. This was a shame because England have never, before or since, made it to such an important final, or achieved top-three status in Europe.

Despite the dull match, it was a memorable day, not only because of England's success but because I timed out with scores of people I had played with or against in years past. One of them introduced me to John Buffer, England's (then not yet legendary) coach. Alfred was much in demand. I hadn't realised until then how much of a volleyball celebrity he had become, partly because he had captained Manchester University so successfully for a couple of years in the early 20s, but more so, I would guess, because of his position in the Nigerian team which had won the African cup three times in five years.

Gemma, as beautiful as I remembered her, showed up that day too. It surprised me that Alfred should have stayed in touch with her. She brought her husband, a musician of West Indian origin who sported dreadlocks platted with orange beads, and three boisterous children. Needless to say none of us – not Alfred, Gemma or I – alluded in any way to the dreadful memory we shared of an accident in which a friend of ours – Melissa – was sent into a coma and from which she never recovered.

Alfred may have won plaudits for his volleyball playing but, by the early 30s, he had not yet found his professional niche. Unfortunately, his father, who had been a successful diplomat some two decades earlier, had lost favour and position with the change of regime that had brought Ojoru in as deputy prime minister. Without friends in high places, even Alfred's top degree in political science had been no passport to power. He joined the army, trained as an officer and took his turn on peacekeeping duties in the restless parts of Africa.

After seven years, he accepted the best civilian post he could find, assistant governor in a region of the country where ethnic disturbances were not uncommon. Given his experience in the army, the governor used him as 'a bucket of water to put out fires', Alfred said, whenever the fires (racial friction) threatened to spread. He hated it. However, instead of throwing in the towel, as it were, he worked assiduously and achieved results where and when he could. His success with the Nigerian volleyball team had allowed him to earn extra income for a few years by appearing in advertisements for a Brazilian car company. He also avoided marriage and saved ruthlessly. Which was how, in 31, he had sufficient funds to return to the UK and pay the uni postgrad fees.

Jumping ahead a few years, I like to recall that I personally engineered a meeting between Alfred and a Nigerian colleague, a personal appointment of Ojoru, who worked in Enterprise 35. And it was this connection that resulted in Alfred being appointed to a senior federal government job on his return to Nigeria after completing the PhD. From there, he went on to work directly for Ojoru in Abuja as one of his many, many advisers. Much later, I also found a place for his skills in the IFSD's Abuja office.

CHAPTER 5

IN WHICH I TAKE MY CHILDREN TO DRACULA PARK

And now for something completely different (a phrase that has stuck in my head since Tom used it often during my childhood; it seemed to have a life of its own, as though it were amusing in itself). My third trip that autumn took me on a package holiday to Dracula Park in Romania. I do not think Gillian or I would ever have chosen such a holiday for our children of our own accord, but when Doug and Miriam told me of their plans and suggested Crystal, Bronze and I tag along, the idea somehow took hold.

By this time, Crystal was already seven, and Bronze was a few months off five, and they were both comfortable with Doug and Miriam's girls (Lucy and Susannah). I expected Gillian to object, but she did not care. Crystal, on the other hand, had never been so enthusiastic about an idea of mine. Most children have a dream holiday preference for one of the mega-adventure holidays sights, such as Spain's Wild West, France's Disneyworld or Romania's Dracula Park. In Crystal's case it was definitely Dracula Park, but I had had no inkling of this. Miriam, though, who was closely attuned to her own children appeared to know more about my own daughter than I did, which is why we had been invited.

I have lots of snaps of that holiday, taken by snap-happy Miriam, and several good memories. The best are of Bronze laughing and giggling often, whether because Susannah was teasing him, or because of the excitement of the Transylvania helter-skelter or the giant Frankenstein puppet show. Although we spent most of the week in the park, as a group we did a day's sightseeing in and around Tirgoviste.

Our guide to the famous ruins of Dracula's Palace told us, in gory detail, how Vlad Tepes, the real life Dracula, became known for his brutal punishment techniques. He relished ordering his enemies to be hanged, skinned, boiled, decapitated, blinded, roasted, hacked and buried alive (the list may have shrunk in my memory over the years). His favourite method was impalement on stakes, hence the surname Tepes,

Romanian for 'the impaler'. Having won control of the region, with help from the Turkish, Dracula took revenge on the local nobles for having killed his brother. The older ones were impaled in the palace courtyard while he watched from a high tower above. The younger ones were enslaved to build a new castle at Poenari. Legend has it, the guide added, that Dracula returned to Tirgoviste in 1989 to drink blood from the bodies of the dictator Ceaucescu and his wife after their executions.

On several evenings, Miriam and Doug went out to eat alone leaving me to watch over the motel apartments and our sleeping children. In exchange, I was to have a whole day on my own to explore a bit further a field – but this was not to be. Crystal had started out on the holiday friendly enough, excited with expectation, playful, similar to any other kid. But, after three days, her selfish demands had got the better of Lucy. Despite Miriam's constant instructions to 'be nice to Crystal', Lucy had given way to a resentful crying fit. Miriam, having felt I was too lenient by far, lost her cool, and gave Crystal a piece of her mind. Apologising to me later, she defended herself by attacking Gillian, who she had never met. I said nothing. As a consequence of this mid-holiday crisis, I decided to take my moody, thumb-sucking daughter with me on the day-trip, leaving only Bronze with the Turnbulls.

We took a bus to the Dracula centre north of Curtea de Arges from where one can look up and see the spectacular and forbidding Poenari castle built by the ex-nobles under the whip of Vlad Tepes. We could have opted to take the cable car that lifts the very young, the old and faint-hearted through the pine trees, but I decided we should walk the 1,500 steps. It took a long time. I carried Crystal on my shoulders some of the way, and for the rest we stopped every 50 paces so Crystal could rest. She appeared impervious to my irritation at her laziness. Once near the top, however, the stunningly gothic outline of the castle perched on the mountain top revived my spirits, and the narrow bridge across the gorge to the castle itself scared Crystal back into real life, into being there at Poenari instead of swamped in her own psyche. Inside, the thrill of peeking over ledges to witness the sheer drops kept her interest alive. On the way back, she repeatedly asked whether it was 'really really really true' that Dracula's first wife had jumped to her death from the south wall so as to avoid being captured.

I should mention one odd occurrence which may or may not have had a bearing on future events. Of the many rides and entertainments at Dracula Park open to seven year olds, only one had as many as three skulls (five being the maximum for teenage/adult rides) – the Vampire's Lair. On the last day, Crystal begged us to let her go on the Vampire's Lair one final time. Lucy and Miriam agreed to accompany her. The ride is little more than a modest roller coaster for 90% of its length. Then it climbs to a maximum height of about four metres and the shuttle car rolls downward smashing through an apparent rock face (a huge heavy material screen) into a dark custom-built cavern and an immense pool of blood (water dyed a frighteningly realistic dark red colour). The car then skims along the surface of the pool, spraying blood out sideways to splash several grotesque life-sized figures on the pool's edge. Carefully placed spotlights light up the faces of the figures, so you can see the blood dripping down. Never mind four or five skulls, the ride should have been x-rated.

As chance would have it, on this last occasion, the car, with its 20 or so inhabitants, halted suddenly in the middle of the pool for no apparent reason. While Miriam opened a conversation with her neighbour about the possible causes or consequences of the breakdown, Crystal, somewhat waif-like, wriggled out of her harness, climbed out of the shuttle car and onto the rail board, which in this stretch was just covered in red fluid. She knelt down, and, with one leg, gingerly tested the depth of the pool. Discovering it was only a foot deep, she climbed in and started wading towards one of the plastic statues. Another child shouted 'look at her'. Everyone turned, and, for a moment, Miriam was horrified. Then, at about the same time, an engineer appeared from a corner of the cavern and saw the whole situation. He spoke firmly and carefully in

English telling Crystal she was safe, to stay calm and not to move. As he began to stride through the pool to rescue her, Miriam, having realised there was no danger, pulled out a camera and took a flash photo of my daughter. I have it buried in Neil, but I do not need to view it now, nor do I wish to.

I can see her, a miniature figure, dressed in jeans and a pink blouse, her arms slightly splayed out to the side so as not touch the pool's surface, more than knee-deep in a flash-lit carmine sea. Later, Crystal reported she had wanted to know if one of the figures reclining on the pool's edge was alive, and Lucy had dared her to find out. Lucy denied this.

***

When I told Jay the story yesterday, he asked about Crystal's clothes and whether they had been stained by the blood-water. To my surprise, I remembered that Miriam had washed out Crystal's jeans with her own light-coloured trousers (which had been dripped on) and the red had come out much more readily than she had expected. Jay did ask to see the photo, but Chintz came in with my meal – tomato soup and basil soufflé dumplings – and I was able to ignore the request.

I wish Miriam had never taken that photograph, and I wish I had never given a copy to Crystal, and I wish Gillian had stopped her framing it, and putting it on display. The image became an icon, one which she employed for several years as a way of reinforcing her individuality and separateness from others.

CHAPTER 6

IN WHICH PRAVIT WINS ME OVER FOR ENTERPRISE 35

At the Beijing World Summit, which I've already mentioned briefly and which took place during the late summer of the same year (2032) before these various trips I have recalled, the world's nations with few exceptions agreed in principle to a major enlargement of the International Fund for Sustainable Development. Ojoru was a prime mover. He had not only strengthened the African Union, but, with much trepidation among Africa's Christians, found common cause with the Arab world against the West. Moreover, his domestic and international successes led, during the early 30s, to Benin, Togo and Niger voluntarily becoming, as a result of referenda, part of a renamed Grand Nigeria Federation.

Incidentally, Ojoru also initiated and enabled a commercial and political alliance between Nigeria and Brazil, on the basis of many common characteristics, not least that the two countries dominated their respective continents and should therefore help each other practise leadership. This bilateral bond – forged between two great leaders Ojoru and Neco Corazon, or Neco the Prosperous as he came to be known later – proved surprisingly powerful over the decades. It helped both countries form a strategic grouping, with China and India, to act as a non-aligned counter-weight to the group of 13 industrialised countries and the Islamic nine. For Ojoru, the link with Brazil, and by extension with all of Catholic Latin America, had the additional benefit of demonstrating his ongoing balanced allegiance to the Christian minority in Nigeria.

The Beijing Agreement covered the following: a revised and more progressive set of principles for the IFSD, and consequently a much wider mandate; for most developed countries, a new and additional contribution based on 0.2% of GDP; a commitment to further increases 'bearing in mind the proposal of the EU for four further additional incremental contributions of 0.2% of GDP and the very heavy burden this would place on the economies of some developed countries';

and carefully defined categories of countries eligible for different kinds and levels of aid.

The media busied itself with cries of 'too much' or 'too little'. Right-wing pundits in the US predicted it would be the biggest waste of national resources since the Patterson education reforms. Left-wing analysts, by contrast, likened the Beijing deal to a worldwide Marshall plan which would invest US money with far better return than various 20th century endeavours such as the Vietnam, Korean and Cold Wars, not to mention the most inefficient and misdirected war in modern history – the war against terrorism.

For those who have lived as long as I or for those who have a cursory knowledge of history, it may appear odd that I pick out and highlight certain developments and not others. But I gave up being a historian on leaving the London School of Economics, and it would take someone far cleverer than I and with far more time to give a better balance and shape to world events. All I can hope to do in my Reflections is to flit hither and thither in my memory while endeavouring to keep a sense of chronology.

I focus on the Beijing Agreement because it became as important, historically speaking, as the Kyoto Protocol, but also because it had such a direct affect on my own career. Within the IFSD, it led to the formation of Enterprise 35, a group which aimed to bring about the practical application of the agreement by the end of 2035. It also led to my moving to the Netherlands to be part of the Enterprise 35 team. Jude, my department head, must have been involved in discussions while I was away in Romania, for she called me into her office immediately on my return. She needed to recommend someone to be seconded to Enterprise 35 for two or three years. I was her number one choice but, knowing my domestic situation, she was far from persuaded I could, would or should go. I had three days to think it over before she would need to consider other potential candidates. I put the offer to the back of my mind and worked solidly through the morning.

During my lunch break, I took a bus to Regent's Park and wandered round the boating lake. There weren't many people since it was cold and grey. I decided to consider the job from three angles: work, friends and family. I had discussed with Jude how the move might affect my civil service career, and she had said it was impossible to say. If all went well, it would do me no harm, and my willingness to accept such a big move on request would definitely count in my favour. If, as some suspected, the whole scheme were to become bogged down in disputes, directly or indirectly because so much money was at stake, it could prove tricky to extricate myself cleanly. On the whole, I reasoned, my ten years in the civil service had been rewarding. Even so, I had never escaped the feeling that my work, representing a single nation's interests, was parochial. My experience in the European Parliament had given me a taste of higher objectives. Enterprise 35 offered a chance to get back into an international arena.

Since my dating efforts had failed miserably and I remained very much unattached, there were no significant social obstacles to my leaving London. Thus, I soon narrowed down the decision to one concerning my relationships with Gillian, Crystal and Bronze. I could foresee no hindrance to my travelling back to London every second weekend for a day or two (I should have known better), although I did perceive that my absence might make things more complicated for Gillian. This was because, after our separation, I had proved a useful stand-in for nanny coordination and other duties whenever she was ill or opted to travel on business. Moreover, as I would have no London base of my own and it would be impractical to rely on friends and family, I'd be obliged to utilise Lacey's Lane to spend time with Crystal and Bronze.

Regrettably, in making my decision, I never considered my children's well-being, only how the practical arrangements might work in the future. In my defence, I believed they had grown so distant to me that nothing I did could have had any influence on their development. Our week together in Romania had not altered that opinion. Would their lives have been any less distressed if I had not moved so far away? I do not believe so. But then again, I know full well how we are all capable of manipulating and moulding convenient reasons for our more suspect actions and setting those reasons in concrete over time, so as to protect our psyches and a decent self-image for ourselves.

I tried talking to Crystal about the fact that I might move to Holland, without eliciting any interest. Gillian proved supportive. She advised me strongly to accept the job, not for any selfish reason, I'm sure, but because she genuinely considered herself my career adviser. As for the practical aspects, she could not see any insurmountable problems. Bronze had started school that autumn, and the current nanny was reliable and helpful. There would be no problem in me using Lacey's Lane, and, with a modicum of planning, I could organise holidays to cover when she needed to travel.

Julie proved less enthusiastic and worried about seeing less of me and her grandchildren. Tom thought it a great idea, and promised that Fragrance and he would visit regularly. As usual, I also sought advice from Alan, although on the professional, not the personal, side of things. Those working in non-governmental organisations, whether involved with development per se, the environment, or both were universally excited about the Beijing Agreement, and Alan was no exception. He emailed: 'Go for it. Your talents need an opportunity; and Enterprise 35 needs you.'

By January, I had installed myself in a slightly cramped but well-lit third floor apartment, with beautifully polished near-white wood floors, on Weissenbruchstraat, and Enterprise 35 had begun its work in earnest in a rented office a block away from the IFSD building.

Pravit Krishnamurty, a brilliant Indian Muslim, only in his mid-40s, who had briefly studied 20 years earlier under Triti Madan, led a staff of 30, some from the IFSD itself but most of them seconded from various parts of the globe. Pravit reported directly to an executive board, made up of two IFSD vice-presidents and several elected foreign and environment ministers, which itself acted on the directions of a steering committee set up under the terms of the Beijing Agreement.

Having talked to us all at length, Pravit quickly set about creating teams, team leaders and various programme tasks. Along with an Egyptian academic, who had once been a junior government official, and a maverick South African, I was assigned to a team led by Boris Kiselev, a 60 year old Russian who had already been with the IFSD for several years.

The task given to our team was to examine the feasibility of the four further additional incremental contributions (each of 0.2% of GDP) by developed countries giving. As per the formal wording, we had to take 'due consideration to the heavy burden this might place on the economies of some developed countries'. Thus, I was not to be in the main stream – the heat of the battle, the eye of the coming political storm (as Brian Vetch had once, long ago, described our work on the Euronet Regulation) – of Enterprise 35's work but, for want of a better description, in the let's-write-a-fairy-story unit. I took the news badly, and confronted Pravit.

'I haven't decamped from London, moved across the water, and left my children 300 miles away just to sit around contemplating pretty scenarios for the future.' Brian, and his boss the once influential MP Lionel Cox, who we called Firey, and even Gillian would all have been proud to see me so assertive, aggressive almost. But, truth be told, I had not yet taken my measure of Pravit, and he looked young, not that much older than me. The man smiled thinly, and shook his head ever so slightly as though recognising some mistake of his own.

'Where is the struggle for the future? What battle do we have to win?' His calm manner diverted me almost immediately.

'We need to convince the doubters that the extra money is absolutely necessary and can be spent wisely, or wisely enough; and we need to do so quickly. That's the mission of Enterprise 35.'

'Yes, I agree. But when you say "extra money", what extra money do you mean?'

'The 0.2% of GDP. It has been known for a newly-elected national government to increase a country's ODA by an increment of 0.2% but such a rapid increase has never been agreed across the board, nor have such large sums been channelled to one agency. That seems a big challenge; and I thought I'd come here to work for that.'

'Yes, I am happy that you did. You were very clear about it when we spoke before. You impressed me.' He paused such a long time that I had begun to think I should say something. 'But I see things slightly differently. To my mind, the 0.2% increment is a deal that's done – a done deal. Yes, yes, we have to wrap it up well with the fancy paper of political intentions, the strong twine of realistic, practical implementation details, the right address and correct postage. Meaning what? Hah, my flowery English always failed me at Cambridge. Meaning we have to address the package in the right way to the right leaders with the right weight to each. Yes. But that is not the struggle. I see the real struggle as the rest, beyond 35. To me the "extra money" you mention is not this first 0.2% but the additional four times 0.2%, the 0.8%.

Can we bring the West up from gifting 1% of its Gross National Income to 2% – can we give wider international credence and power to the European Union's vision? Is it possible? Now that is what I call a challenge.

And you Kip Fenn – such an unusual name, a pleasant one – do you want to be a packager or the man who devises the next parcel so astutely that we'll need our packagers long into the future. Hah, excuse my extended metaphor, it always goes on too long.' He paused again. His voice dropped to a confidential tone. 'Furthermore, I must confide, I may need you for higher things. Our Russian friend is dicky.'

Disarmed. In less than five minutes, Pravit had me completely disarmed and turned from a potential renegade into an Enterprise 35 devotee. If I harboured slight suspicions that he had achieved this through charm rather than sincerity, these were completely dispelled a year later when he chose me to take over as team leader. Boris, 'our Russian friend', had spent more time pursuing his private business than those of Enterprise 35 (we made progress despite, not because of, his leadership) and had, eventually, been recalled to Moscow. I suspect Pravit's threats to sack him finally penetrated the Kremlin's thick walls.

His replacement, Ninel Horeva, far younger and more committed than her predecessor, became a valuable member of my team. I should mention that she made a simple pass at me one Friday evening, not long after her arrival. I then spent a sleepless weekend terrified that my refusal would undermine the new working patterns I had been striving to establish. But it was a redundant fear stemming from my own insecurity and inexperience. She was as bright as ever on the Monday morning, and, within a few weeks, had hitched herself to a Frenchman working in one of the other teams.

CHAPTER 7

IN WHICH I FALL IN LOVE WITH DIANA

I declined Ninel, not because of a lack of attraction, nor because we worked together, but because, by this time, I had fallen in love with Diana.

For several months after arriving in The Hague, most of my weekends were spent either travelling back to London, working or shopping – equipment for my rented flat, a scootbike and so on. I did find the time to meet up with my old college friend and flat-mate, Peter de Roo, who, with his wife Livia, was living in Amsterdam. After concluding a postgraduate degree in energy economics at LSE, Peter had taken a post in a government agency providing advice to the environment ministry. Livia had completed a postgrad course in fabric science, and was working as a researcher for a large outdoor clothing manufacturer on the outskirts of Amsterdam. They had two children, Rudy and Ulla.

One Sunday, in late April, Peter and Livia invited me to join them on their barge moored at a pretty location not five kilometres from Alphen aan de Rijn, near a lake and a café-restaurant called Stoffers. Unfortunately, the fine spring weather had broken the day before, and the air was cold and full of drizzle. By the time of my arrival, a small gathering had collected in Stoffers rather than on the lake shore. After greeting my friends, who gave me a general introduction, I sat down in a spare seat next to a woman dressed in two tones of green velvet. She turned to speak to me. This is where and when I first met Diana.

'You are English?'

'Like Livia.'

'She is Cornish.'

'It's not a separate country yet, I don't think.'

'But it should be. Scotland is a country, but it has no language. Cornwall has a language. It should be a country.'

'I see you've been a friend of Livia's for some time then.' She laughed. Her large hazel eyes, framed in a round cherubic face (I don't know how else to describe it) by a fringe of dark hair and two dangly silver earrings, latched onto mine with playful interest. I grinned back.

'A few years. I have a boat along the bank from Peter's. That's how we know each other. Well, it belonged to Karl, but he went back to Berlin, and I decided not to sell it.'

'And Karl is?'

'Karl was. Karl definitely was.' She had a very good command of English, although with a heavy but, to my ears, attractive Dutch lilt. For an hour or more, as we ate and drank, I let Diana monopolise me with talk about her work in theatre design and her enthusiasm for travel to faraway places. I told her briefly about Gillian and my children. In my limited experience, Diana stood out as an exotic radiant creature, albeit one slightly older than me.

As the afternoon lazed on, Rudy, Ulla and a few other children, who had eaten at a separate table, managed to engage several of the adults in a game of Dump-the-Chump, which, as it happens, I knew well for it was one of Bronze's favourites. Diana proposed we walk along the river. The drizzle had all but halted, nonetheless she carried an umbrella to protect us on our way. She showed me Tic-tac-toe, a converted and motorised snik, beautifully painted. We sat in the narrow galley, drinking the coffee she brewed and talking about the boat, and then about Karl Engelhard. Somewhat naively, I can say in hindsight, I took it as a sign of friendship and intimacy that she opened up about her relationship with Karl. Over time, during the early years of our relationship, the barge, which was a permanent reminder of the man, became a constant if mild irritation. It was only after we decided to have a child together that Diana agreed, for symbolic reasons if no other, to sell the boat.

On the walk back to Stoffers, Diana suggested we meet for dinner a fortnight hence. She chose a tulip palace restaurant since I'd never been to one – which is how we came to be at Keizerskroon the night William Caxton, my bête noire, was assassinated, about which I've already written. We had drunk a bottle of wine between us, and Diana had rambled on at some length about Karl again, unashamedly (or provocatively whichever way you care to look at it) revealing fairly intimate details about the sexual side of their relationship. After the news broadcast, I began to explain why I hated Caxton, but I had not thought through where the story would lead. I certainly did not expect myself to go as far as confessing sexual frailties. But I did. I made a full and honest confession about Lola, and about the *Daily Truth* article. Diana listened attentively, encouraging me to explain more fully. She then asked candidly when I had last been naked with a real woman.

'A long time ago.' I felt as though I was at school again, standing outside the shower room waiting for the door to open.

'A long time ago is too long.'

Like Peter, Diana also lived in Amsterdam although in a very different part, next to the Noorder AmstelKanaal on Jan Van Goyenkade. Her flat, which filled the two uppermost floors of a five storey 20th century building, appeared a wonderland to someone as conventional as me. In the lounge area, exuberant masks and exquisite puppets jostled for space with Indonesian wood carvings and Nepalese weavings. In the large attic space above, which we accessed by climbing a steep ladder, model theatre sets (old, new and half-built) crowded part of the floor space, while framed and unframed photos of theatre stages covered the walls. Pens, paints, crayons, brushes, knives, scissors, tweezers, unused strips of coloured modelling clay, rolls of braid, coloured tapes and twines, jars of buttons and beads, tubes of glue and the rest filled a large set of mailroom-type shelves at the back of a wide, relatively tidy, work area. To one side, a glass desk backed by a sizeable wallscreen held a multicoloured keyboard and computer console.

'Welcome to the world of Diana Oostlander,' she said, before extravagantly removing her ruby bonnet and bowing towards me. 'And now, the bedroom.'

Back on the lower floor, this was a much quieter, calmer room suffused with a sweet scent of vanilla. A large bed, covered in a striking lacy or crochet-style cream bedspread, was placed by a wide low window, giving on to the trees that lined the canal. To one side, on a small table, there was a vase full of tall apricot-coloured lilies. On the other, a huge palm in a square copper-glazed pot stood on the floor. A large mirror and dressing table occupied one corner of the room; a wall-screen (showing an abstract art soother) hung across another; and half of one wall was taken up with built-in wardrobes and cupboards.

'Welcome to the bedroom of Diana Oostlander.'

We returned to the lounge, and she offered me a joint. I hesitantly admitted I never smoked, so she poured us both a whisky instead. I was very nervous and stiff. I imagined that Diana was wondering if she had made a mistake. She fussed around for a while with the console, finally selecting a Louis Armstrong concert to play in the background on sound only, and then disappeared. I sank deeper and deeper into the silky cushions on the sofa, considering when and how I should say goodbye and leave. I may have been asleep or slipping into the music when I felt myself jolted. Diana had joined me on the sofa wearing only a white kimono carrying a trace of the vanilla perfume I'd detected in the bedroom. We kissed, and while we kissed she undressed me; and then she led me through to the shower. There she massaged me with soap, and encouraged me to do the same for her, but I was too tense, too impotent for an erection. Neither could I do much in the bedroom. Evidently, abstinence had not improved my ability to perform. When I tried to use inadequate words to apologise, Diana swore quietly in Dutch.

'Sex is for fun, for pleasure, don't go all English on me. What do you enjoy, what would help, what is your cup of tea? Don't be shy. English men, they are always shy, afraid the world will suddenly collapse when someone finds out they tried on their sister's tights once or caught crabs in a Manila brothel or bought a blow-up doll. Don't be shy with me, English man. You've done the tough bit – talking. What do you fancy? A striptease. I tell you I'm not very good, and I'm getting self-conscious about my flab. Or some porn. We have some good porn in Holland, maybe you have heard. Maybe this is why you are here.'

How can people be so different? How could Gillian be so different from Diana? How could I be so different from Karl. This plasticity of human behaviour has never ceased to amaze me. Professionally, I have met men and women of many different races and cultures. The religions, customs and patterns of behaviour differ hugely from country to country, and these are often emboldened in our mind by stereotypes. Yet what matters most in personal relationships, whether in a marriage or round the business table, is an individual's character, and this varies most from extreme to extreme within each race and nationality.

And as for falling in love, we understand little more today – give or take some inconsequential neuro-psychological science – than the great British poets Donne and Shakespeare did 500 years ago. Would I have fallen for Diana without the experience of Gillian behind me? Possibly, probably, given the chance? But, the converse is not true. Without Karl, Diana would not have looked at me twice.

I woke early, my mouth dry, my bladder full, and my head buzzing with emotions, memories of sensations, feelings of satisfaction and anxious projections about the future. I moved quietly through to the bathroom and then to the lounge, where I promptly fell asleep on the sofa. Before nine, Diana had dressed and made us both a milk coffee. We took a tram to Leidsestraat, and, hand-in-hand, walked slowly along Keizersgracht. The sun's warmth meant a light mist hovered over the canal. I remember feeling happier than I had for many, many years. At Leliegracht we cut across to Cafe't Smalle to scoff pancakes on the terrace. It was a restaurant we returned to often in the coming months, until a new owner cheapened the decor and food to attract more students. Afterwards, Diana made some purchases at the cute cheese and organic produce market that hung around the base of

Westerkerk, before putting me on a tram back to Central Station.

I had meant to spend the Sunday working, but instead of returning to Weissenbruchstraat I walked a kilometre or so to the Mauritshuis near the parliament, thinking to divert my lively mind with the Vermeer classics that a colleague had recommended I see. It didn't work. I kept thinking about Diana, and particularly about how I should proceed to woo her, not wanting to be too keen, and not wanting to be too English. We had parted without another definite arrangement and I was worried she might perceive me as a one-off entertainment, a show that closed after the first night.

On my way out, I noticed that a side room was dedicated to old photos of the Mauritshuis itself and the surrounding area. This gave me an idea. When I got home, I spent hours on the net educating myself about 19th century Dutch photography and downloading onto Neil a menu full of favourites. But it was the Asser photo of Keizersgracht (the one I have already mentioned) that I picked out to print and send by courier to Diana with a note thanking her for such a lovely evening, and promising to call.

A few days later I received, also by courier, an old French postcard with a crude sketch drawn using contours of red and green lines. In the envelope, curiously, there was a square of transparent red plastic. I have the postcard picture on my screen now. It shows a smiling man standing in the sea (right side) looking towards a young agitated woman on the beach (left side). She is dressed in a gown and has a bow in her hair. The card reads: 'Qu'à donc la Baronne à courrir si vite?' (Why is the Baroness running so fast?) When the square of red plastic is placed over the left-hand side of the card, it has the effect of removing the red lines leaving only the green ones visible. The woman now appears naked. She has large breasts and a huge derrière, not unlike Diana herself. A new caption says: 'Pourvu que l'on ait rien vu.' (Hopefully, nobody saw anything.) On the back, Diana had written, very lightly in pencil: 'Don't lose the red square English man.'

Over the next few months, she sent me a collection of cards from the same set. And she also helped me find a way of copying them onto Neil: after scanning we used art software to separate out the red and green and to create a simple key command for removing the red. I must show them to Chintz later on.

Our love and friendship progressed at a measured pace. It took a few months for us to be comfortable with, and confident in, each other. Thereafter, we found a routine which involved me spending part of every other weekend at her apartment in Amsterdam, and us meeting occasionally during the week, perhaps in Leiden for dinner or a film, or, if she was not too busy, in The Hague.

I usually made the effort, for my pleasure as much as to support Diana, to be present at any of her mid-week opening nights, whether in Amsterdam or elsewhere. Occasionally, I would be travelling or too busy at the weekend in which case I opted to sacrifice a tedious trip to London rather than time with Diana. Gillian objected to my inconsistencies and would then make subsequent visits awkward for me. After a while, neither she nor the children noticed if I only showed up once a month.

At times, Diana became feverishly busy, even at weekends, spending long periods in her studio engaged in cam-phone conversations, art work on the screen, or model building. Nevertheless, she liked having me there in the apartment. I would bring papers from The Hague, and read or write in the lounge; sometimes, if the weather was fine, I would walk across to Vondel Park with a report or a problem to mull over. Diana preferred to design for the theatre but, occasionally, took on festival and opera projects when they paid better. During her youth, she had often worked abroad, especially in Germany with Karl; by the time I met her, though, she had become tired of too much movement, and preferred to save her travelling for pleasure.

In the summer after my move to the Netherlands, I returned to England for two weeks, which was the minimum time I could negotiate with Gillian for being in charge of Crystal and Bronze. We stayed with Julie for one week making various excursions to the coast and adventure playgrounds. We saw Tom twice choosing the cinema for our entertainment both times. For the other week, I packed Crystal and Bronze off to an expensive camp while I visited friends and work colleagues. I also took two days for a stay in Bradford to explore the recently-expanded National Media Museum (with which I was to have a closer association later in my life). This pattern remained similar for most of the 30s, although during one summer I looked after Crystal and Bronze in the Netherlands for two weeks, and, during another, Diana and I suffered a foursome holiday at a rented cottage in Devon. I hate to admit it, these were periods to be endured. Crystal took on a positively antagonistic attitude towards Diana, and, when reproved, slipped all too easily into a Gillian-type sulk, while Bronze lurched from one asthma attack to another with allergy rashes in-between.

Assuming I stick to my outline plan, I will have much more to say about Crystal and Bronze in later chapters.

CHAPTER 8

IN WHICH WE ARE LUCKY TO SURVIVE A CYCLONE

Diana and I took our first joint holiday, to Toulouse, in the autumn of the year we met. The following May, to celebrate our anniversary, we signed up for a 15 day group tour to the Andes. Neither of us had been away on an organised tour before, but with so little time (two weeks was the longest continuous holiday I could take) and travelling so far away, it seemed only sensible to make the most efficient use of it. We chose a British company recommended by one of Diana's friends, and were not disappointed by the guide or the itinerary: Lima, Cuzco, Machu Picchu, La Paz, Lake Titicaca, the Andes themselves. Subsequently, Diana employed an Inca motif for one of her play designs; and I added to my collection of Marc Ferrez's 19th century photographs of Rio by finding and copying a few early Peruvian photographs, such as those taken by the Courret brothers, Abraham Guillén and Martin Chambi, all roughly contemporaneous with, or slightly later than, Ferrez.

On that tour, Diana and I engaged with most of the other participants politely but as infrequently as possible. However, we did choose to spend free time with a Canadian couple, both journalists, from Montreal – Ike and Augusta Davidson. Diana and Augusta stayed in touch after the holiday, and, on Augusta's suggestion, we decided to use the same tour company for a similar activity holiday 18 months later to East Timor and Indonesia's eastern islands. We were lucky to return alive.

There is much about that holiday which I could recall: the Hindu festival and the hot springs on Bali, strange green birds seen during a trek up Rindjani on Lombok, Ike's oddly aggressive tantrum over the mosquito spray on Flores, and our visit to the impressive mangrove plantations in West Timor developed to help with shoreline protection. My purpose, though, in mentioning the holiday is not to provide a travelogue but to lead up to 28-29 December 2035. We nicknamed the storm, which hit us that night, Cyclone Kip in honour of my birthday which began a couple of hours before the storm's eye. It was not officially recorded as a cyclone, nevertheless it did more damage to East Timor than any other disaster since the Indonesian army had sacked the already ruined country before its independence, more than 30 years earlier. Until global warming started messing with the world's climate, Indonesia had remained largely outside the cyclone zone. Two or three true cyclones had come dangerously close to Timor during the previous decade, but not to the extent of worrying the tour companies.

We lodged in large wood huts, built on stilts, 300-400 metres back from a delightful beach at Osolata. Although appearing traditional, the huts had been built solidly for tourists with glass windows and plumbed shower rooms. When planning these trips, I positively insisted on not taking the budget option, and even Diana, with more experience of travelling than I, would agree that the extra expense could be well spent. That evening, the 12 of us on the tour ate and drank well at a restaurant designed to cater for the tourists staying in the mod-con huts. As the meal progressed, so the wind outside grew in force. Our waiter even closed the shutters; and the restaurant owner told us, with a huge smile, that 'a beeeeg storm' was coming.

Later, Ike, Augusta, Diana and I all linked arms to walk back to our huts through the howling wind and rain. Diana proposed Ike and Augusta return to our hut, but they wanted to get out of their wet clothes and go to bed. Diana and I went to bed too, cuddling together more than usual, but nervously talking about our friends and the laid-back guide, and how good it would be to get home soon. Suddenly, the door flew open and banged violently backwards and forwards. I had to drag a chest of drawers through the water, which had begun to puddle inside, to ensure the door stayed closed. By the time I'd dried myself and got back into bed, Diana was convinced the house was not only shaking slightly, but beginning to wobble. It felt sturdy to me, but I began to feel it might be safer if we got up and dressed. I collected our passports, money, phonepads and credit cards, placed them in a plastic bag, and put the bag down my trousers.

When the eye of the storm came, and with it a peaceful silence, we both drifted off to sleep using sheets and cushions on the cane chairs. Less than half an hour later, I was woken with an almighty bang as a small tree crashed into the side of our wooden veranda. From nothing at all to full force, the storm came back within minutes. I suggested to Diana that we might be safer outside or at the restaurant which had concrete-built walls, but she nodded towards the door which I had barricaded, indicating it would be difficult to get out. Instead, we took our sheets and cushions and struggled to hide under the bed. We had only been there a few minutes when the house exploded.

I remember screaming involuntarily and somersaulting through the air, and simultaneously Diana shouting something. Then I must have been unconscious for a few seconds. As I regained awareness, instinctively I lifted my head slightly but the wind was so powerful and carried so much debris (stinging sand, bits of wood) that I pushed my face sideways towards the sandy, muddy ground. I tried yelling for Diana, but had no idea how far my voice would carry over the howling and swishing of the tempest. I could see nothing through the darkness and I was unable to orientate myself relative to the hut or where it had been. Without moving my legs – I was afraid they might be broken and did not want to test them – I groped around with a hand until I caught hold of a heavy piece of wood (which proved to be part of the bed), and pulled this over my head for protection. I continued shouting for Diana until my throat went sore. I was terribly afraid that her failure to hear me or answer meant she might be dead or badly injured. I tried to think through where she might be or what might have happened, and whether there was any means of finding her. Even if I could run through the deadly wind, though, I figured I hadn't the faintest idea which direction to take. I also realised, after a while, that although neither of my legs were broken my left knee was injured and bleeding. As time wore on, the water level rose slightly and I began to shiver with cold. While the raging wind and flying debris continued unabated, I convinced myself that I must have been the lucky one and that Diana and our friends were dead.

I lay there for two or three hours, regularly shouting into the gale and peering into the darkness looking for movement or lights or the shape of a tree. Several times I thought I heard human voices but when I couldn't hear the same pattern again, I assumed it had been a noise mirage. Only with the first rays of light, and when the wind had quietened to nothing more than a strong gale, did I feel able to try and stand up and – with a very heavy heart – search for Diana. The gash in my knee stung viciously, and I gave momentary thought to the possibility of infection. But I had to find Diana.

She was no more than 20 metres away, uninjured and, compared to me, in relative comfort. She too had been thrown through the air but not so far. She had held on to a cushion, landed near the mattress and managed to crawl under it. Like me, she had undergone mental torment thinking I must be dead.

A few metres away, where the hut had been, a single wall stood crookedly at an angle supported by fallen beams, broken planks and piles of crushed furniture looking not unlike a bonfire prepared for Guy Fawkes night. When I felt down inside my trousers, I was relieved to discover the plastic bag still in place. For a while longer, we lay together under the mattress hugging each other very tightly. Diana kissed me repeatedly as though needing to reassure herself of my living presence, and I couldn't help from saying to myself over and over again 'thank god' as if the words had meaning.

With more light and less wind, we made our way – I hobbling and Diana supporting me – along the debris-strewn walkway, manoeuvring over or round the roots and branches of fallen palms to where our friends had been staying. Although the veranda had gone, the structure of their hut had otherwise remained in tact. Inside, Augusta was shaken, but Ike, whose comic talents were not always appreciated (by me especially), greeted us (or me in particular) with this line: 'I thought you guys were doing something about this stuff.' Only then did he perceive the state we were in and the blood running down my leg. Augusta apologised for her husband and rushed me to the shower room where she had plenty of first aid paraphernalia.

Osolata, and hundreds of other towns and villages across Timor, suffered terrible damage as a result of Cyclone Kip. But, as far as I could find out from enquiries later, only a handful of people died as a direct result of the storm. Obviously, there was huge coverage of the disaster in the East Timorese press. The Indonesian media, though, was not so interested in the plight of the East Timorese people but in whether there might be a trend for tropical storms and cyclones to move west and hit Bali or Java.

In Dili, the following day, and on the plane home, and for weeks after, I thought often about how so much of the damage was local, to villages and local infrastructure, and I wondered how repairs and replacements would be paid for. I imagined that some individuals and small organisations would be clued up enough to seek compensation from the authorities, and that some aid agencies would provide assistance to others. But tens of thousands of individuals would have lost their homes, and/or their livestock, and/or their crops, and/or their possessions, and the vast majority of them would just carry on as best they could, more impoverished than before. I was no stranger to this issue: how to make aid work at a micro level across the globe in millions of villages and rural areas where the poverty, health and environmental problems were at their worst, as opposed to employing the easy option and depositing huge grants on bribe-fuelled inefficient governments willing to kowtow to Western demands.

Fortunately, I never had the wound on my knee stitched. It healed with a two inch scar, and, thereafter, I was able to embellish on my Cyclone Kip adventures whenever it was noticed by friends or family. The adventure firmed up our (or more accurately Diana's) friendship with Ike and Augusta; and, perhaps, it also strengthened my relationship with Diana.

Two days after our return to Amsterdam it was 1 January 2036. But this was no ordinary New Year's Day. It was a Tuesday.

CHAPTER 9
IN WHICH I RECALL NEW YEAR'S DAY 2036

Since the influential United Nations report on the state of nations and the emergence of the First Tuesday Movement (FTM), only one New Year's Day had fallen on a Tuesday, and that, coincidentally, was in 2030, at the start of a new decade. From Buenos Aires to Nepal, from Paris to Manila, from Kinshasa to Oslo, cities across the globe witnessed some of the largest demonstrations in their history. In European metropolises such as Munich, Marseilles and Birmingham there were violent skirmishes between Muslim and Christian hooligans. It was estimated that nearly a billion people worldwide may have marched or protested against their government or multinationals or racism or pollution or poverty. That was the day, though, that led governments everywhere to take serious notice of the FTM: not only did the size and breadth of the protests scare the authorities, but some cities, especially in the developing countries, witnessed widespread looting and a significant number of injuries and deaths.

The FTM did not vanish thereafter, far from it; but, in the subsequent six years, there was no single Tuesday which brought out so many people on a global scale again. There were several explanations for this. Governments certainly succeeded by a variety of means (appeals/propaganda, firm prohibition announcements, far stricter controls, armed police etc.) in reducing the FTM's ability to attract protesters. A few countries with autocratic governments managed to stamp the protests out completely by imposing marshal law and shooting those who ignored it. Moreover, many of the demonstrators, having seen the extent of the unruly behaviour that day, decided not to march again. But, it was widely believed that the main reason for such a mass turnout on 1 January 30 was because of the conjunction of a first Tuesday with New Year's Day.

The movement itself had no concrete identity. It never had any formal headquarters, nor any leaders; coordination of meetings, marches and protests emerged organically through netsites or inadvertent signalling by the media. Authoritarian attempts to censor the net failed, and often backfired. At the command of the EU's member state governments, for example, the Euronet Agency looked into whether it would be possible to impose a ban on propagating FTM information through Solar, the open Euronet, but concluded it would be impossible to police. Where governments elsewhere did try, their efforts often proved counter-productive and led to bigger and wilder first Tuesday marches than usual.

So, on our return from Timor, the media was full of speculation about what would happen on Tuesday 1 January 2036. In European cities, immigrants of all races and all colours were FTM adherents mostly because they felt, as the working classes had done in the first half of the 20th century, downtrodden; pensioners marched to the FTM tune because, for more than a decade, they had been cheated out of a comfortable old age; and youths were ready to use the FTM banner to protest about anything and everything unfair (unemployment, racism, war and gene technology to name but four targets).

In the developing countries, where reasonably democratic governments had failed to silence the FTM, street spokespersons were anxious to rail against the riches of Europe, Japan and the US (especially their governments and businesses) and, like the youths in the West, wanted a fairer world; or else they wished to protest against their own poverty or lack of medicines or government corruption. Many of these would-be protesters could be seen in newsclips wearing the adaptable FTM logo, often with the middle T converted into a gallows hanging the dollar, euro or UN symbol.

Globally, the FTM attracted its biggest ever multitudes that day, and its worst. Looting and violence – Triti Madan's predicted 'endemic social terrorism' – was the norm, not the exception, in many cities.

In Amsterdam, as usual, crowds flocked to Vondel Park to hear spontaneous soap-box speakers, to sing protest songs and then to bring half the city to a standstill by marching to the Central Station. This time, though, the crowds were tenfold the usual numbers on a first Tuesday, and the marchers managed to cause a huge amount of damage on their way. Two children drowned in a canal. In London, the police used water cannons and plastic bullets to break up massive crowds which had dispersed from the official march routes. Nineteen people died from violence of one sort or another. In Paris, Brussels, Hamburg and many other European cities and towns, inter-racial clashes led to deaths, hundreds of injuries and thousands of arrests. In Cairo, Nairobi, Karachi, Djakarta, Mexico City the ransacking of multinational business premises was the worst it had ever been, and heavy-handed police may have killed up to 1,000 all told. In other cities such as São Paulo, Caracas, Moscow, and Seoul looting under cover of the city-wide chaos caused by the FTM resulted in billions of dollars of stolen goods and damage. Events that day led, eventually, to several requested interventions by the UN and European armies, not least the one that caused the Jamaica Skirmish in 2037.

It was in the United States, though, that the most dramatic change between 2030 and 2036 was evident. The FTM had been slow to build in the US and Canada (partly because the late 20s and early 30s had seen a very slow recovery from recession and unemployment) but by 2034-35 the FTM had taken off, fuelled, as in most other Western countries, by youthful disillusionment with capitalist ideals. The underprivileged masses, which in the US were still the black and Mexican peoples, joined the protests on 1 January 2036 in their millions, protesting partly for themselves but also against their government's arrogance in world affairs. The next day the headlines did not reflect the protesters' objectives but the rioting, looting, violent clashes and deaths. Of the large nations, only Japan and China remained relatively untroubled, but then they were among the countries to suffer most from the suicide epidemics a little later, in the 40s.

New Year's Day 2036 proved to be the FTM's zenith. Spontaneous first Tuesday protests continued around the world for many years but never again to the same extent.

CHAPTER 10

IN WHICH RICH NATIONS MAKE MAJOR COMMITMENTS

The year 2035 had come and gone without Enterprise 35 achieving its goal – a fact that had certainly provoked FTM protesters on New Year's Day 2036. No one, though, could blame Pravit Krishnamurty. He was a slave to the cause, and inspired most of his staff, including me, to be the same. The problem, inevitably, came from politics and the interplay of demands by various important donor or receptor governments. In the autumn of 2034, there had been a follow-up meeting of world leaders aimed at transposing the Beijing Agreement into reality. As a result, they had publicly promised to reach a conclusion the following November (35) in Vancouver.

Secretly, or in the fine print of the preparatory accords, though, they had made so many contradictory demands that a deal looked doubtful. We all worked feverishly towards the Vancouver summit. Some weeks it appeared as though Pravit never left the cam-conference room, having to listen and negotiate with so many different factions. There was less pressure on my own team because, whereas the others were engaged in preparing financial and legalistic detail for a formal agreement on how to spend the extra 0.2%, we had only to draft a set of recommendations.

Vancouver proved an embarrassing failure for the European proposal, the UN, and for the IFSD in particular, not because Enterprise 35 couldn't deliver, but because certain countries (the US, Germany, Japan, Russia, Nigeria and Brazil) were at logger-heads over several basic issues, and because of a serious stand-off between the Christian and Muslim worlds. A decision was stalled and a new summit scheduled for the following autumn in London.

I believe the United Nations would have reached agreement in London on the primary issues without the FTM chaos of 1 January 2036 but, possibly, it might not have responded so positively to my own team's recommendations for future expansions. Under cover of the laborious and aggressive bargaining on details surrounding the committed 0.2%, my group had quietly beavered away with our hugely ambitious and optimistic plans to transfer four times as much money again from the rich to the needy.

In this respect, Pravit continued to be an inspired strategist. While he consistently pandered to the IFSD executive board on the main issues vis-à-vis the initial 0.2%, knowing that its members were simply reflecting the views of their national governments which were, in any event, being played out at all the negotiating conferences, he managed to minimise their attention to the drafts of my report. Naturally, the executive board, and the steering committee did examine my team's work from time to time, and, at the summit preparatory meetings, we were always fully exposed to every nation's negotiators. Nevertheless, through Pravit's management, we managed to press forward in a kind of camouflaged ideological haze in which no rich nation wanted to be seen as anything less than beneficent towards the future well-being of the planet, so long as no real final commitments were at stake.

To divert for a moment to the personal, I wish to recall a particularly gruesome encounter with Rike Thomas, the oily man from the overseas aid section of the UK's Department of External Affairs. Not needing to contact him regularly was one bonus of my leaving the Department of the Environment, not that oily people didn't grease my Enterprise 35 office on a near daily basis. In private, Rike may have been an agreeable person but, somehow, he got up my nose more than most. When I was at Shropshire House, he would beg favours or ask for information, and demand to take me out for lunch or a drink in recompense. He gossiped continually, and had a childish name-dropping habit. He must have been good at his job, or how else would he have survived in it for so long.

Unfortunately, after moving to The Hague I didn't lose sight of him completely because, on some issues, he was involved, as the UK's representative, in preparing the EU's input into the Enterprise 35 process. Prior to one meeting at our offices, he called to invite me to lunch. When I declined politely, he said he had a 'message' for me, and insisted on a private meeting. I gave way and agreed to a light snack at Jaspar's, near the gloriously nicknamed 'tits and penis' town hall. I ordered and ate quickly while Rike rambled on about how his wife's horse shared the same stables as a horse ridden by the wife of a cabinet minister; and how, unusually, he had actually been present at a meeting with John Lyndquist, the prime minister, and so on. I wasn't really listening until, through Jaspar's hum of banter, some words came into focus.

'... and, so you see, His Majesty's Government, HMG, your paymaster, is calling you to service. It's an honour really.'

When I got to the bottom of Rike's meaning, it wasn't so much an honour I uncovered but a threat. I was being leaned on to tone down the scale of Enterprise 35's ambitions. Rike suggested there might be a senior civil servant's job waiting for me 'back home' if I did as advised, but that if I was 'stupid enough not to listen' I would make 'a lot of important people unhappy'. My secondment to Enterprise 35 might be brought to a swift and unpleasant end, Rike warned.

Even today, thinking about the snake makes me squirm. I never discovered how much he personally had elaborated on the 'message', but it was a clumsy and ill-judged manoeuvre. I knew the left wing of the Conservative Alliance could never have approved it (my friend Horace confirmed this later by talking to his friend Terrance Spoon); and the Green Party, which was also part of the governing coalition, would rather have left the coalition than be involved in any attempt to weaken the IFSD. In short, the UK's finance minister, a Lyndquist loyalist positioned well to the right within the Conservative Alliance, had become alarmed by the latest draft of my team's report, and perceived a real danger that Pravit's tactics, especially after 1 January 2036, might eventually lead to a yet bigger drain on the UK government's purse. One of his over-keen advisers had then worked up a ploy or two.

The main reason I mention this unsavoury episode is because I decided, as I was walking back from Jaspar's to the office, that I would, when the time was right, leave HMG and seek a permanent posting with the UN at the IFSD.

At the London summit, in October 2036, the Western world finally agreed on all the myriad conditions and parameters for most developed countries to provide within three years an additional 0.2% in overseas development aid, half of it directly to the IFSD – this was an enormous sum, billions of dollars, to fuel our work. The recipient countries, for their part, all made further commitments to deal with corruption and inefficiencies, to spread the incoming wealth to rural areas, to open up ownership and trade rights, and to tackle crime against foreign-owned property.

Astonishingly, moreover, and in response particularly to the work done by my team, the London summit participants signed up to a further total increase of 0.5% in two stages, raising the level by 0.25% each, starting in 2039. While the wording on this was not as firm and committed as the Beijing Agreement had been on the first 0.2%, it was still far more than most pundits had expected after the Vancouver failure.

'What do you British say? Hah, I have it. Bingo,' Pravit whispered to me in a corridor when he knew for certain the content of the agreement. 'I believed, in my heart of hearts, there would only be one further increment of 0.2% – not so much work for the packagers. And now look how well the gods have treated us.'

The gods indeed. He might have been referring sarcastically to the world's leaders or to the fact that the additional 0.5% deal came largely as a result of growing religious (Muslim-Christian) conflict in Africa, Central Asia and Europe, which stemmed, the Arab/Africa lobby believed, from the odious inequality of riches. There is no doubt that the worldwide FTM disturbances at the start of the year contributed to the Arab/Africa cause, as did the escalating climate problems which regularly seemed to kill so many more poor people in poor countries than rich people in rich countries.

I am tempted to go on at length about the work my team did, and the content of the 0.5% deal, but this is a matter of public record and the UN's archives surely contain our final report delivered to the London summit. Besides, I will have much more to write about the IFSD and my role therein. Suffice it to say that the original European Union proposal to raise development aid by 1.1% in five stages (the initial 0.3% and four further increments of 0.2% each) had been whittled back to a 0.7% increase in three steps (an initial 0.2%, followed by two further increments of 0.25% each), but that, nevertheless, the Beijing and London agreements together constituted one of the UN's greatest ever achievements.

After the London summit, the IFSD disbanded its Enterprise 35 department, and most of the seconded staff were offered permanent posts within a new Future Policy Division created to prepare the way for the next two expansions. I was recalled to Shropshire House for a meeting with the Department's most senior official and Jude Singleton. Rike Thomas's threat clung to me like an irritating boil that demanded squeezing but wouldn't subside, so I expected to be told I had let my country down and other disagreeable things. In fact, the reverse was true. My seniors had anticipated that I would want to stay on at the IFSD and were ready to entice me back with a grand lunch at Jude's club, and a significant promotion to section head (overseeing the environmental health of the country's waterways) within the Department. It would have been impolitic to refuse on the spot, so I said I would consider the offer. I took the opportunity, though, to gossip about Rike's dirty stick-and-carrot in the hope that the story might be spread round.

Half-jokingly and half-deviously, I tested the job offer on Pravit. He had been appointed director of the newly-created Future Policy Division, and was in the process of devising its structure. He had already invited me to be a unit head, but I was still officially a British civil servant.

'Pravit, I've been offered an excellent post in the UK's Department of the Environment. Do you think I should take it?'

'I have been thinking about you Kip. Are you well?'

'Yes.'

'Are you happy here in the Netherlands?'

'I could be happy in London too,' I lied, thinking about Diana.

'And me. Am I happy?'

'I hope so. Enterprise 35 achieved more than you dared hope.'

'You know and I know it is not enough. It will never be enough. We can only do our best. But that is not why I am unhappy at this minute.' He looked very serious, almost forlorn. I couldn't tell whether he wanted me to speak, and there was a long pause before I responded.

'Why are you unhappy, Pravit?' Suddenly and transparently, his expression lifted.

'I cannot decide who should be my deputy director.' A pause. 'The hints come from above and from the side, but I plan to make up my own mind, be my own man, as you British say. And then, finally when I make up my mind, the very person I have chosen – a highly intelligent thinker, a loyal colleague, a hard-working efficient administrator, and a nice fellow to boot – tells me he is leaving. If you can be happy in London, then, Kip, you must go. Yes you must go. Hah. You never know where you are with the British.'

Thus it was I became a UN employee, and stayed one for the best part of 30 years.

CHAPTER 11

IN WHICH I LAUNCH TOM INTO SPACE

Flora has been absent for the last few days. I thought she might have had a relapse and been confined to her charpoy (which she insists on calling it, though her bed is nothing like one), but she just whirred in, and talked with such excitement I thought she might fall out of the Easy. She wanted to tell me about a stream of unexpected visitors – how does she cope with them? – some maharajah she had once known, and his daughters, visiting the UK; a great-grandson over from California; and the daughter of a niece who wanted to record her talking about her life history.

'I said no, no, no, my name's not Kip Fenn! And I dislike her intensely, she only suggested it because she wants me to remember her in my will.' And then, forgetting my low tolerance threshold, she prattled on about life in India with her husband, an expert in pharmaceutical manufacturing processes, 50 years ago or more. I closed my eyes until I heard her hum away.

And Tom slipped into my mind.

I want to introduce Guido, but before him, I need to give Tom, a send-off. The last film we saw together was on or near my 38th birthday. During the afternoon we took Crystal and Bronze to one of the West End superscreens to see Aaron Lambert's *Marcella's Bullet*. There had been the usual commercial hype but, despite this, the film had attracted rave reviews. There were long queues to buy popcorn and to enter the auditorium. Unusually, both my children were content at the choice of film, and even I was interested to see what all the fuss was about, having missed the first Marcella film and only see one of Lambert's early adventure flicks.

Marcella was billed as a modern female version of Batman, James Bond and Pacific Prince all rolled into one. Having inherited a fortune from her corrupt father (lots of flashbacks and opportunities for side plots), she had become a special private detective helping the unfortunates of New York gather evidence against their rich oppressors. In several of the stories – such as *Marcella's Bullet* and *Misty Marcella* – the International Police Authority persuaded her to close her Harlem office for a week or two and help them unravel a complex plot against the world, or capture some colourful villain. The formula worked splendidly, partly because Lambert was a genius storyteller, and partly because Lyra Hampton (who needs no introduction, even to youngsters today) brought intelligence, compassion, a touch of Irish humour and a cartoon sexiness to the role.

Tom loved the film. Crystal was inspired enough to forget to sulk afterwards and complain precociously about Marcella being nothing like a real person. And Bronze kept asking questions because the plot had been over his head. After milkshakes, we took the children back to Lacey's Lane where their mother Gillian was as formal with us always; and then Tom and I went on to have an Indian meal in Willesden Green. He looked grey and tired; and he hadn't taken much care of his dress. He told me Fragrance had walked out on him and filed a legal suit for alimony. I guess, in retrospect, she killed him, she and drink.

Tom certainly drank heavily that night – drank and coughed. I decided to go back to Epsom with him rather than, as planned, head for Godalming to stay with my mother, Julie. He fell asleep in the taxi, and I had to manhandle him into the house. The next morning, he apologised on his way to the loo, and then went back to bed. He was sleeping when I left.

A few weeks later, one day around lunchtime, he called to tell me he'd had a heart attack and been admitted to Kingston Hospital. I took an early evening flight, and spent the night in Godalming. In the morning, Julie, who hadn't seen her ex-husband for ten years but still carried some kind of dim torch for him, wanted to come too. Tom was dozing when we arrived. A nurse explained he had advanced cardiomyopathy, and then a doctor advised heart surgery. We waited nearly an hour until he stirred. Once fully awake, he was in good humour; seeing Julie, though, gave him a shock.

'Bloody hell! Have I passed to the other side?' But it was said with a touch of the old charm, and he followed it up with warm words. I could see he was genuinely delighted to see Julie. He confessed that he had no intention of agreeing to any surgery. 'Never trusted doctors, and no intention to start now,' he said with conviction.

Julie drove the two of us back to Godalming, and then I borrowed her car to return later in the day and spend another couple of hours with Tom. He had become maudlin, morbid almost.

' "I see earth, it's so beautiful." They were the first recorded words spoken by a man in space. And then, in his statement afterwards, Gagarin said, "There was a good view of the earth which had a very distinct and pretty blue halo. It had a smooth transition from pale blue, blue, dark blue, violet and absolutely black. It was a magnificent picture." I've been wondering if life's a bit the same. By dying relatively young and in a crash, I reckon Gagarin missed out on the dark blue and violet, but me I've been there. And now I'm heading for the black.' He closed his eyes for a few seconds before slowly drawing out the familiar words, 'Well fucking say something.' Before I had chance to offer my usual rejoinder, he carried on with another Gagarin story, as if to cheer himself up.

'Did you know that in the official Soviet records there is no mention of Gagarin using a parachute ejection system, although he ejected at seven kilometres above the earth's surface to avoid the deadly impact of the capsule landing. The international aviation rules at the time stated that a pilot had to remain in his craft from launch to landing. Officially, he could have been disqualified from his record.' Tom loved this piece of trivia. 'He died, you know, before Armstrong got to the moon. I hope I don't go before Martian Seven.' I reassured him that he had many years to live. A taxi would be taking him home the following day, he said, and he'd be fine. It sounds corny, but I gave him a kiss on the cheek before I left, not because I didn't expect to see him again, but because he had appeared so sad, so vulnerable.

60

Four weeks later, his local doctor called me, as next of kin, to inform me that Tom had died from a massive coronary earlier that day. He had been sitting in his car about to go somewhere, and a neighbour watching from a window had seen him slump over the steering wheel.

The funeral took place at Croydon Crematorium. Wreaths, a few warm words and he was gone. Julie and I were the only two truly mourning. Gillian came with our children; Fragrance was there with a boyfriend, although she never spoke to me; and there were a few colleagues from Euroil. His will left bequests of 10,000 euros each to Crystal and Bronze, and the rest to me. After expenses and duties, and a negotiated deal with Fragrance, I inherited around 300,000 euros. I spent more than a quarter of it to launch Tom's ashes into space. The extortionately priced package came complete with an elaborately framed certificate and a three minute camclip of the moment the ashes were released into space with a view of planet earth behind. It was an irrational gesture for which I offer no explanation. Gillian thought it was madness, but Diana, who only ever worried about money in terms of the budget a director had given her, said I had surprised her – which was a compliment. I have the recording on Neil, and I've asked Jay to save it with all the rest of the family paraphernalia for future generations.

CHAPTER 12

I WHICH DIANA AND I HAVE A SON

Guido. Here, on my screen, is a photo of him, aged but three weeks. He is wearing a bright blue all-in-one, centimetres too long for him in the feet. And here is a photo of the Guido co-op standing atop Peter's barge. It was Guido's fourth birthday, in December 2042. Guido himself, who is perched on a raised hatch, is wearing a dark suit, a white bow-tie, and a top hat. (Diana loved dressing him up when he was young enough to put up with it.) Behind him, the four us – that's Peter, Dominique who was Diana's younger sister, Diana and me – are all leaning slightly back in an arc and pointing fingers at Guido as if to say 'you're the man' or similar. I have a camclip from the same day of Guido making paper aeroplanes, and Dominique's two older children looking decidedly unimpressed. I do not like to view it, though, because it always brings Dr Jessop to mind. There is a moment in the camclip when Guido's face is at a half angle to the camera. The first time I saw it, I was reminded of someone, but I couldn't think who. The image of Guido stuck with me for days until I woke in the night startled by a dream in which I had gone to a doctor's surgery and seen a framed camstill of Guido standing on the doctor's desk.

This is my favourite photo: Guido, at five and a half years of age, and I holding hands and laughing while running down a grassy hill towards the camera. It was taken, with Diana's camera, on the English South Downs by Veronique, Mireille's older sister, in June 2045. I almost decided not to mention this photo now because it will be too complicated to explain, yet here I am delving back (or forward whichever way you care to look at it).

Straightaway I should explain that Guido married Mireille, some 20 years later, after that photograph was taken. Veronique and Mireille (16 and seven years old respectively at the time) were the daughters of Didier and Helene Rocard, a Parisian couple involved in the theatre, who were among Diana's closest friends.

That summer in 2045, we went first to Southampton, where my old friend Horace Merriweather had won a fifth election victory. After making his first celebration party in 2027 (with Gillian), I had missed the following three, and there was no pressing reason for me to go to this one in particular either, other than that Horace had especially urged me to be there. Perhaps this was because I had recently taken over Pravit's role as director and the UK media had highlighted my appointment; or perhaps he wanted to show off his recently-acquired grand house or his new partner. I should stress that, by then, Arturo had moved out of Horace's Camden Town pad ... Oh, this is making no sense. I knew the photo would lead me places I do not yet want to go.

In any case, the timing of the journey was good for Diana and me. After Horace's party in Southampton, we visited Julie, who by then had opted to follow her mother's route and retire in Parsonville, before heading to Brighton for a couple of days. Veronique had recently arrived in Brighton for a long summer of English study, and Diana had arranged for us all to meet on the West Pier. On the second day, Veronique, Guido and I went for a walk on the South Downs (when the photo was taken), while Diana stayed behind to discuss a future project with a director at the famous Candyfloss Theatre.

Driving on towards Dover, at the end of our short holiday, we heard on the radio that prime minister Terrance Spoon (of the Progressive Party which was still the dominant partner within the Conservative Alliance) had appointed Horace as minister for business. This was his first – and last – government job.

Viewing these photos, however, is a digression from my main purpose of introducing Guido. On returning from London in November 2036, after the meeting with Jude, I announced the job offer to Diana as though I were seriously considering it (just as I would to Pravit a day later) – which I wasn't. Diana's immediate reaction was one of indifference; she wanted to talk about the weekend's arrangements. When I admitted, later in the evening, that I had no intention of going back to work for the UK civil service, she got angry with me for playing games.

'Go, stay, I don't care,' she said, barely containing an edge of spite in her tone as well as her words. This hurt, and I was left for days reassessing the nature of our relationship. It had been about three years since we'd met, and, I believed, we had established something firm and real between us. On the rebound from Karl, Diana appreciated my stability and loyalty, my grounding in the 'real world', and, I suppose, my intellect.

Karl, a successful German theatre director who dabbled in film, had been instrumental in Diana's own creative development, but he had also abused her professionally once too often. In their personal relationship, he had played fast and loose with her love, and left her several times for young actresses. For my part, I adored Diana. Whereas my time with Gillian had been like a promised feast with nothing to eat, life with Diana was a rich picnic full of sumptuous tastes and unexpected delicacies – although not one without its ants and wasps to contend with.

Sex was one irritating problem, Karl was another. Sex had always been an important part of Diana's life and, with effort, we enjoyed each other. But we did not have the need or passion to make such an effort very often. Despite her liberal attitude to pornography, for example, it was only acceptable to Diana intermittently. Cannabis, which I would take occasionally, and drink helped, but even so Diana made the running. She grumbled about this, which led occasionally to me sounding off about being in Karl's shadow. Too many conversations ended with some reference to him, or Diana's past. Moreover, Diana was far less intellectual than Gillian so I missed being able to discuss my work in any depth. But, as I say, life with Diana was a glorious picnic. For her, though, life with me must have seemed quiet, placid and safe, after years of being caught up in Karl's nervy unpredictable domain.

Some weeks after the 'I don't care' argument, when I had already signed my new United Nations employment papers, I began to consider moving to a larger and better-situated apartment. Thinking I could reassure Diana about my love and commitment to her, I tentatively asked if she had ever thought we might live together some day. Again Diana put the conversation to one side, not wanting to be diverted from some creative process or other.

A few days later, a small package arrived at my Weissenbruchstraat pad. It contained a British postcard from the 1950s of a man sitting on a chair with a baby lying across his lap. Here it is on my screen. The man, who has a cigarette hanging out of his smiling mouth, is in the process of tying up the baby's nappy. On the floor stands an upturned red lady's hat adorned with a yellow ribbon. There is something dark and indiscernible inside the hat. Behind the man, a woman in a dark green dressing gown is screaming, 'Don't give me guff! You knew damn well that was my new hat!' On the back Diana had written in pencil, 'What's guff?' And the package contained a paperback entitled *Co-ops – a better way to bring up children?*.

My immediate reaction was to imagine that Diana was pregnant but, after a moment or two, I realised she would not have told me this way. Instead, she was enlarging my question about living together into a much bigger one. Although she had never talked about it, I had no trouble in understanding why she had not opted for motherhood before. I had also noticed that, unlike some women of her age, she had not positively decided against having children. Most of the time I had found her neutral on the subject, without an opinion.

I emailed her back that same morning. If I embroidered my language a little, it was surely because I'd taken on some of her ways, some of her confidence in our relationship. I received a reply before midday. I have copied this correspondence for an appendix to this chapter.

Having thus made the huge decision to have a child at the age of 39 (in fact she was 41 when Guido arrived), Diana spared no effort in making sure everything functioned properly, if I can put it that way, during her fertile spells. When her first two or three periods came, she did not mention them; but, by the time of the fourth, she had begun to express disappointment and concern, which soon turned into anxiety, and visits to the doctor. I thought she was being unreasonable, but logic did not work well on Diana. Moreover, she had had two abortions when younger, and she knew several women who were unable to conceive.

Through this period I continued to suggest we look for somewhere to live together. Diana, who had wanted to wait until she was pregnant before making a commitment on this, changed her mind in the spring of 2037. Her sister Dominique, with children herself, suggested it might help in some way to prepare her psychologically for conceiving.

By August, we had moved into a modern-looking three storey semi-detached house in Leiden, 25 minutes walking – less than ten cycling – from the train station. We had looked at older traditional properties, and if Diana had insisted on one or if we had found a house suitable for our joint purposes, we would have taken it. But this one, on Oldwijkgaarten, won both our hearts. It was part of a 12 house (six building) complex built around a large green with car parking terminals on its outskirts. To arrive at the front doors it was necessary to walk through the communal garden, past the complex's central wind turbine with a kids' climbing frame around the base. Each building, individually designed with silver-coloured solar energy glass (a precursor of s-glass) and charcoal grey absorption tiles, had two private secluded gardens, one for each dwelling, accessed from the lounge areas at the back. I could afford the mortgage for the house on my salary alone, so Diana opted to keep her Amsterdam pad and rent it out, in case, I suppose, things didn't turn out well between us. Within two years, though, she had sold it to the tenant, and had taken over part of the capital and mortgage base on the Oldwijkgaarten house.

Inside our new home, there was sufficient space to allow Diana and me separate areas: Diana took the two top-storey rooms for her studio (with the door between them removed), we took a bedroom each on the middle floor, and allocated the third room to our unborn child. On the ground floor, I took the eating room as my office – we usually ate in the kitchen or, with guests, in the lounge. The private garden was – what shall I say? – petite, but had been carefully tended with mature fragrant roses, miniature apple and plum trees, and attractive clematis climbers on the border fences.

It is possible that Anders was conceived the first time we made love in the house, but, even if he wasn't, Dominique's advice worked, whether it was prophetic, salient or serendipitous.

But, life rarely offers such an easy ride. Eighteen weeks into her pregnancy, we already knew our child would be a boy. Diana had asked if I would mind calling him Anders as it was the name of her mother's father who she had adored as a child. I agreed, thankful I had been consulted – my first wife Gillian having never bothered to discuss children's names with me.

With this settled, we invited, on two successive evenings, the couples we hoped would be part of the Anders co-op: Diana's sister Dominique and her husband Waltar Meijer; and Peter de Roo and his wife Livia. Both Dominique and Peter had already indicated they would consider it a privilege to be part of the co-op, but we wanted to discuss it more seriously with their partners as well.

I had learned, from the book Diana gave me, that ours was the simplest form of co-op, not far different from the old-fashioned parents and godparents model. Nevertheless, by accepting a co-op role, Dominique and Peter knew they would be expected to make a positive contribution towards Anders' future. Should Diana and I separate for any reason, or if one of us were to die, then their involvement might have to increase substantially. Neither Waltar nor Livia admitted any objection to the commitments made by their partners, although Peter intimated later that Livia was not wildly enthusiastic about the whole concept. Nor was I. Yet I didn't care.

Diana and I were living as man and wife, and that was enough for me.

A week after these serious meetings with our friends, Diana began experiencing sharp pains. Within a further two weeks she had miscarried. There was a horrible scene in the bathroom, with blood and histrionics in equal proportions. I was unable to bring Diana any comfort. The external festivities – Christmas was two weeks away – emphasised our sadness. A local priest organised a short simple funeral service in a nearby chapel. Only the four of us from the co-op were present.

As scheduled, I then went to spend the holiday period in England finding little consolation in seeing my mother, or Tom, or my children (apart from the outing to see *Marcella's Bullet*). Diana went to stay with Dominique and her family. Less than three months later Tom died. Around the same time, Diana fell pregnant again – against the advice of her doctor. Guido (a name with no significance) Tom Oostlander-Fenn was born, a healthy plump chap, on 22 December 38. Only then was the Guido co-op formed out of the vestiges of the stillborn Anders co-op.

POSTCARD PICTURES AND CAPTIONS

Diana Oostlander to Kip Fenn

May 2033

Without the filter

A woman leans over to tie her shoes; a bowler-hatted gentleman behind spreads his hands across her rump.

Caption: Oh! Quelles formes appétissantes. [Oh! What an enticing body.]

With the filter

A naked woman has turned round and is slapping the man in the face.

Caption: Zut! Ma femme. [Drat! My wife.]

July 2033

Without the filter

A portly man in a beach gown looks towards a bathing hut.

Caption: Que fais donc ma femme – elle est bien longue? [Why is my wife taking so long?]

With the filter

Inside the hut, a naked girl is embracing a young man.

Caption: Ça y est je l'suis. [Oh I get it.]

September 2033

Without the filter

An old dear sits on the beach looking out to sea.

Caption: Que fais donc ma fille, sous l'eau avec son cousin? [What is my daughter doing in the water with her cousin?]

With the filter

In the sea, a topless girl, with the perkiest of cartoon breasts, embraces a boy with an excellent leer.

Caption: Voilà!

EXTRACTS FROM CORRESPONDENCE

Kip Fenn to Diana Oostlander
October 2034, Last night

I've discussed the fabrics with you at length. I've contemplated all manner of projections on your screen. I've seen the model. And yet the final results left me breathless with surprise. Last night's show was wonderful. The colloquial Dutch was a bit impenetrable here and there, but it didn't matter I was too busy admiring your genius.

One reviewer says (I translate badly), 'It is impossible to imagine any other designer but Diana Oostlander doing this play such justice.' Another says, 'Although Van den Bossche's intelligent excursion into the heart of Dutch man and Dutch land makes this a great play, Oostlander's set with the Inca motifs lifts it into one of the very best of recent years.'

I agree.

Diana Oostlander to Kip Fenn
October 2034, re: Last night

Darling, I've got up so late this morning – the party went on and on. I wish you could have stayed in Amsterdam last night. I haven't looked for the reviews yet, but I could feel the success in the theatre. It was very exciting. And I want to say something. I want to say that part of this is because of you. We were together in Peru, and your comments on my work made a big difference. You think I dismiss you as a businessman with no art (except for a few old dirty photos!!!) and I make you listen and then never listen back.

But I do, darling – so there.

xxx

Kip Fenn to Diana Oostlander
January 2037, Guff

Guff means nonsense, humbug. Also, I didn't know this before I looked it up, guff means a smell or a stink in Scottish dialect. Actually, I'm not bad at changing nappies, and I can promise I would never misuse any of your hats, however out of fashion they were, and however infrequently you wore them. As for a co-op, why do I always feel you are not content to tint my traditional values, but want to dye them a new colour altogether. I'll read the book tonight, if I can control the buzzing in my head, and the pumping in my heart.

Diana Oostlander to Kip Fenn
January 2037, re: Guff
Darling, I promise you that all my red hats will be available for guff duty – so there!!! But I am very glad of your reply, I've been anxious since I sent the packet.

Kip Fenn to Julie Fenn
June 2033
I was delighted to watch you in that education promotional film. You were the star. But did I read somewhere that the Conservative Alliance is planning to prune back the Independent Education Authority because its ideas are too 'progressive'? Won't this undermine all Jones' efforts even before anyone can prove the IEA's worth? You look smart and kind, the type of head any school kid would want – except for me! I can't think why I had a problem with you as my deputy head. Now you've done the film, isn't it time for a book.

I should mention that I've met someone. She's called Diana, and she couldn't be more different from Gillian. She's a successful theatre designer, and a bit older than me, but attractive and fun and warm. I've attached a photo of us taken in a tulip palace (the same night Caxton was killed – good riddance). It's early days, but I really like her. See you soon. The second week-end in July?

Julie Fenn to Kip Fenn
June 2033
Thank you for your note and the photo. Diana does look very attractive. I hope things go well. I hope to meet her soon. (By the way, Gillian rang the other day and asked me if I would

look after Crystal and Bronze for a week in the summer. Did she discuss this with you?)

Yes, you are right. I am very worried about this government. Unfortunately, the right-wingers are running scared and only see education in a 20th century kind of way. A reassessment of the IEA's role was part of the Conservative Alliance's manifesto, but it's a question of how far it can or will go. The Authority may have made some mistakes, and it's still learning, but it would be a shame to stop it now. It's already made a number of important additions to the curriculum: basic democratic/community responsibilities, sustainable development, the understanding of cultural/national differences, simple money management, news monitoring, and healthy/sensible lifestyles among others. They could make such a big difference to people's lives in the long run.

Alan was here for a few weeks. He says he's going to start work on a book about floods. I remember him saying the same things five years ago. But it was lovely to see him.

All my love.

Kip Fenn to Julie Fenn
January 2036
It was good to talk with you on the camphone last week. It was some trip, as you gathered. Diana says 'sorry' for dragging me to faraway places. It's true I would have been happy to spend the two weeks on Bali, but Diana has a need for adventure – she got her money's worth this time.

See you soon.

Julie Fenn to Kip Fenn
January 2036
Do you know there are children in my youngest classes who have never seen snow. I don't know if that is a good thing or a bad thing, but I decided it was time we had an assembly on climate change. I made you the hero of the day, explaining about your Timor adventure and about your work there in The Hague. I was also surprised to discover that out of 350 chil-

dren in my school more than 10% claimed they had experienced an extreme natural event of some kind (mostly tropical storms, but also floods and earthquakes).

I can't believe how far the FTM went on New Year's Day. I think teenagers and young adults are so sad and distressed at the moment. I feel it's our fault – teachers and leaders.

I'll see you next weekend, yes?

All my love.

Kip Fenn to Julie Fenn
January 2037
Do you remember telling me a few years ago about one of your teachers who had formed a co-op for her first child. A Dorothy maybe, I can't remember exactly? How is she and the child?

Julie Fenn to Kip Fenn
January 2037
She's still with me, one of the better teachers in the school. She has two children by the same man, both co-ops I think. I don't know much else. Why are you asking?

Kip Fenn to Julie Fenn
January 2037
Diana and I intend to take the co-op path. She really wants a child before it gets too late, and I want to have one with her. I don't think we'll get married. Here's the blurb from the back of a book called *Co-ops – a better way to bring up children?* by Caspar Melville Junior. Yes, he's American, but it's not a one-sided tract by any means.

'Co-ops, in a recognisable form, began around 2010-15 as an alternative model for raising children. The concept originated in the UK, but spread more rapidly in the Netherlands, Scandinavia and the US. Although no country yet recognises the legality of co-ops, both Finland and Norway are looking at the possibility of legislation. In the US, the Christian fundamentalist movement is too strong to allow for legal recognition but co-op arrangements have, nevertheless, won important battles in the courts.

The idea with a co-op is for a group of people, usually the mother and father (but not necessarily) and other relations/friends, to make a firm commitment to a child and his/her lifetime development and well-being. Thus, rather than a child being brought up in a family centred on the life and wants of the parents, he or she is brought up in a co-op entirely focused on his or her needs. Some sociologists believe the child co-op system is more suitable to a culture in which long marriages are now the exception rather than the norm, and in which individuals often choose to have children with different partners. Other experts believe the propagation of such ideas can only harm us by further undermining marriage, one of the cornerstones of Western society.

Lifetime studies, which began in the late 10s, have already begun to demonstrate that in many situations co-op children can be more popular, self-disciplined and successful in school compared to children brought up in traditional families. Far from accepting the ethos of co-op children uncritically, this book looks at the pros and cons, and how these might apply to individuals in differing circumstances.'

I'm not sure I could be an advocate for co-ops but, for Diana and me, it might be a good idea. Diana has no track record and I have a dreadful one, so bringing close friends into a co-op might help us both be better parents.

Any how, I wanted to give you early warning.

Lots of love.

Julie Fenn to Kip Fenn
February 2037

It's not for me to pass any judgement on your choices. Tom and I have nothing to be proud of – but you. Sometimes I worry so about Crystal, and about Bronze. I blame myself for much. But I can't see what any of us could have done or can do. Gillian tries, she does, I know. If they have problems, I believe it was in the chemistry between their genes, chance and the misfitting of you and Gillian together.

But Diana is a lovely lady and I've no doubt you'll make good parents together. And another grandchild is always to be welcomed.

All my love.

Kip Fenn to Julie Fenn
April 2038

I thought the funeral went well considering. Tom had become a sad man, and I don't think he enjoyed retirement at all. I was considering what you said, about being sorry for what was, and grateful for what wasn't. That's not like you at all, it's far too pessimistic a view. As you said in a letter earlier this year, how can we know in advance the way a thing will turn out. We do our best, that's all we can do.

But I'm writing to tell you that Diana, whose birthday it was yesterday, is pregnant and joyful again. In the summer or autumn, when you've retired, will you come and visit us?

Julie Fenn to Kip Fenn
July 2038

It's funny, but I think more about Tom now he's dead than I did when he was alive.

The school gave me a grand send off; I kept bursting into tears. I've attached a short camclip, although I'm a bit embarrassed by all the attention I was given.

To stave off the worst of retirement I've accepted a part-time (voluntary) advisory post with the Independent Education Authority. Now Ireland's reunification is finally complete and off the Westminster agenda, I'm hoping Garth Fuller's administration will refocus on domestic issues, and boost the Authority's mandate again. It might also do something about the stranglehold of the Academics.

I hope to have time to visit Leiden soon, or should I wait to the spring when the new baby will want to see its Gran?

All my love.

PART TWO

Crystal, the Pearly Way and Promotion

'There is no truth around me, not in love, not in charity, not in happiness, nor even in friendship. We are insignificant animals. Ants. We float around thinking we are gods, but we are no more or less than human ants, enslaved to selfishness, hope and money. We wallow in hypocrisy. I am suffocating. I write this book to breathe.'

No Reason to Live by Pearl Worthington (aged 15) (2041)

CHAPTER 13

OBSERVING MY GREAT GRANDDAUGHTER, MARIA

I know for certain I have one great grandchild. Her name is Maria Silva Magalhães. She is dark-skinned, so pretty, with mischievous eyes, high cheek bones, and thick glistening hair set up in a twig. She came yesterday, with her father, Juliano, one of Arturo's children, and her mother Eliane, who is from Recife in North Brazil.

Whereas most people might have trouble sorting out their family connections behind them, thanks to Arturo I have difficulty working out those in front of me, as it were.

Sometimes, on Saturday afternoons, I allow Chintz and others to make a special effort to transfer me from my fixed bed into a portable contraption so that I can be wheeled, preferably if the weather holds, into the gardens, or, if not, into the theatre room where some third-rate entertainer tries to raise the dead with comedy, magic or storytelling. The few times I've persevered through such shows it's thanks to Flora's creative and inspired heckling more than the quality of the entertainment.

Yesterday, though, it was a warm bright day, and I was taken out into the rose garden which is my favourite spot in early summer. Left alone for a few minutes, I closed my eyes, which was an odd thing to do: here I am, stuck in bed and in my room 24 hours a day, mostly communicating with a wallscreen or sleeping, and the instant I am brought out into the garden, I close my eyes. Sight can be too powerful a sensation. I sense more without it, the heat of the sun on my cheeks, the light breeze catching the edge of one ear, the fragrance of roses, and the chirruping of greenfinches in the laurel hedge or in the willow tree beyond. It is these sensations, more than any emotions towards Jay, for example, or Guido's children, or Maria, or surviving friends of mine, that cause me to regret the impending end of life. I mean no disrespect to those I love and those that may love me, rather that these sensations are a direct link to the essence of being alive, and thus draw attention somehow to what it must be like to lose that essence.

Since I settled here at Willow Calm Lodge, Jay has acted, with perfect generosity, as a coordinator for my visitors. And, since my death date was decided, he's cautiously contacted more distant friends and family with a view to encouraging them to make at least one visit during these final months.

To my knowledge, I have four grandchildren through Arturo – although I suspect there may be more. I never knew Arturo's first wife Edna, but I did meet their (or his) cloned daughter Alicia once. She disappeared in her late teens. I have, though, met his second wife Fatima and their three children, Ignacio, Juliano and Tina. Juliano is the only one of these three to have married and started a family. Of the whole clan, Tina, the youngest, is my favourite. She must be about 30 by now. When I saw her as a teenager she reminded me strongly of Gabriella, a composite Gabriella in my mind that is, part Amado character, part Gabriella on the bus all those years ago in Brazil, and part Conceição, Tina's grandmother. Jay tells me Tina may come to England in the autumn.

I am conscious of the fact that I have not yet even introduced Arturo adequately, so it is fortuitous I don't have much to say about Maria or her parents. Jay, who had sponsored their air fares (with my money), had also advised them that, given my condition, they need not stay long. Conversation was awkward since my Portuguese was poor, and their English was little better. When Jay was speaking, I let my eyes wander to watch Maria race across the lawn chasing after a ball. She tumbled over her own feet. This triggered in me another type of sorrow, not the self-pity I had touched earlier, but a contradictory one born of angst for the future. If Maria's world is going to be similar to the one I have experienced, suffering of some kind at a personal and a public level will never be far away. But then she scrambled to her feet, straightened down her bright pink top in a precocious way, and carried on running to kick and chase the ball. A few minutes later, she ran back to where we were sitting. I asked her to climb gently up on my lap, so Jay could take a camclip of us together.

On leaving, Juliano and Eliane each gave me a kiss on the cheek. Their kisses made me feel as if I were already a corpse propped up in a coffin. Having seen them out, Jay returned to the rose garden and asked if I wanted them to visit again at the end of their week-long package tour around the British Isles. Only if they must, I said.

'I liked them,' Jay volunteered.

'Me, too. I'm glad they came, really I am. I'm very happy to have met Maria, and to know she has seen me in the flesh, or what's left of it.'

'I don't think Ignacio will make it this year. As far as I can tell, he's devoting himself to local politics, in Pernambuco with Grupo Hijo de Jesus, the Son of Jesus group. His emails come with flyers about the movement. Did you know it has 20 million members in Brazil, 35 million in Mexico and nearly as many in the US? I'm only a click away from salvation.'

'Can I ask,' I said, 'that you send Juliano one of the cam-clips, the one with Maria on my lap, and me brushing a hand through her hair. I bet she was grimacing.'

I let my eyelids fall, thinking I might catch the bird song again, or the scent of floribundas; but Jay was in a talkative mood.

'For a straight guy, Pa, you've created a right motley crew of kids, with one exception. Which is ironic.' I like that Jay calls me Pa. It was a tradition in his mother's family. Lizette called her father Pa while he was alive, and after his death she never talked about 'my father', only ever about 'Pa'. Jay went through a stage, in his late teens, when he thought himself too old for the familiar term, but he came back to it.

'Not ironic, if you follow the science of the matter and attribute this, er, "motley" gene to my DNA.'

Jay, a good 15 centimetres shorter than I was before old age shrunk me down, but with more handsome facial features, is not my blood kin, no more than I was Tom's. Lizette was already with child when she and I fell in love, and it was partly because of my experience and influence that she agreed to the idea of nurturing Jay with me through a co-op.

'I'm not convinced a motley gene would be enough to explain Crystal's troubled life.' This was Jay prompting me, since he knew I had been planning to write about her and thought I might want to use him as a sounding board.

'No, not at all. A motley gene? I doubt it. Swathes of bad luck, definitely, for she was certainly caught in a cultural swirl; but, most important of all, incompetent, derelict parenting, mine and Gillian's.'

'It's a long time ago now.'

'Over 50 years.' I lowered my eyelids again.

'Are you tired? Do you want to go in?'

'Jay, I wish you'd find someone new. It's not as if you are as young as you were once.'

'What brought this on?' he asked. I kept my eyes closed lightly and began wondering if I could evoke any of the fragrances from the Taunton House garden. 'As it goes, I've heard from Vince. We're meeting next week. He broke his back two months ago doing some mad-fool stunt skiing in Austria, and now he's convalescing. He sounds repentant. You look tired, Pa, shall I take you in?' Jay asked again.

'I'm pleased. I worry about you living alone, being alone.'

'I'm OK Pa.'

'I know you are. But I've been remembering too much about Crystal; that weekend she came to Leiden, in May 43. Without the pill menu, the memory enhancers, I'd never be able to write these Reflections, and sometimes I wish ... I doubt if I should be doing it.'

'The visitors were tiring, you'll feel better later. You don't have to carry on, Pa, you can stop at any time.' Jay can be mildly patronising, but it's too late to fight it or change him. He means so well, and I wouldn't want to hurt his feelings.

I let Jay wheel me inside. He stood watching as I was ably transferred back into my bed, and then, when I pretended sleep, he departed quietly. The medication may be helping my memory, but without Jay's support, his love, and his companionship I doubt I would have the resolve and the perseverance to make headway with these Reflections, too many of which are difficult, dark and painful.

CHAPTER 14

IN WHICH CRYSTAL SHOWS UP IN LEIDEN

Crystal, my oldest child, dropped out of college when only 17. I had been given no hint of an impending problem, and the first I knew about it was a simple email from Gillian – this was in the autumn of 2042 – telling me that our daughter had left home and was living with a boyfriend called Vidrio, an artist. The two were no better than Scavengers, Gillian said, and there was nothing to be done.

I tried calling and messaging Crystal to no avail. When I flew to London a few days later, she refused to answer my requests to meet. By interrogating Gillian, I discovered our daughter had been spending most of her time playing intensive screen games or roaming the streets with graffiti artists. She had shown no interest in qualifications, and, since starting college the previous September, had threatened to leave home. Only the lack of money had prevented her. Then Vidrio came, and led her into the night.

Despite many emails to Gillian and to Crystal over the subsequent months, I learned next to nothing about Crystal's activities, until, that is, she turned up unexpectedly in Leiden a few days before her 18th birthday, in May 2043. By then, Diana and I had been living in the Oldwijkgaarten house for nearly five years, and Guido was three and a half. These were busy, productive and mostly happy times. During Guido's early years, Diana had trimmed back her working life, but, when we entered him into pre-school, she re-integrated herself into the theatre world with gusto. I looked after Guido when I could, taking full advantage of the flexi-time laws (and over-working in compensation). When either Diana or I were away, we relied extensively on a caring and generous widow called Elly, who lived nearby and missed her own children. Incidentally, Elly's nephew ran an excellent local cheese and produce store.

Crystal materialised late on a Thursday afternoon. The previous night I had flown back from Washington, and, for various reasons, I was not due into the office until Monday.

Diana was at a theatre somewhere, and Guido and I were in the Oldwijkgaarten common area showing our neighbours how to play cricket. I did not recognise the girl walking towards us. Dressed entirely in shades of grey, with a scarf covering her head, and a black material bag on her back, she could have walked out of a late 19th century photograph of gypsies I'd seen once. There was no smile of recognition, nor did she stop for a moment to allow a pause in our playful antics; instead she walked right to me, and, as if we were but acquaintances, put out her hand for me to shake.

'Hi Dad. I'm not too good. Can I stay for a day or two?'

I called Guido over to say hello to his sister, which he did dutifully before rushing off to collect the cricket ball and continue playing. I led Crystal inside, thinking we might drink tea and talk, but she only wanted to bathe and sleep. I called Diana to fore-warn her, before going back out to find Guido screaming with laughter, and the cricket bat being used in a tug-of-war.

I have tried consciously over the years to hold on to the memory of that long weekend, for it is the best I have of my only daughter. I had taken Friday off work partly to attend an auction of vintage photographs at Swann's in Amsterdam, so I cajoled Crystal into accompanying me. On the train, she remained mute and self-absorbed, responding to my few questions with single syllable answers. Her ash-coloured headscarf, with its mottled pattern, vaguely resembled a moonscape, and I remember thinking my daughter might as well be on the moon. I distracted myself from anxiety by reading through the glitzy catalogue sent me from New York.

During this harmonious period of my life, and encouraged by Diana, I had assembled a very modest collection of vintage photographs and begun to educate myself on how to store and care for them. I paid three auction companies to send me their paper and digital catalogues regularly. I collected them with commitment, and often copied the larger reproductions into Neil. Only once or twice a year did I actually take part in an auction and make any purchases.

Crystal must have expected to see the old photographs themselves, because, having shown no apparent interest in our journey or its purpose, on arriving at Swann's she suddenly asked what was going on. I explained how the physical auction was taking place in New York, but that roomfuls of prospective buyers in Tokyo, Amsterdam, Milan and São Paulo were participating as if they were there in person. Huge wallscreens on either side of the Amsterdam auction room showed the item on sale from two different angles, and the central screen was fixed on the hammer-man. Bidders could either employ the traditional signal, waving a hand holding a special card which the intellicams would pick up, or utilise a keypad by each seat. It was a bit slow for some compared to a one-site auction, but pure entertainment for an enthusiast such as me: all those fabulous photographs, given a provenance, described in loving detail and displayed on the screens.

Although prices were below the peak levels of a decade earlier, gasps erupted whenever the hammer went down on an item at over $100,000. I might have bought an E J Constant Puyo nude for around $1,000 but Crystal's presence intimidated me; instead I spent nearly $2,000 on three Japanese portraits, albumen prints by Felice Beato, each one hand-tinted. None were in the best of condition, nevertheless, I felt it was a good price. (When they were delivered, a week later, I scanned them into Neil, and Diana used the scans to create and print out a special card for Crystal, a memento of her visit. I waited in vain for an address to mail it to.)

We left the auction house on Prinsen Canal, ate a bagel and drank chocolate, and then strolled along Keizersgracht – all in silence. When we reached the stretch of canal in the Asser photograph, I started rambling on about the area and its importance to me, about meeting Diana, falling in love, and our first morning together walking hand-in-hand. And then, suddenly, as if a gag had been removed, Crystal began to chatter and prattle, barely stopping to take breath, much like her mother at times. Initially, she launched an attack on me.

'How can you do that, spend $2,000 in a moment, on a few bits of paper that mean nothing to anyone? Did you see that beggar on the bridge back there? $2,000 for what? Don't you know how hungry people are in Ethiopia, in Bangladesh? How ill people are everywhere, ill in their bodies, and ill in their minds? You could have given that money to the Red Cross, saved lives. It was obscene, watching you and all those others spend millions for nothing, on nothing. It's evil.'

But she wasn't talking directly to me, she kept her eyes sternly down focused towards the ground, while her head kept bobbing backwards and forwards as if trying to punch out, from inside, the obscenities she was talking about. I did not interrupt, I let her rant on about hunger and religious terrorism and injustice and disease and capitalism. After a while, she began to denounce the specific opinions of her mother or well-known politicians or her teachers, and to reveal a passionate support for the more anarchic ideas of her friend Vidrio. When she paused for breath and I asked her, very quietly, to tell me about Vidrio, she did.

Vidrio (Spanish for glass) was not his real name, but a self-appointed pseudonym. According to Crystal their affair lasted many months but had finished abruptly when, one morning, he had decided Berlin, not London, needed his art and talents. His life's work, I learned, was etching graffiti on glass, usually that found in expensive cars and shop windows. Glass etching had become a real urban problem at that time (one fairly minor symptom of the endemic social terrorism in many cities) largely due to the availability of affordable etching/staining guns. Many countries had lightly outlawed the machines, yet they could be obtained easily enough. Yobbish youth culture, as typified by the Scavengers, tended to view glass etching as the fine art of graffiti skills. Poor Crystal, she saw Vidrio as a cross between Van Gogh and Vi Hoop, combining the artistic talent of the one and the passion for freedom from religious intolerance of the other. Who's to say she was wrong.

Intoxicated by love or poisoned by rejection, Crystal could not stop herself pursuing Vidrio by phone and email. I remember exactly the words she used when, as we walked around Paddington only three months later, I thoughtlessly enquired if she'd heard any more of Vidrio: 'He told me to fuck off. He said I was only his London fuck-chick, and I didn't know shit about art, or cock, or politics. And he'd never have looked at me twice but for my name. That's what he told me.'

We spent the rest of the Friday in Amsterdam – thankfully Dominique was able to cover for me by driving over from Utrecht to collect Guido from school – mostly walking and talking. She told me of her mother Gillian's cycles of depression and boyfriends, and recounted various tales about au pairs she and Bronze had put up with over the years. She had nothing favourable to say about her brother.

When I eased the conversation around to her education and whether there might be any possibility of her continuing to study, she clammed up abruptly. Half an hour later, she leaned over an old iron railing and stared wistfully down at a barge decked out with flowers moving slowly along the canal. This led us on to find a tourist boat and to sign up for an hour long tour complete with an English-speaking guide.

Afterwards, sitting in the quiet of the Begijnhof early evening, Crystal came round to asking questions about Diana and Guido and me. She expressed genuine astonishment when I gave a much simplified account of the IFSD and my work therein. For a minute or two, she looked at me with something akin to respect in her eyes. I was amazed too. How could my daughter have grown up, be almost an adult, and not know me, or who I was, or what I did? Unfortunately, there was no one to blame for this but myself.

CHAPTER 15

IN WHICH WE CELEBRATE CRYSTAL'S BIRTHDAY

Diana and I swept aside most of our joint and separate plans for the weekend, so that I could spend as much time as possible with Crystal.

On the Saturday, she and I took the train to The Hague, and I showed her round the IFSD building and my office. We stopped by the public relations department, where someone was invariably busy, weekdays and weekends, and I asked to be shown a promotion film for a recently-approved aid programme. I was keen to impress Crystal, not so much with my role, but with the fact that important efforts were always being made to help and support developing countries, even if this was not apparent in the daily media. However, she walked out of the screening before five minutes had passed. I guessed she could not cope (or did not want to cope) with the size of the funding figures or the scale of the works being undertaken, and preferred to allow a youthful prejudice against office buildings, full of nothing but paper, screens and computers, to extinguish any spark of interest in my work and the IFSD.

We walked by the town hall, which didn't interest her at all, and stopped for refreshments at Jaspar's. As Crystal had withdrawn into herself again, I thought I might get back on her wavelength if I told the tale of how Rike Thomas had tried to threaten me in this very bar, but she yawned repeatedly and, apropos of nothing at all, interrupted to request we go to a games room. One of the waiters at Jaspar's directed us to Houdijk's, 20 minutes walk away in an area of town I had never visited.

In Houdijk's, a large basement café decorated in black and silver with aluminium furniture and grey terminals, Crystal was perfectly camouflaged. We waited half an hour at the bar for a table and a free terminal. Crystal may have tried to explain her favourite netgame of the moment, Final Oblivion, but her explanations went over my head. When I sat down to watch, though, my stomach churned. The object of Final Oblivion was to commit suicide, and to do so with a mission at one of many levels. The missions included the following: causing as much chaos and destruction against dark forces as possible; assisting an avatar with doubts about the ecstasy waiting beyond; and overcoming personal demons (the Pearl Worthington way).

Crystal skillfully avoided other players' crazed suicides and psychological quagmires, and had clearly developed a real expertise at the game. In the corner of the screen, a counter showed that more than half a million people worldwide were playing concurrently. For the sake of our very recent and fragile friendship, I made no comment.

Later that day we returned to Amsterdam so Crystal could inspect Vondel Park, where so many FTM protests had congregated, and where, in recent years thanks to Dutch government initiatives, FTM festivals had become more popular than lawless marches.

Prompted by a further request from Crystal, this time to walk on a dike, Diana arranged for the four of us on Sunday to drive to Hoorn, north of Amsterdam, where a friend showed us around the pretty harbour. We made various stops on the way there and back, not least at Edam, and near Uitdam, where we fought the wind on dike-top foot and cycle paths. Spread across Ijsselmeer, we could see hundreds of modern yachts, windsurfers, parasailers, and the traditional sniks and skutsjes. Despite the apparently idyllic scene, large parts of the surrounding countryside had, in the previous 15 years, twice been devastated by storms and dike breaches. Many lives were lost on both occasions. Successive governments continued to insist that most areas remained safe, and to pour public money into never-ending improvements of the internal and external sea defences. Nevertheless, large-scale regional evacuations – ordered and spontaneous – had become increasingly common. In the years to come, the sea would reclaim some of the land we could view that day, especially in Flevoland, the largest of the polders which the Dutch had so successfully exploited for more than a century.

I possess a few delightful photos from that day. There are several of Crystal with Guido and/or me, and one, taken by Crystal herself, of Diana, Guido and me. These are the pictures which are most deeply associated with my feelings of love for Crystal, the love that I had never been allowed (by Gillian or myself) to express, and of grief, and of guilt.

On the Monday evening, Crystal's last with us, we went to Dominique's house. Crystal and Dominique had met on the Friday, and Dominique had suggested we all come for supper on Monday. Having forgotten, initially, it would be Crystal's birthday, I had agreed. I suspect Crystal spent most of that day gaming, although she did return to Oldwijkgaarten with a few new clothes purchased with the money I'd given her. I left work earlier than usual, returned home first, and then drove the four of us to Utrecht.

Visiting Dominique and Waltar Meijer and their two lively sons, Jurian and Lukas, then aged around nine and eleven, was always a pleasure, their house being full of easy good humour, gentle activity, bright decorations and a multitude of house plants.

Crystal did her best to relax and join in, responding politely to Waltar's queries about her activities over the weekend. For a while, before dinner, she helped Guido defend himself against the Meijer boys physical teasing, and I saw flashes of a carefree childish Crystal. As a climax to the dinner, Dominique brought out a fantastic cake, topped with lavender-flavoured berries and 18 candles.

Through a haze of chatter and laughter, Dominique asked Crystal to blow out the candles. Guido stood up on his chair and, so cutely, asked Crystal if he could help blow them out too. She stared at the cake and the candles and at Guido. For a second, no more, all the chatter in the room subsided, as if waiting for Crystal to answer Guido. But the sudden silence must have left her feeling exposed and scared for she shoved her chair back sharply, stood up and raced out of the room. Dominique followed but soon returned saying Crystal wished to be left alone.

We barely spoke on the return journey from Utrecht, nor the next morning. As Crystal and I left the house for the station, Diana, instinctively but thoughtlessly, attempted to give Crystal an embrace and a kiss on the side of the cheek, but she shied away offering only a curt 'thank you'.

At the station, I too got a thank you, a softer one.

'Thanks Dad. It was good, wasn't it? I was afraid of coming. If you hadn't of been outside, you know, I might not ... Guido's nice. He looks like you. And thanks for the money. I'm going now.'

'Take care Crystal. Thanks so much for coming, it was really nice to see you. Come again soon. Come any time, any time at all. If you need the money for the plane or train fare, just yell. And write, please please write.'

'I'll try. Thanks.'

I watched Crystal climb aboard the train with mixed emotions. Among them I recognised anxiety about her future. But also I felt relief at having been allowed to experience a humble shred of paternity towards her. As usual, though, I completely underestimated, or refused to face up to, the depths of Crystal's anguish. I would only see her one more time, and then she would be dead.

CHAPTER 16

IN WHICH I TRAVEL TO NIGERIA

The days off work and Crystal's visit had already set my tight schedule back considerably. A pile of paperwork awaited me at the office after the Washington trip; and, by the weekend, I would be in Abuja, Nigeria's capital, for my third trip to the IFSD's African offices there.

I need to backtrack for a moment to put my working life in context. During the summer of 2040, it had looked as though the world leaders, scheduled to meet in Djakarta that autumn, would not be ready to agree on detailed implementing arrangements for the second global increase in overseas development aid and expansion of the International Fund for Sustainable Development. Thus many of us in the IFSD were expecting a re-run of the Vancouver summit failure. However, a week before the Djakarta summit, anti-West and anti-Christian demonstrations flared up so violently across Java and Sumatra, but especially in the capital, that the meeting was hastily relocated to Oslo (conveniently for us). Parallel demonstrations across the rest of the developing and Muslim world were sufficient to persuade the recalcitrant Western leaders (led by the US and Japan) into a politically dramatic u-turn, relinquishing their hard-line nationalistic positions.

The huge boost in development aid resources actually agreed at Oslo (i.e. the second stage 0.25% increase) allowed the IFSD to expand again, in The Hague and in Abuja, and with new main offices in Islamabad and Manila. Thereafter, we, in the IFSD's Future Policy Division, were able to focus exclusively on working towards the third incremental increase of 0.25% – or, as it became known internationally, the Next Step.

In my role as deputy director, Pravit exploited me as his organiser-in-chief for tidying up loose ends, or for modest liaison responsibilities with other IFSD divisions. And he employed me shamelessly whenever he felt a white face could achieve more than a brown one. 'We must work within the realities of the realities,' he would say confident of my understanding. I did not appreciate these tasks, and in the time leading up to the Djakarta/Oslo summit, in 2040, I began to feel I had been sidelined. I watched unit heads, such as Ninel Horeva, press steadily forward and achieve tangible results. I also observed Pravit move from one crisis to another, using his considerable political and diplomatic skills to ease each team's work over apparently insurmountable barriers. By contrast, my own, often bureaucratic, input felt intangible and diffuse. On a few rare occasions, I failed to hold back my grumbles, but Pravit regularly managed to redefine or explain my role and assignments in such a way that I exited from his office refreshed with commitment.

Soon after the Oslo meeting, though, Pravit found his time increasingly absorbed by the IFSD's hierarchy. This was because the agreement in Oslo had been bought at the expense of major compromises which created new and unexpected working complexities. As a consequence, increasingly during 2041 and 2042, he called on me, his deputy, to stand in for him as the head of the Future Policy Division. Thereafter, though the demands on his time outside the Division gradually diminished, he never attempted to reclaim the full power of his position.

In May 2043, a few days after Crystal's unexpected visit, I travelled to Nigeria. During two previous visits to the country, I had failed, through lazy planning, to catch up socially with Alfred. This time, however, work itself brought us together (as it would several times over the next few years). Alfred had moved sideways and upwards within Ojoru's administration and, by this time, had become a key adviser on certain agriculture and environment issues.

I had not seen Alfred in person for seven or eight years, not since he had finished his doctorate and returned to Nigeria. Yet such is the power of childhood friendship, even only intermittently refreshed, that I could barely keep a smile off my face during the flight in anticipation of meeting him again. And, at the airport, we greeted each other like long lost brothers. I had already agreed by email to put myself in his hands for the remainder of the day, Sunday, so first he drove me to my hotel and from there to a sports park in the city suburbs. Normally, on a Sunday night, he explained, he would be busy training the Capital Warriors for great exploits in the all-Nigeria volleyball cup, but, in honour of my visit, the first and second teams had agreed to play a demonstration match.

'I told them it was necessary to show a great English setter how champion Africans play.'

'I don't need reminding how well Africans play, Alfred.'

'Ah, but you should see Sanfry – he's one of the best. He's made the Nigeria team already, and he's only 17.'

Unfortunately, Sanfry (short for Sanfrancissisi, apparently) didn't turn up that night, causing Alfred to spend an angry few minutes on the phone. Nevertheless, the Capital Warriors put on a splendid display, and I told them so. Afterwards, Alfred took me to his modest home, a small, newly-built detached concrete bungalow, with a plot of long shaggy dry grass. He introduced me to his beautiful and very young wife, Fayola, and their two year old son Fela, named after the great 20th century Yoruba singer.

Steering well clear of our own business which would start on the following day, we talked mostly about international affairs. Although I had seen glimpses of the old Alfred at the sports park, his personality had become more sombre than I remembered, weighed down, it appeared, by Africa's troubles. Some years earlier, a terrible drought had laid waste vast regions across the whole of the southern Sahara. All the affected countries (Sudan, Chad, Mali, Burkina Faso, and parts of Nigeria) were still dealing with the long-term consequences of the resulting famines, plagues and migrations. Alfred was intent on reminding me of past horrors, and present troubles.

When I asked about his family and his wife and son, he brushed off such questions and wanted to know whether I approved of NATO (the New Allies Treaty Organisation which had evolved out of the North Atlantic Treaty Organisation) stepping up the terms of its treaty obligations with India.

More specifically, he asked what I thought about the use of the phrase 'a major act of aggression' to define any NATO decision to become physically involved in protecting the remnants of Indian Kashmir. He believed that the United Nations should have done more, from the 2020s, to tackle the growth of Christian-Muslim tension, and that Europe should have done more to curb US tendencies to press NATO to become involved in religion-based conflicts. Every move by the US or Europe to bolster Christianity in Asia and in Africa, he opined, strengthened the Islam cause. In one particularly maudlin moment, before he took me back to the hotel, he turned prophet.

'The IFSD is swimming against the tide. It's only a matter of time before there's a real war. Five years or 20, it's inevitable now.'

I had come to Abuja with a briefcase full of tasks, but my main – yet undeclared – purpose was to investigate why one stream of negotiations, led by our agriculture team, had stalled. The team leader, a German national (with a very French name), Louise Pavard, had repeatedly come to Pravit and myself complaining that Nigeria on its own and the African Union (representing almost all countries south of the Sahara) was refusing to attend low-level negotiating meetings. She claimed that African states were asking for utterly unreasonable commitments on the share of funding to go to African agriculture. Moreover, she said, donors, such as the US and Australia, and recipients, such as the Latin American countries, had threatened to boycott any future discussions if the African states did not moderate their 'illicit demands'. The African Union position in general and Nigeria's specifically were being further complicated by an escalation of internal conflicts between, essentially, the Islam and Christian dominated regions and factions.

All Monday, I sat through a meeting of the committee that liaised between the Future Policy Division and the African Union secretariat. The Future Policy Division's coordinators, based in Abuja, did most of the work. I intervened with explanations or potential solutions here and there, and every-thing proceeded as normal. Only when we came to the subject of agriculture did the meeting fall apart, mostly because the African Union's own representatives contradicted each other. I sensed, as it was my job to do, that something else was going on. Alfred, who was there with observer status, remained silent throughout the meeting, and left before I could catch him afterwards. The next day, I was due at the Nigerian Ministry of Agriculture for a courtesy introduction to a new minister and for discussions with his advisers (including Alfred). However, before I had shaved, my phone rang. Alfred, all formal and business-like, told me that my meetings had been cancelled, and, against my protests, offered no explana-tion. He did, though, say he would be arriving in one hour to take me on a guided tour. I didn't seem to have a choice about the matter.

CHAPTER 17

IN WHICH ALFRED INTRODUCES ME TO OJORU

A guided tour of Abuja University! To get there, we drove through a few respectable neighbourhoods, some dominated by residences and office blocks in the neo-Tropical style. These were generally free of traffic jams. Most of the journey took us through areas typical of those to be found in many African cities: dense traffic, squalid and not-so squalid street shacks and semi-slums, unrepentant bustle and noise, and patchworks of colour in the midst of much grimness. However, Abuja was not as bad as Lagos, which, despite Ojoru's many advances (and the famous IFSD-funded 'golden' dikes protecting Lagos Island) had failed to lose its 'shitty city' moniker.

Life of all sorts – student traffic, games, teaching circles, snack sellers – teemed around the university buildings. Alfred began my tour at the tallest block, for teaching medicine. He showed me the well-stocked library, the lecture rooms, and the well-equipped laboratories, all supported by UN agencies. Then he showed me the artistically-furbished, but very different, Christian and Islam foundations, and explained that they were financed jointly by the federal government and the churches. A few other parts of the university appeared no poorer than a badly-funded European college, but Alfred's purpose was to bring me to the impoverished agricultural science and technology block, a concrete shell of a building with its rooms all empty but for a few broken chairs and tables. We stood outside in the muggy heat, and, finally, Alfred came to the point.

'Education, my friend, education. We need intelligent farmers, people who can read and write and understand money, and who know how to learn to look after their lands in good and bad times. We need farmers who are neither stuck in traditional ways nor taken in by Western salesmen, who can deal with suppliers and government agencies, who can read and research for themselves, who understand the importance of long-term sustainability, who can look ahead and manage their crops and animals with confidence and foresight. It's not that this building doesn't have the facilities of an Oxford college, you know as well as I that much of the teaching is done at home through the net. Yet this building says it all for me. We've had dribs and drabs of help from the UN for agricultural science and education; and there have been projects up and down the continent, but they've petered out, or collapsed in the face of financial and cultural difficulties.' Alfred looked tired and worn out, but there was hope in his eyes, a touch of zeal wanting out.

'Our belief now is that these efforts have always failed because they've never been implemented on a large enough scale. The IFAD and Unesco have never had the muscle. There has been no momentum on this issue. Only the IFSD has the resources and the clout to make a difference. Yet, my friend, as you know better than most, education and training are not considered part of the IFSD framework; they were not included within the Fund's mandate, because of IFAD, because of Unesco. This was a terrible mistake.' A group of unruly students rushed by. 'We've tried before now to open discussions on widening the IFSD mandate, but have been blocked at every turn. This time we're determined. Very determined. Now, come, I want you to meet someone. We must be punctual.'

We drove to the president's Palace. It took about half an hour to get there and another half hour to work our way through security and into an ornately decorated reception room. We waited a further hour which gave me plenty of time to examine the European-style portraits (I could only recognise Ojoru), the exquisite traditional hangings (batik-style), and the beautifully intricate wood-carved sculptures and panels by a famous 20th century artist called Lamidi Olonade Fakeye. Alfred refused to chat, or to confirm for whom we might be waiting. Then, he took a phone call, ushered me to my feet and guided me towards the centre of the room.

Ojoru, surrounded by three assistants or bodyguards, entered the room in a gust. He came within a metre of where I was standing. He was slighter than I expected, and more human. I had only ever seen him in the flesh from a distance. I confess that I was slightly awestruck. All I had the presence of mind to notice was that his eye whites shone (like an actor's) and that he was dressed in a trim cream-coloured suit with crimson darts.

'Alfred has talked of you, Kip Fenn. He says you are a man of faith in people, and a man with foresight. I am glad of that. There is much to be done.'

'Yes, sir.' For several seconds Ojoru continued to peer into me. Everyone in the room remained motionless and silent. I debated internally whether to mention that I'd been there, in the European Parliament more than 20 years earlier, when he had delivered his famous mantra, but I felt too intimidated to speak further. It was as much as I could do to hold his gaze. Suddenly, he made a decision and put out his arm towards me. Instinctively, I stepped forward to shake hands with him. He had a very firm warm hold.

'Thank you for coming,' he said. Almost immediately he turned about and, with his entourage in perfect step, exited. Curiously, for a moment I thought not of Ojoru, but of Crystal's cold and formal greeting a few days earlier in the Oldwijkgaarten garden.

Over lunch back at the IFSD building, Alfred loosened up. He explained that if I could find a way of widening the scope of the exploratory negotiations for the Next Step (this, as I've said, was how everyone came to talk about the third planned increase in Western overseas development aid) to include agricultural training and education, certain unreasonable African demands and differences might disappear.

I thanked him profusely for the honour of being introduced to Ojoru, but protested that he was overestimating my position, my responsibilities and what could be achieved at my level. Alfred thought not. He promised that a substantial and convincing plan, backed by academic research and intellectual analysis, would be forthcoming if and when it would be given proper acknowledgement and IFSD-backed circulation privileges. He also forecast that, if the idea gained legitimacy, the vast majority of beneficiary countries could be persuaded to gather in its support.

There were other meetings, and other business which I forget now, and a couple of meals out with Alfred. One evening, he persuaded me to borrow a pair of shorts and trainers, and knock a volleyball about with friends, including the tall, agile and smiley Sanfry, on an outdoor court near his house. The heat troubled me within minutes, the ball caught my left index finger badly, and then I fell, scraping a knee on the earth. I declared enough was enough and that my volleyball days had ceased long ago. Nevertheless, I did experience a buzz of pleasure seeing Alfred take so much enjoyment from the game.

On the flight home, I considered how I could achieve the mission that, in effect and thanks to Alfred, I had been given by Ojoru, one of the greatest men of the 21st century. It did seem an impossible task, especially since there had been previous failed attempts to enlarge the IFSD's aid framework to encompass education. Moreover, none of us at the IFSD were looking for new battles, and the entire Future Policy Division was working towards an objective – the Next Step – that many sane and intelligent intellectuals and politicians thought could never be achieved. And, while Western national leaders steered clear of being too publicly negative or defeatist about the chances for the Next Step, their opponents – international think-tanks, independent members of many parliaments, media commentators and others – had no such qualms. Nevertheless, somewhere over the Mediterranean, an idea did emerge.

The following day I secured a late interview with Pravit who listened to my verbal report with patience. I had intended not to tell him about the encounter with Ojoru (after all nothing had actually been said), but then found I could not properly communicate the importance of the matter without doing so. I proposed that it was all a mistake, brought about because of my friendship with Alfred, and that it needed an older, wiser and more senior head than mine to find a way forward.

'Kip, you become trickier by the day. I do believe you are a tricky one, are you not?' Long pause. When he put such enigmatic questions, I usually found it best to remain silent. On this occasion, though, it was not the right tactic. 'Am I waiting forever then? All right, all right.' He was not in the best of moods, for otherwise he would have allowed us to saunter leisurely for a few minutes through the roles of master and pupil. 'My head is going to hurt tonight. Tell me your plan.'

And so I did. I have no wish to get bogged down in the nitty gritty of my working life, but, briefly, the plan – which in time partly succeeded inasmuch as any draft plan ever retains its original shape – was this. Firstly, it was necessary to deal with Louis Pavard, the team leader, who had repeatedly rejected all requests to circulate documents relating to agriculture education. She had refused to accept declarations on the subject citing the Next Step's mandate word for word, as if it were the Koran. Pavard was in the pocket of the German government which, most of the time, used its muscle to undermine the EU's generally positive approach to the IFSD. So, Pravit moved, through a German director of the IFSD board, who was not a closet nationalist, to replace Pavard with a younger more malleable and idealistic team leader.

Secondly, Pravit and I began to propagate, through our respective contacts within and without the organisation, the idea that we should not be falling back on defensive positions for the Next Step but that, conversely, a new bold idea would help inspire support for it. And education – at least in terms of farming practices – was that idea. It was no longer feasible, we claimed, to believe real sustainable development of land resources would be possible without earmarking a very significant proportion of aid for teaching farmers (not a few hundred here and there, but tens of thousands, hundreds of thousands) how to profit from and, crucially, care for their land better.

Thirdly, over the next six months I travelled extensively to the capital cities of many Western donor countries, mostly those that were positively interested in seeing the Next Step succeed. At meeting after meeting with ministerial advisers (where I could get them), senior civil servants and all kinds of experts, I explained our current difficulties, our need for a new momentum, and the reason why a revision of the existing Next Step mandate was now being proposed. Often it was a thankless and dispiriting task, and, especially in the autumn during the weeks after Crystal's death, I lacked the necessary diplomatic energy (as Pravit would call it) to do the job effectively.

By the end of the year, however, doors began to open more freely, and a growing sympathy for our approach was evident at many of my follow-up meetings. In advance of the April 2044 negotiating session in Mexico City, I took a gamble and attempted to coordinate a large group of donors who were prepared to ask for a revision of the mandate. In parallel, Pravit braved the IFSD board.

There were all kinds of attempts to derail and block us (not least those stemming from other UN agencies, such as the IFAD and Unesco, involved with agriculture and education respectively). For the first three days of the Mexico meeting, I was apprehensive, believing they might have succeeded: some of the support I had so carefully fostered appeared to be drifting. But, while I had been arguing the case with the donors, Alfred's team had been hard at work too. When it became clear, on the fourth day in Mexico, that there was near unanimous support from the recipient countries for 'the role of education and training in sustainable development of agricultural practices' to be considered for the Next Step, more donors than I expected hesitantly pressed their green buttons. The opposition, suddenly isolated and spot-lighted, fell away tamely.

For the next two years, until the second Djakarta summit (not relocated this time, thanks to highly controversial policing methods), 'the role of education and training in sustainable development of agricultural practices' became one of the main motors for the negotiations. It was during this period that Pravit retired suddenly for health reasons, and after a short period as 'acting head', I was promoted to head of the division.

It is possible, I should say, that Pravit retired slightly earlier than he might have done so as to allow for my promotion prior to a change of government in Britain. Already in 2044 it was evident that Fuller's centre coalition would not last a third term; and Pravit understood that a future Conservative administration might not provide the necessary behind-the-scenes national support for my promotion.

CHAPTER 18

IN WHICH ALAN'S WORK ON FLOODS IS PUBLISHED

Before my promotion, though, my heavy work load led to a series of conflicts with Diana, and the most uncomfortable period so far in our ten year relationship. In the summer of 2043, Diana and I had promised (or casually planned depending on the point of view) to visit our Canadian friends, Ike and Augusta Davidson, in Montreal. So, when I declared, several weeks after the Abuja visit, that I would no longer be able to take a full vacation in the summer, Diana responded angrily. Following much discussion and argument about alternative arrangements, we decided that Guido and she would go without me.

As part of the same decision, and somewhat resentfully I judged at the time, she objected to joining me in London for a family-oriented weekend in early September, soon after her return from North America. My mother, Julie, and her brother and my Uncle Alan were the focus of that weekend. On the Friday, I went to Alan's book launch, and on Saturday Alan and I helped Julie celebrate her 70th birthday with a lunch party. I also spent Sunday afternoon with Bronze at the cinema; and I delayed my return trip to the Monday morning so as to accede to an unexpected request from Crystal to meet up that evening in Paddington. As I've already disclosed (why is it so difficult to keep the chronology in order?) the latter was a distressing encounter.

Alan. I have all kinds of regrets about my life. Only stiff people, who live by imprinted route maps or hand-cuff themselves to pre-packaged religious models of being, can get to the end without regrets. Or so I like to believe. One of my regrets is that, over the years, I did not spend more time with Alan. He invited me to St Petersburg, where he lived for the last 20 years of his life, on numerous occasions, but somehow I never got round to going. He was one of the most intelligent and warmest and kindest of men I ever knew.

Officially, he had retired from WWF in the late 30s. Yet he continued to work as intently as ever, not only as an adviser to

WWF and others, but on his ambitious book. It took him more than ten years all told, and was finally published in September 43. *Floods: past, present, and future* (two atlas-sized volumes plus a major netsite) gained immediate plaudits from across the world, and soon became a standard reference work. Not only was it full of geographical and scientific explanations, cultural anecdotes and detailed historical notes, but it was replete with extraordinary photographs and illustrations, albeit often of tragedies. For the next decade, until old age slowed him down, he enjoyed a certain amount of fame, travelling far and wide to give lectures based on the book and the information he had amassed for the netsite.

Alan had arranged for the book launch to take place in the same week as his sister's birthday, not only for his own convenience but because he thought Julie would enjoy a touch of reflected glory. The publishers, Universities Press Inc, in conjunction with WWF, had engaged the International Geographical Society in a marketing deal which included use of the Society's premises for the launch. A maxiscreen displayed a slick slide show, moving occasionally into camclip footage; large-scale photographs from the work and of Alan adorned the walls; and the books themselves had been piled up with architectural skill on publisher glam-stands. Constrained by looking after my mother, I managed nevertheless to talk with Anna Mastepanov (Alan's partner) and Jude Singleton (my old boss from the Department of the Environment) who recounted a pleasingly awful anecdote about Rike Thomas. I also encountered Matt Fortune, an influential left-wing backbencher MP who, as a tireless campaigner for the IFSD cause, I already knew, and a sharp environmental journalist called Bobby Jespersen.

Part Danish and part American, Bobby had made a name for herself in Brussels by careful reporting on green issues for the *Wall Street Journal* and the London *Times*. She had written two books, one on European-US environmental policy conflicts, and another which analysed in detail how Europe had won the battle for the initial expansion of the IFSD. I knew she had excellent contacts in the IFSD, as elsewhere, but I personally had never spoken to her before. With a short squat body, far too much make-up, layers of odd clothes, and unkempt long mousy hair, she could have been 40 or 60. She was abrupt, almost rude in the way she interrupted my chatter with Julie; and she had no fluff talk at all. Despite her coarse outer shell, Bobby had a gift for probing intelligent conversation and also for listening purposefully and attentively. While declining to answer a barrage of questions about progress on the Next Step, I did agree to grant her an interview later that autumn. No sooner had she bounded out of earshot in search of further contacts, than my teacherly mother deemed her an 'oddball', which was the best she could do to disguise her dislike of the woman.

I only mention Bobby because some years later she and I developed a useful synergy, which I shall come to. Incidentally, she gave Alan's book a superb write-up.

After a couple of zinis and several short speeches, Julie and I took a cab to The Plains in Chelsea. Alan and his Russian partner Anna had invited approximately 30 friends to join them there for a post-launch late lunch. Julie sat next to a charming man she had encountered through Alan many years previously, and who lived in Ireland. As a consequence of this re-acquaintance, the two of them became correspondents to the end of my mother's life.

Halfway through the meal, Monique, Alan's old girlfriend, who had looked after me so well in Rio de Janeiro all of 20 years earlier, appeared. She had missed the launch party because of a four hour security hold-up on trains through the Channel Tunnel.

Having spent 12 years in Brazil, I learned, Monique had returned to Paris where her rainforest expertise was much in demand by international groups, including my own organisation, the IFSD. She had helped Alan on his book and was proud to show me, with exaggerated pride, her name listed as a key contributor. At one particular moment, she turned to watch Alan stand and affectionately embrace two people who were leaving.

'I love that man,' she said.

'Me too.'

My mother's birthday party, at the Dog & Pheasant in Brook, Surrey, followed on Saturday. Here on my screen is the camclip recorded by a friend of Julie's who had travelled from Edinburgh to be there. It is precious for being the last clip I have of Alan, Julie and me together. Alan's friendly face is rounded by a trimmed white beard. He is laughing and raising a toast to his sister. Julie herself looks gloriously happy, and far from old. My first wife, Gillian, is scowling, and not communicating with anyone. She was invited largely to ensure the attendance of Bronze, so that, as a minimum, one of Julie's grandchildren would be present. And there I am in the camclip, making an effort to communicate with Bronze, whose face is covered in acne. I remember he wouldn't eat, and he complained about having to miss a religious march taking place in central London. I should have been grateful that Gillian and he came at all, at my request, but neither of them wasted much time being pleasant to Julie or me, and so I was relieved when they left early.

Later, I managed to spend an hour alone talking with Alan and Anna about the book, their plans and their life in St Petersburg. Anna spoke English moderately well and with an elegantly light accent. She must have been about 50 then. The two had first met in Kiev on a Ukrainian flood-relief project when she was 25, already with two children and a husband. Only later, after the marriage had disintegrated, and the two children had found high-paying jobs in far-flung corners of the Russian Federation, did she find Alan again. It was Anna who had persuaded him to slow down and settle permanently in St Petersburg. And, presumably, it was she who had provided a platform of domestic stability that allowed him to persevere for so long and complete the mammoth work on floods.

At the turn of the century, according to Alan's book, on average 1.5 million people were suffering in some way every year as a result of floods; in the late 20s and early 30s the figure peaked at around 5 million a year; and by the early 40s, had fallen back to around 2.5 million. Alan explained, in the book, how the turnaround had come about largely because the flooding cycles had increased to such a frequency that government policies and people themselves began to shy away from the most vulnerable areas. Furthermore, he showed how infrastructure investment, often led by the IFSD, had been instrumental in safeguarding important agricultural regions and many urban areas – there was even a sunset-lit picture of the Dutch-built dikes around Lagos Island.

CHAPTER 19

IN WHICH I LOSE MY DAUGHTER

We were not, though, living in happy times. While the cost in human life of flood damage may have been receding, other trends indicated that the golden era of oil and chips was fast coming to an end. Floods apart, man continued to be battered by increasingly unpredictable weather fronts with hurricanes bringing untold damage in a matter of hours, and droughts causing famines and plagues that lasted years. Religious conflict and intolerance were rising and arising day-by-day, and at every level whether in local communities or in the UN organisations. International affairs and diplomacy were often bogged down in efforts to bridge the growing religious divide. Many feared that NATO, its member countries under permanent verbal attack from the International Islam Brotherhood for Peace, was moving inexorably towards a defender of countries dominated by Christian peoples.

By this time, the First Tuesday Movement had already disintegrated into a patchy framework for religious protests, demonstrations and riots. Only the American continents, dominated by Christians faiths, were largely free of this particular affliction. Even there, though, in cities such as San Francisco, Quito, Rio and Buenos Aires young people regularly demonstrated their anger against US arms being sold to so-called friendly regimes or to freedom fighters in North Africa and the Middle East which just happened to proclaim secular or acceptably moderate religious objectives.

Many ordinary citizens, faced with the growing chaos in the world and a belief that a decade of popular protest had achieved nothing, turned inward seeking spiritual or religious solutions. Cults of all types found new adherents, while traditional religions, in all their variants, swelled their numbers. This served to further exacerbate and polarise religious strife. According to the social historian Gregory 'a worldwide plague of pessimism' emerged, especially among those who could not find solace in imaginary gods.

There was one non-religious cult, the Pearly Way, which brought a most terrible despair to millions of families. Gregory's *Suicide in the 21st Century*, published in the 60s, claimed that suicides worldwide increased from less than one million at the turn of the century to around two million in 2040. By 2043, this figure had grown to three million. It went on multiplying until it peaked in the late 40s at around five and a half million.

My daughter was but one single individual in these vast statistics.

But a girl named Pearl Worthington was more than just another statistic. In 2041, her recently-published book, called *No Reason to Live*, won a major US award for its insight into youthful despair and tragedy. On live television, minutes after receiving the award, and while still on the presentation stage, she pulled a plastic gun from her bag and fired a bullet into the side of her head. Cameras caught each horrifying moment in close-up detail, and the camclip made headlines in all the media, from Beijing to Santiago and from Helsinki to Cape Town. A week later, *GlobeOne* magazine ran an in-depth feature on suicide, with three words on the cover: 'The Pearly Way'. Pearl's book became an instant bestseller, and was quickly translated into dozens of languages. Across the world, but especially in Japan, Brazil, China, India, the US and the Scandinavian countries, unhappy men and women, young and old, followed Pearl's example, if not with a gun, then with pills or gas or by throwing themselves in front of metro trains or from tops of buildings and cliffs.

Pearl's mother, Xanthe Worthington, however, managed single-handed to turn what might have been a dreadful, but short-lived, fad into an appalling, tragic and permanent feature of our world. Xanthe, having started her adult life as a call girl, amassed a huge fortune by marrying and outliving a series of rich and very rich husbands. Pearl ran away from Xanthe mansion (or wherever) when only 14 and never spoke to her mother again. Her book, *No Reason to Live*, came to be seen as a suicide note, condemning society and the author's mother in roughly equal measure.

Following Pearl's death, Xanthe spent several months trying out psychiatric programmes and psychotherapists, but emerged one day, with the appearance of a nun not a queen, to tell the media she had decided to use her fortune in remembrance of Pearl. With a team of amoral and greedy businessmen, software engineers and security personnel, she moved to the renegade Martinez islands in the Caribbean and set up hundreds of netsites in dozens of languages. Some of these glamorised the idea and practice of suicide, providing information on simple and effective ways to kill oneself, and making funds available for regional propaganda. Others offered free downloads for playing simple individual screen games.

And yet others provided portals to the addictive netgames Final Oblivion I and II. Both of these were commissioned by Xanthe from a creative young game developer in Korea who later tried, ineffectively, to use his natural copyright (having sold the legal one) to close them down. Xanthe advertised the games widely, allowed the playing software to be distributed freely, and made no charge for involvement in the gaming universe. As the playing numbers increased exponentially, so her team worked round the clock to provide the necessary infrastructure in every continent.

It took Europe nearly three years, until 2046, to place an effective ban through Solar (the open Euronet) on the Oblivion games (by classifying them as Unacceptable Content), but efforts to prohibit them in the US and at the UN level failed altogether.

Xanthe herself died in 2048. It's possible she was poisoned by one of her employees, but the facts were never established. Thereafter, her associates fought among themselves, and the mini-empire quickly fell apart. By then, though, Xanthe's bitter and vindictive objective had succeeded all too well. Even in the Arab world, which suffered least from the cult because of the strictures of Islam, there were increased numbers of suicide bombers, disease-spreaders and fire-raisers, all ready to appease their anger and find glory wherever and whenever they could. In India, China and Southeast Asia there were epidemics of those dying slowly from hunger or quickly from earth burials. Mostly they were protesting against low pay, inhuman working conditions and poverty. In Catholic Latin America and Southern Europe, the suicide statistics were dominated by those eager to get to heaven and experience oblivion.

In Northern Europe and the US, we had them all: the oblivion seekers, the nihilist black-hole-and-outers and the Pearl copycats who used suicide to protest, whether against their lovers, their family or society. And, across the Western world of course, there was an explosion in the numbers of those ready and willing to make a quick easy escape from the trials of old age (plastic surgery sags and other cracked-mirror syndromes, pension failures, or body/brain dysfunctions).

Crystal killed herself on Wednesday 23 September 2043, only three weeks after she and I had walked through the streets of Paddington. She was found by a friend called Donna at a Scavenger's house in Streatham, South London. She had cut her wrists and was lying in a bath of blood and water. A note, in her handwriting, said only: 'All is annihilation, all is oblivion. I do this entirely on my own, and of my own free will. Crystal.' An autopsy found her stomach full of prescription pain killers and mood calmers. This, and evidence from the distraught Donna, were sufficient to convince the coroner that Crystal had taken her own life. She was cremated in Croydon at the same crematorium as her grandfather, Tom.

While the sun had shone for Tom, it only rained for Crystal. Apart from Diana and me, there were a handful of mourners: Gillian and a man friend, Bronze, Julie and three odd-looking acquaintances of Crystal. We all went our separate ways soon after it was over. I did attempt to exchange a few words with Bronze, to establish how he was coping, and whether he needed anything. He had become a fervent evangelical Christian by then, and believed his sister had done the right thing and gone to a better place, and that, therefore, there was nothing to grieve for.

'R. I. O., rest in oblivion, Crystal,' he said to me without a trace of irony.

My relations with Diana, which had been under strain since the summer, deteriorated during the journey back from London. On receiving the news about Crystal's death, she had been sympathetic, and generously agreed to accompany me to the funeral. On the train journey to London, she had allowed me to grumble, as I had done in the early days of our friendship, about Gillian. But Diana had a selfish streak – greatly tempered, I should add, by being a mother – which I never wished to acknowledge, let alone stand up to. During the return leg, Diana's thin shell of forbearance towards me crumbled. I was probably re-living the weekend Crystal had visited Leiden, or re-dissecting our walk and conversation in Paddington, when Diana snapped. I do not believe it was anything in particular I said, rather that she had waited until a nearby passenger moved so we would not be overheard.

'It's no good going over it again and again. She's dead. She was unhappy, and now she's dead. Bronze is right, she is in oblivion.'

'I don't believe in oblivion, you know that.'

'You left her a long time ago, it's your fault, it's Gillian's fault, it's the world's fault. What is done is done. Let it go.'

'No.' I felt offence. 'She was my daughter. She lived in pain. She died before she was even an adult. Whose fault is that? You want me to deny she existed, stop thinking about her, stop talking about her, forget about her altogether?'

'Yes.' This stark word stunned us both into silence. I felt she meant it literally and turned away towards the window. The request – or was it a command – felt threatening, not in itself, but because it meant I might have to re-evaluate the person who had made it, and from there, possibly, reconsider why I was loving her. It was easier to contemplate the rain battering the glass, and the rivulets streaming from one side to the other.

It took Diana a minute or so to continue her meaning, and to try and deflect her apparent callousness. 'Yes. Yes, stop thinking about her for now, stop talking about her. Please, for me. Not to forget her. Remember that you ruined the summer, that you are working too much, that you are always travelling. You want Guido to become like Crystal.' Instantly, she realised she had gone too far again. She apologised verbally, and physically too, by taking hold of my hand. Silently, I made yet another resolution to control my working hours and be more available for Diana and Guido. Yet, as with previous efforts, it was soon forgotten – for this was the time I was busy on my mission for Alfred, Ojoru and Africa.

Before leaving the subject of the Pearly Way I should add that I, personally, knew at least five other individuals who committed suicide in the 40s. They were: a Russian IFSD employee who had been caught trying to blackmail his line manager; a Japanese civil servant who negotiated in the IFSD committees on conditions and funding for solar energy and who had been passed over for promotion; an actress acquaintance of Diana who had been screamed at once too often by a director and who had never got over abuse by her parents; the mother of Waltar Meijer who was suffering from multiple sclerosis; and Rob, the brother of Melissa.

Rob had found his way to the house in Lacey's Lane several times in the 30s, evidently seeking the kind of financial handout Gillian and I had given him once. On each occasion, according to Gillian's emails, he had stated he was looking for me, so she had given him my address in Leiden and a few euros. He finally made it to Holland one weekend that same summer (2043) while Diana and Guido were in North America. He arrived with Imogen, a woman ten years his junior who acted like his self-appointed social worker. He had changed beyond recognition from our last meeting, about the time of Bronze's birth in 2028. Physically, he looked much tidier than when I'd last seen him, although his unbearded face carried several shaving nicks, and his suit would have fitted a taller, fatter man. Mentally, he reminded me of a dull and doltish teenager, one devoid of character.

The nervous and shy Imogen explained that Rob had talked of making this trip for so long that she had finally consented to organise it and accompany him. They stayed for one afternoon only (thankfully), during which time we took a short walk around the Leiden sights, and ate ice cream in the touristy Mars Bar, one of Guido's favourite places, on Nieuwe Rijn.

Rob struggled to talk at all, so Imogen raised the topic of Melissa for him. Rob's memory of that fateful afternoon had become so distorted or muddled up with other memories, I learned, that Imogen did not even know for sure whether he had had a sister, or how she had died. So, while sitting on a bench by the quieter Oude Rijn, I described, in as much detail as I could remember, the picnic at Sweetwater Pond and what had happened subsequently. Rob's eyes quietly watered as I told them of my final visit to the hospital and hearing of the decision to let Melissa go.

Imogen put her arm around Rob. I was touched by the friendship of these two. But that is all. I had travelled a long way, and, at this busy time in my life, I had no spare emotions. Imogen and Rob were intruding, and I was being polite. At the station, Imogen thanked me profusely once, and then again when I gave her 200 euros. Six months later I received a short letter from her informing me that Rob had died from a deliberate overdose of heroin. She explained that he had not been an addict for more than five years but then a chronic kidney disease had flared up and left him in pain, so he had decided to take the Pearly Way.

My own attitude to suicide has undergone several revisions. When young I believed in a liberal euthanasia policy, such as that evolving in several European countries, and I would not have argued against an individual's choice to relinquish his or her mortal coil (so to Hamlet-speak). Gillian, whose extended family, both present and past, had been scarred by more than one suicide, led me into several prolonged debates on the subject during our time together. She believed that condoning suicide was problematic because of the impact on friends and family, and because individuals rarely remained suicidal for long. I allowed myself to be persuaded. Over time, I suspect, Gillian's views hardened and she became fervently intolerant of liberal views on suicide, which may or may not have affected Crystal's course.

In the weeks and months after Crystal's death, I deflected the pain of the grief and the guilt, as many other parents of suicides did, through anger. The media was full of debate and comment about Xanthe Worthington, her netsites and games, and the various offshoot cults she had fostered. Most governments considered laws and initiatives to try and curb the escalation in suicide attempts – for every successful one there were several failures which put enormous strains on health services, and caused psychological traumas among relations and friends. And, everywhere, the Pearly Way was a topic of intense discussion in families, at social gatherings, and at workplaces.

My anger switched easily to and fro between Pearl/Xanthe Worthington and the media which did so much to propagate the Pearly Way ideas. For two or three years, I took the view that any legal acceptance of euthanasia was wrong and that such laws had opened the floodgates, allowing citizens to deny their citizenship, and abdicate their responsibility to families and communities alike. Diana, who did not usually have any firm views on major political or social issues nor did she much enjoy discussing them, expressed surprise when she heard me pontificate these views. It was only in the late 40s, when Diana and I witnessed the pain and struggles of Dominique and Waltar with regard to Waltar's mother's illness, that my moderate liberal opinion returned.

Even today, 50 years later, thanks in part to the Pearly Way epidemic, I had to navigate through an endless rigmarole before receiving legal approval for my own death date.

Horace said once, during a school debate on the phenomenon of suicide terrorists (this may have been an argument I personally originated, but I only remember Horace speaking it), that one of the best arguments against anyone, including a desperate religious fanatic, committing suicide was that life is full of surprises, possibly good ones. If Crystal had held on for a few further weeks she would have been presented with a fully-formed, fully grown half-brother – Arturo – and who knows what influence he might have had on her.

CHAPTER 20

IN WHICH I GAIN A SON

For me, Arturo turning up so soon after Crystal's funeral seemed akin to some god's crass attempt at providing a replacement or compensation; it was as if Crystal's tragedy had entitled me, unknowingly, to a ticket in a lottery of miracles, and I had won a dubious jackpot.

The first time I saw Arturo he certainly looked a million dollars, as they say, with his light tan-coloured skin, short wiry bleached hair, and a bold handsome face made-up with mauve lipstick and purple-dyed eyebrows in the re-invented he-fem cat-walk style popular at the time. He wore an immaculate shiny two-tone jacket and pressed trousers. It transpired that he had gone to Godalming and charmed my address out of Julie – without so much as a call to me to check if it would be all right. He said he was the son of a friend from Brazil and wished to surprise me, which, I suppose, was no deceit. While Arturo lacked (I would discover in time) other qualities – I could mention integrity, morality, decency – he was not short of charm.

It was a mild but overcast Sunday in October, Diana had taken Guido with her to Theatre Stadsschouwburg in Amsterdam to monitor work on the set of a play she was designing, and I had spent the morning at the IFSD office in The Hague. I returned at about 2pm, and was strolling through the communal gardens thinking about what I would eat and drink when I saw the jazzily-dressed young man sitting on one of the benches. His gaze followed me to the front door, and, as I was turning to close it behind me, I saw him approaching. I waited.

'Mr Fenn?'

'Yes.'

'My name is Arthur. Your mother give me this address. I wish to talk to you.' His English was adequate – in the present tense.

'And my mother is?'

'Excuse me.'

'My mother? What is her name and where does she live?'

'She live in Godalming. She call herself Julie, naturalmente.' He smiled. He looked harmless, and carried no bag, and so, mildly curious, I let him in. I led him through to the lounge area at the back of the house, and offered him tea.'

'Coffee, do you have coffee? I wish to drink coffee.'

'Coffee it is.' I went to the kitchen to put the kettle on. 'Where are you from Arthur? You sound Spanish or Portuguese from your accent. It sounds familiar.' I spoke loudly so he could hear me in the other room.

'Brazil. I am from Rio.' And when he said the words 'Brazil' and 'Rio' he said them in the way of his own language, which I did then recognise as Brazilian Portuguese. This was a further clue to what the man might be doing in my house, but it only took me as far as thinking he could have some connection with Monique, who I had run into at Alan's lunch six weeks earlier. I took the coffee and biscuits through to the lounge, sat down opposite the man, and poured out a cup for each of us.

'It is pretty here, artistic,' Arturo said.

'My partner, Diana, is very artistic.'

'And that?' He pointed to a poster-size portrait of me temporarily hanging on the door to the kitchen. It was no likeness, except for the long legs and lanky body.

'That's by Guido, our son. He thinks I'm three metres tall.' I kept wanting to say 'so, Arthur what brings you here', but he continued to edge in, asking questions with his broad lipstick grin.

'You have a son. How old?'

'Five in December.'

'Five. Do you know how old I am?'

'No.'

'I am 21 last April. I finish my degree, in biological sciences. I finish it quite young you know, and I get top mark.'

'Congratulations.'

'Where is Guido today and Diana?'

'In Amsterdam. They're coming back soon. I don't mean to be rude, but why are you here, Arthur, how do you know my mother or me, how did you get my mother's address?'

'You know Brazil.' It wasn't clear whether this was a question or statement.

'Yes, I've visited Brazil, but Arthur why are you here?'

'You have a good time in Brazil?' Now I began to feel impatience, and saw no alternative but to show it.

'Arthur, please answer my question or I will have to ask you to finish your coffee and leave.'

'Naturalmente, Mr Fenn, but please my question, then I answer.' Arturo's smile vanished, and he suddenly become intent.

'Yes, Arthur, yes, I did have a good time in Brazil. I liked Rio very much.' And I waited. Arturo looked around the room. There was an expression on his face, and he carried a look that made no sense, no sense at all, and for a moment, until he spoke, I began to feel wary, under threat.

'Conceição. You remember Conceição?' And still I would not tune in. I have been trying to think how to explain what was happening in my head, and the best I can do is to compare the process to that of Tom trying to find, but only half-heartedly, a radio station on an old analogue receiver, moving through bands of low-level interference, crossing louder bands of hissing and static, and making no serious effort to find the correct wavelength where sound and information could be heard and understood crisply.

Hearing the name Conceição provided a moment of relief, for, at least, the mystery was explained. But then I realised that if this Arthur had come visiting on the strength of his relationship with a woman I'd long forgotten, I had absolutely no interest in him or his business with me.

'Vaguely, very vaguely. I met her briefly. I hope you haven't come all this way to tell me something about Conceição, because, quite frankly, I wouldn't be very interested.'

'Excuse me.'

'I mean ... I'm sorry, I remember the name, but I don't remember her at all. It has been a pleasure to meet you, but I do have things to do. So, if you don't mind.'

'She is my mother.'

'I see.'

'She dead, died, two years ago.'

'I'm sorry.'

'Something related to AIDS.'

'I am truly sorry.' I was beginning to long for the return of his supercilious mulberry smile.

'I am, was 19. The compensation pay for me to carry on my study. Is more coffee?' I poured him another cup from the coffee pot.

'Please take your time, I'm going to phone Diana.' I went upstairs to call her in case she was close to arriving home. When I returned to the lounge, Arturo was standing by the kitchen door and examining Guido's poster.

'I am born in April 2022, you know. April 2022 is nine months after July 2021. Do you think I look like your mother? I think I have her nose, but your chin.' And back came the smile.

All the hissing, all the crackling, all the interference vanished. In an instant I was digitally tuned in despite my very best efforts to flounder around in an analogue haze: the man was claiming to be my son. A true *Eastenders* moment, if ever there was one in my life, only there was no emotion within me to guide my words or actions. Instead, with Arturo's comically alien face staring at me, waiting for some acknowledgement, I fixed on doubt as my way forward.

I asked him how he knew I was his father, when Conceição must have slept with other men before and after me. He pulled out a piece of paper from the inside pocket of his jacket and passed it over to me. It was a certificate declaring that Arturo Fenn Magalhães was born on 10 April 2022. He said that Conceição had told him it was a question of dates and possibilities, and that there was only one possibility. She would not have put my name on the certificate without being certain that I was the father.

And why hadn't she contacted me before now, if only for financial support? Because she did not want my help or involvement. She recognised it had been her mistake, and she had no desire to interfere with my life; also I was far away. And why then had Arturo shown up now? Because he wanted to know his father, and to study in England, and to see Europe. His backpack was at the station, and he didn't have much money.

Naturalmente, I told Arturo he should stay for a few days while we find out more about each other. I insisted, and he agreed without question, that we should take a DNA test as soon as possible.

It would be dishonest of me to deny that, in the days before the test and waiting for the result, I did not entertain a hope that it would prove negative, and that I would be able to cast out the stranger from my life without remorse. It didn't and I couldn't, so, from that mild October day in 2043, Arturo became a part of my life and stayed one, intermittently, for more than 35 years until his death in 2079. Indeed, through his varied off-spring, he has remained one – as witnessed by the visit of his son, Juliano, and granddaughter, Maria, a couple of weeks ago.

***

Flora, bless her. She has more life than all the staff (except Chintz) put together. Not long after observing me with Maria in the rose garden, for example, she rattled into my room demanding to know who she was. No sooner had I told her, than she launched into a never-ending eulogy for her own seven great grandchildren. Since then she's been hyperactive, visiting too often and staying too long. I confessed to Chintz this evening that I might have to ask Flora to cross me off her touring list. But Chintz hinted that she was not as fit as she appeared, and that too many others inmates had already shut their doors on her. When Chintz asked if I had any good flicks lined up for viewing, I got out the popcorn (metaphorically speaking) and launched Joaquima's *The Last Great Puppet Show*, a film based on the 2048 Barcelona World Puppet Festival.

CHAPTER 21

IN WHICH ARTURO MOVES TO LONDON

I suppose, from the standpoint of my emotional response to Arturo, I could have shut the door on him, even though he was my genetic son, not with a slam but with firm and persistent pressure. And yet I didn't, I left it open, wide open. Perhaps if he had arrived before Crystal's death and the guilt and pain I felt about that, I would have been less accommodating. Perhaps not.

Superficially, Diana tried to accept Arturo's presence with reasonable humour, and my invitation for him to stay with good grace. But she was not one to hide her feelings for long. On a near daily basis, I sensed her communicating that she resented his existence, his presence, and his ongoing residence, especially given my frequent absences abroad on IFSD business. My relationship with Diana was already under strain, and Arturo only served to exacerbate the effects of the distance between us. I did not blame her. She was probably being more tolerant than many a partner might be under such circumstances.

On the plus side, Arturo proved a reliable and trustworthy guardian for Guido, relieving logistic and time pressures on Diana and me. He played with Guido more empathetically than either Diana or I could manage. He was polite, and charming, thanking us for meals and the loan of our various vehicles. On the downside, he was chronically untidy, regularly asked for money, and used the house as if it were a hotel. I signed him up for English language lessons. I tried to get him a part-time job in the Mars Bar or similar, but the immigration laws had been made water-tight, and only a few quasi-legal enterprises, which never survived long, would risk employing those on tourist visas. By the end of November, his presence was proving too great a strain on our small family.

In early December, I sent him on ahead to London, with all the relevant paperwork, to organise a British passport. He stayed in a cheap hotel. I followed a few days later and the two of us went to my mother's house. By then, Arturo and I had altered the past to make it more palatable for Julie: I had had a holiday romance with Conceição, a student, and she had recently died from cancer. I let Arturo improvise in response to more detailed questions. Over the course of a long weekend, and daily train trips into the capital, I introduced Arturo to various people, not least Gillian and Bronze (that was a gaggle of laughs), and to the Turnbulls.

After Dracula Park, Doug and Miriam Turnbull had never invited me on vacation with them again, but they had remained friends. I was accustomed to dining with them whenever I visited London, initially with Bronze or Crystal until they reached their teenage years, and thereafter on my own. The daughters, Susannah and Lucy, had matured into attractive and active young women. Susannah had gone through an anorexic phase while doing her 16 exams, and Lucy had finished her 18s and was studying at a music college. I guessed they might find Arturo interesting and/or amusing, but Miriam, with the insight of a protective mother, saw danger. She kept our visit short, and brushed aside my suggestion of a meal out or a visit to the cinema.

It was my friend Horace, perversely, who resolved the dilemma of what to do with Arturo. I knew he wanted to study genetic engineering at a British university the following year, and that, until then, he needed to concentrate full-time or nearly full-time on improving his English, but neither he nor I were clear as to where he should do this. We had discussed various alternatives, but I had hoped that one of my friends, such as Doug Turnbull, would offer to help him settle in London.

By the Monday, my last day away (I was due to travel somewhere on Tuesday evening from Amsterdam), I was no nearer deciding what should be done with the boy. I'd arranged to meet Horace at the Houses of Parliament, partly because he had contacted me recently wanting my news, and partly because I thought Arturo might like to be taken inside and shown around by an MP. Arturo had dispensed with the lipstick at my request, but he looked no less alluring.

Once inside, and in Horace's hands, so to speak, Arturo piled on the youthful charm. In the guest's Tea Tavern, Horace announced, for I had not known this, that he owned a third-storey studio in Camden Town, in addition to the Kensington apartment and the Southampton house. It had been inherited from his parents. They had died within a few years of each other and left Horace and his younger brother Tim several properties which they rented out. A year previously Horace had taken the Camden studio back from an unscrupulous agency, and lent it to a struggling artist. That artist had now gone overseas and the flat was free. True or not, it was Horace's story.

Arturo, Horace offered, could have it for six months at a nominal rent. I tried to intervene, to thank him, and to say we would discuss the matter and get back to him, but Horace was talking to Arturo, and Arturo was responding with enthusiasm. If I, personally, had any doubts about what Arturo was getting himself into, I did not have any that he thought he knew what he was doing. I can't put my own mind about the matter clearer than that.

Arturo returned with me to Leiden to collect his backpack, and a second bag we gave him to carry the new things he had bought. On the way we discussed finance. I offered to pay the rent and education fees, but he would need to work to cover his living expenses. Apart from the English lessons, I insisted he enrol in a local college and work towards two university entrance exams. If he passed them with a reasonable grade and achieved a university place, I said, I would pay his fees and cover his accommodation expenses for up to four years.

I hoped life at home would improve with Arturo's departure. For several weeks, it felt as though it had. I made a conscious decision to preserve the Christmas holidays for Diana and Guido, and I paid for Arturo to fly home for two weeks, so as not to feel obliged to invite him to Leiden. But, no sooner had the year 2044 started than I was travelling again, and working all hours in the run-up to the negotiating session in Mexico I have already mentioned. There was a brief respite after Mexico, when Diana, Guido and I managed a week-long holiday on the island of Rhodes in May (which was entirely overshadowed by the news of the terrible earthquake in San Francisco), and a holiday with the Rocard family in Italy during the summer. Then, from the moment I became director of the Future Policy Division in October 2044 to the final Djakarta summit in December 2047, work took me over completely. There were a few breaks, such as the one to England in June 2045 to Brighton and to Horace's party in Southampton, but they were usually short and rushed.

CHAPTER 22

IN WHICH DIANA AND I ARGUE

Diana and I did not have many serious rows, but one argument stands out in my memory. In early February 2046, I was labouring 12-14 hours a day in preparation for another negotiating session, this time in Cairo. Diana was working towards a big show in Antwerp. We had our diaries and schedules and Guido-caring responsibilities clearly planned out in advance, as was always necessary whenever Diana was in the final stages of a project. I was due to leave on Tuesday afternoon for a day of meetings in Geneva on Wednesday. Diana would be working in Antwerp that day and evening but would return by 10pm. Elly, our dependable childminder, would collect Guido from school, take him to her house for supper (where he played with a daughter of Elly's neighbour), then bring him to Oldwijkgaarten, put him to bed and wait for Diana.

On Monday afternoon, Elly left a message to say she had contracted a chest infection and would be unable to collect Guido the following day. She was excessively apologetic, as if mindful of the trouble her illness might cause. Diana and I began arguing over who should make the calls to find covering arrangements. Under normal circumstances, Diana would do this. She was more social, she was better on the phone, and she had a much clearer idea of who might be able to help. On this occasion, though, she demanded that I do it, and would not relent – I didn't know why.

Neither Dominique nor Peter from the Guido co-op, who were often available and willing to help out if they could, were busy. Peter's wife, Livia, did assist a little by offering to collect Guido on the Wednesday. I phoned two alternative childminders we had used in the past, but neither of them were free. I contacted other friends, and I even walked round to some of our neighbours in Oldwijkgaarten, which was mildly embarrassing since we did not have that kind of relationship with them.

When I told Diana later that I'd had no luck, she was furious and blamed me for not having asked the right people, or for not having asked them in the right way. And she insisted I would have to delay my flight to Geneva until the morning. I said that was impossible because I had important meetings. I suggested it would be much easier for her to come back early from Antwerp than it would be for me to postpone my flight.

Although I was annoyed by Diana's lack of logic, and unable to fathom out why she was making such a big issue out of it, I wasn't surprised, since we had had similar niggling arguments on many occasions. This one, though, would not end. Our voices got louder, and we swung from Dutch to English and from English to Dutch. Diana accused me of being a workaholic, of not caring for Guido, of not supporting her in her work, of following the same pattern as I had with Crystal. I defended myself by arrogantly trying to take the moral high ground and implying that my work was more important than hers – much, much more important. I called her attitude selfish and egotistical. I might be a workaholic, I admitted, but at least I was working for a worthwhile cause not a vain one.

'Nothing will stop me going to Geneva tomorrow, nothing,' I shouted.

'Don't bother coming back,' she screamed. Never before had either of us let loose a thought that implied there could be an end to our relationship.

The argument came to a sudden halt when Guido, in his Oink jamas, came bursting in to ask that we stop shouting, and that we kiss and make up. He was crying and demanded a family cuddle. Diana bundled him up in her arms, and took him back to bed. I went to my office to do the work I should have been doing earlier. I forget what arrangements we finally made, though I'm sure I did not change my flight.

A week later, the play – Angelika Stockmann's *The Children's Land* – opened to excellent reviews. Stockmann was certainly one of the best German playwrights of the 21st century. This play, which had been a great success in her home country two years earlier and which had been translated into several other languages including Flemish, helped develop that reputation. Classically structured, and Ibsenesque (or, more accurately, Oakleyesque), it tells the story of the battle for a piece of land, situated in a housing estate dominated by immigrants, earmarked for a children's playground. Unrelentingly, Stockmann strips down the characters of the planners, the developers, the officials, the immigrant campaigners, the religious and altruistic do-gooders and so on to reveal the upper, middle and lower orders of hypocrisy. Only the children are left unblemished.

Given the distance of Antwerp from Leiden, Diana suggested I not accompany her to the opening night, but that we make an evening of it, with Peter and Livia, two days later on the Saturday. Diana's set was impressive. She had managed to create a central waste ground space which cried out for the promised playground. In each scene where adults met to argue with, or bully or bribe, each other for using the plot of land in some other way, there was a symbol of adult recreation (such as a cycle exercise machine, a punch ball, or a carpet golf strip) nearby, while across the stage, a child would be kicking the inevitable tin can or throwing stones.

We did not get back to Leiden till one in the morning, but it was not a good night for me. Peter noticed early on that Karl, Diana's ex, was listed as the play's director, and asked after the man who had been his 'barge neighbour' years earlier. He was not in the theatre that night, at least not obviously thanks, I have no doubt, to Diana's planning. I did not want to think about Karl's reappearance in Diana's life, or why she hadn't told me he was directing the play, but couldn't help doing just that all through the evening. I wondered, too, whether some arrangement Diana had made with Karl was at the root of the argument we had had earlier in the week. Cowardly, I chose not to confront Diana about Karl, and her deceit.

The next day, Guido, Tom's spirit and I, along with the rest of the world's population except Diana, sat glued to the screen watching Minty and Wayne Nolan walk on the surface of the planet Mars. Nearly two years later we would again unite with most of the earth's population to wait tensely for the Martian Seven module to return safely into the earth's atmosphere. As is well known, the craft's power had been exhausted in the last desperate navigational adjustments, and the scientists, with all their billion dollar computer facilities, were unable to predict if the module would burn up or land the orphan brothers safely in the Pacific Ocean. The Nolans – what heroes!

CHAPTER 23

IN WHICH THE NEXT STEP SUCCEEDS

Life as a team leader and as deputy director in the IFSD had been a cakewalk compared to that as director.

In one obvious sense, the success of the Next Step and the third expansion of the IFSD was in my hands. It depended on the way I handled the people I met and how I dealt with the paperwork on my desk. The responsibility was on my shoulders. But, when all the wheeling and dealing was done and dusted, I can say honestly that, personally, I made a negligible difference to the 2047 Djakarta deal, the Djakarta Settlement as it came to be known. The IFSD board, and in particular its director-general, monitored every significant step we took; and, ultimately, the world's nations decided for themselves how far they were prepared to negotiate on every detail. The plain truth is that by 2047 the world was teetering on the edge of a global conflict essentially between the Christian West and the International Islam Brotherhood for Peace (IIBP).

The IIBP, already under the influence of Imam Al Zahir, had begun talking about the need for the rich to pay Zakat – meaning that the West should be contributing a full 2.5% of their GDP in aid to the developing countries not only 1.5-1.7% – which was approximately what the percentage would be for the top rank richest nations once the Next Step negotiations were concluded and implemented.

By this time, all international negotiations, whether in the UN agencies or at the world group summits, were constrained by a simple need to keep peace. And the only effective way to keep the peace was for the West to bribe the East, the rich to bribe the poor, especially the Muslim poor. Thus, no one any longer believed the West would renege on its original offer of a third big increase in overseas development aid (i.e. to the IFSD), it was more a question of how the aid pie would be sliced up among the beneficiaries, or, in other words, how much the West would give in to the threatening demands of Islam nations.

The US championed giving a large share of the new funds to Catholic Latin America and it was the most hawkish voice in NATO (by then the umbrella for most of the developed world's armed forces). Japan lobbied for its Far East neighbours, both Muslim and non-Muslim. Europe, as usual, was dominated by doves and tended to take a middle ground. It did also insist on fair play for all countries, which meant providing the most support to the most needy countries, i.e. those in sub-Saharan Africa, many of which had not yet aligned with the IIBP, thanks largely to the continuing effectiveness of the Ojoru-led African Union.

Last night I showed Jay a panorama photo of all the heads of state at the Djakarta summit. I pointed out a few of the historical names he would recognise, not least Terrance Spoon, the GB Conservative prime minister at the time. Ironically, he was wielding one of the widest smiles. I explained the irony: while the Garth Fuller-led coalitions, between 2037 and 2045, had actively supported the IFSD and pressed for the Next Step, Spoon, who brought the right wing back into power in 2045 thanks to coalition support from the newly formed Christian Faith Party, attempted to stone-wall the European policy, like Lyndquist had done in the mid-30s. This was one instrument in his tool box of policies designed to convince a domestic British audience as to the strength of his commitments on fiscal prudence. I caught a 'so what?' expression on Jay's face, whose disinterest in history has been tested by my anecdotes on many occasions.

So what? In the spring of 2046 – a year before the Dajkarta summit and agreement – my friend Horace Merriweather, minister for business in Spoon's government, had taken time out from a busy European tour to invite me for lunch at my choice of restaurant. This was a low moment for me personally because of the friction with Diana. Moreover, the IFSD had recently been rocked by the uncovering of various fraudulent activities. None of these, I hasten to add were in my division, but the problems inevitably put a spotlight on the organisation's administration and the size of its bureaucracy rather than on its many excellent works. They also provided ammunition for opponents of the Next Step.

I chose the quiet Indonesian restaurant Lake Toba (which, despite several changes of management, served me well for decades). It proved to be an appropriate venue since Horace's prime motive was not social but to quiz me about the current situation on the Next Step and progress towards the Djakarta summit scheduled for the following year. In particular, he endeavoured to extract information on any vulnerable points in the negotiations which Britain might be able to exploit to dilute the financial impact of the Next Step on European countries. This is my interpretation, but when – in a teasing light-hearted way – I accused him of such deviousness, he protested his innocence with inappropriate vigour. As minister for business, the Next Step negotiations were way off Horace's patch, but Spoon must have decided it would be worth trying to exploit Horace's friendship with me.

Jay showed little interest in my story. His thoughts had been diverted. What he really wanted to know was how things had worked out between Horace and Arturo. The honest answer is I never knew, not exactly. Once Arturo had installed himself in Horace's Camden Town pad and his regular allowance was in place, I heard from him less than once a month; and I was generally too busy to respond to his emails, or to enquire further as to his well-being. Besides, my own role in the situation did not bear much scrutiny. If the two of them did engage in a mutually beneficial arrangement, then I, who was paying only a nominal rent to Horace (on his insistence), was, in effect, pimping my own son.

I did discuss the situation with Diana on several occasions: when Arturo and I returned from London, and later when Horace's name cropped up in the occasional email from Arturo. Her attitude never varied. They are grown men, she said, let them get on with their lives.

This I do know. Arturo lived in Horace's flat not only through to the summer of 2044, but for the first six months of his time at Imperial College. Then, a few weeks before the

British general election in 2045, he emailed me a new address, in Kentish Town. Thereafter, Horace's name was never mentioned again. I saw Arturo a couple of times that year, when I was visiting London, and once when he came to stay a few nights as part of a holiday round the Benelux countries. I believe he had a fling with Lucy Turnbull, although neither of her parents, Miriam and Doug, ever referred to it. I did not volunteer the information to them, nor that Arturo might have been sleeping with a Member of Parliament at the same time.

In 2048, Arturo graduated with a good degree in bio-engineering. He returned to Brazil where he joined a large, but highly secretive, organisation called O Futuro, or, in English, The Future.

As I say, I was only ever an administrator. I oiled wheels to help the political trains run a little more smoothly, and I greased the points to help those same trains avoid collisions. If I personally made any more specific contribution over and above this, it was through the Ojoru mission which I'd undertaken when still deputy director. Following the decision in Mexico to widen the mandate, our objective, as first proposed to me by Alfred at Abuja University, took on a life of its own and did in fact become a key element in the Djakarta Settlement. Perhaps I am being too modest. The final documents contained scores of drafting subtleties that, over the years, I had prepared and proposed to the chairmen of negotiating sessions. That said, they also contained text proposed and discussed and negotiated by thousands of other individuals.

In many ways, the Djakarta Settlement (for the third incremental increase in rich-to-poor overseas aid) was a significantly more advanced agreement than its predecessors, which had been modelled on old methods and patterns of aid that had been creaking at the seams for decades.

Without getting bogged down in detail, one of the many improvements in the Djakarta deal related to how tightly and directly the donors controlled the purse strings. It became far more difficult than hitherto for nations to tie their aid to trade deals or political considerations (other than a set of clearly stated conditions relating to war, terrorism and human rights). Moreover, it allowed for more wastage and inefficiency to occur before triggering a blockage of project funds and the aero-hovering in of Western-trained trouble-shooters.

If I am to claim any other slight influence over the agreement, it must be in relation to this latter aspect. During the 40s, there was a growing body of research and analysis, from the least developed African and Asian nations, which demonstrated clearly how inefficiency, bribery, wastage were cultural norms and could not be eradicated over night, or in one generation or two. By continuing to impose impossibly high standards on project implementation, Western donors and their agents (whether companies or non-governmental organisations) had often acted as the final arbiters over what actions, projects, initiatives the recipient countries needed (as opposed to wanted). And, as a broad generalisation, these actions, projects and initiatives tended to fit well with what expertise or equipment the Western nations wanted to sell, and with their domestic politics. I pressed my staff to be aware of the importance, especially to the most undeveloped nations who often had the least effective negotiators, of this issue; and when it came to preparing drafts for negotiating sessions, I paid special attention to the clarity of the language for certain types of amendments!

After the Djakarta Settlement, it took a year for the IFSD to implement its expansion. A new director-general, appointed in 2048, overhauled the entire structure. The Future Policy Division, which had had less than 100 staff, was disbanded. In 2049, I was appointed director of the Environment Division, one of the top seven posts in the organisation, accounting for over 700 staff employees (400 of them in The Hague), and over 1,000 additional contracted personnel around the world. It was responsible for nearly one quarter of all the IFSD's outgoing funds.

CHAPTER 24

IN WHICH WE ALL GO TO A PUPPET FESTIVAL

And so – as a finale to this chapter of my life – to Barcelona, May 2048, where and when Diana, Guido and I spent a most happy two weeks staying in a large apartment with the Rocard family.

Didier Rocard and Diana were old friends having studied for a short while at the same theatre school in Berlin. On returning to Paris, Didier began working as an actor, but his inventive imagination and ability to motivate others soon led him on to directing plays, especially large open air spectaculars. And then, for one reason or another, he diverted out of mainstream theatre to run a puppet theatre. At about the same time, he married Helene, a childhood sweetheart from their home town of Arles. To many, including Diana, it had seemed a strange match at the time. Outwardly, Helene, an accountant, appeared far too conventional and harnessed to a world of numbers and business, while Didier was an artistic explorer living in a world constrained only by his imagination and ability to self-promote.

By the time I met the Rocards, which must have been during my first year with Diana, no one could doubt the success of the partnership. Their differences and different worlds had not led to them drawing apart, making different friends, having different ambitions (as Diana had expected). The reverse was true, their partnership, their love and friendship, or whatever one might call the rare magic they possessed, had guided them into an exciting and successful venture which lasted more than 20 years: the publication of a series of works called *Le Monde Fantastique de Marionnettes*. Each 'work', which focused on a particular historical or geographical aspect of puppetry, was 'published' as a largish crafted wooden cube containing a collection of objets d'art: a replica puppet, a lavish book, further miniature puppets, photo-posters, and an uncopiable memory story for a screen show full of texts, camstills and camclips on the particular puppet topic.

Initially, these gorgeous works of art were published in a single limited edition of 500 and sold for 500 euros, but, for later works the limited editions number rose to 1,000, and the price to 1,000 euros, making each one a million euro enterprise. A few years ago – not long before Lizette died – I read about a Rocard original, not in the best condition, selling in auction for 100,000 euros.

Didier designed the packages and employed the artists, and Helene managed the projects, organising the finance, printers and manufacturers. For the first two works, she demonstrated an astute instinct for marketing and promotion. By the third one, though, marketing was no longer necessary since demand had begun to exceed supply (incidentally, opening the way for other companies to make good money producing similar but lesser products). Diana had three Rocard originals on show in our Oldwijkgaarten house, with the main puppets cleverly self-supported above or in front of the attractive cubes. One of them, the first of the series, Diana had been given in lieu of her help in designing the box; and the other two she had purchased at a reduced price.

But I digress. In the autumn of 2047, Didier had invited Diana to work with him on a large well-funded school project within the framework of the annual World Puppet Festival in Barcelona the following spring. He had been offered a fancy apartment in the old quarter, and, after various on-off discussions, it was agreed that we would all go for a full two weeks, even though it would mean taking our children out of school for one of them. I warned Diana that if the Djakarta summit unexpectedly failed to deliver, and a new one was convened for June, say, I might not be able to go. Diana suggested, with a naivety I found both endearing and disturbing, that I make sure the summit did not fail. I obliged.

There were seven of us in the apartment. The Rocard girls, 19 year old Veronique and ten year old Mireille, took the attic bedroom with its one window view across the roofs of old town Barcelona; nine year old Guido made himself comfortable in a tiny box-room; Helene and Didier took the master bedroom, with an excess of mirrors; and Diana and I had the most charming room, L-shaped and decorated with rococo-light wallpaper, a style we thought had faded out in the 30s.

Soon after arriving we decided communally to confine eating to the large kitchen, and project work to the dining room, which left the, thankfully spacious, lounge for, well, lounging, entertaining and entertainment. We used a pot-pourri of English, French and Dutch to communicate, which was no problem for the five of us adults, but Guido and Mireille had to communicate in pokes, tickles, signs, surprisingly proficient mime and schoolgirl English.

Didier, who made several preliminary visits, arrived a week in advance of the rest of us. Until his show was over at the end of the first week, he worked from dawn to midnight. Diana had been supplying ideas and designs by email, and also contributed her time for the first half of the holiday; only thereafter was she able to relax. Indeed, for the initial week we were all involved in the project to one extent or another.

To explain briefly, Didier was using a school and upwards of a 100 children to create what I can only describe as a public hide-and-seek game. It involved giant puppets, twice life-size, each with two children inside, and extraordinary drapes and material/paper creations to transform the school buildings and infrastructure. All three of our children made definite choices to take part for the three days of performances, while Helene and I were more than happy to help out with whatever preparations were required of us.

This was a blissfully happy time for me, a make-believe world far, far away from the IFSD and all its tensions and responsibilities. Some evenings, we fought our way through crowds along the Ramblas, always finding something new to examine in the artisan stalls displaying puppet-related arte-facts, toys and books. Then we would stuff ourselves with paella or tortilla, and drink too much wine before allowing (or not) Veronique to bully one or more of us along to a late night plaza performance or pop house or sound/light multiscreen extravaganza.

During the second half of the holiday we formed groups varying in size from two to seven to explore Barcelona and to see as many shows as possible. We were guided so expertly by Didier and Diana that we had the good fortune to be present at live performances of four out of the five shows that featured in the famous film *The Last Great Puppet Show*. It is worth remembering that the film was originally going to be marketed as *The Greatest Puppet Show on Earth* or similar, but Joaquima changed the title after the organisation, that had fostered and developed the festival for 15 years, became subject to an ugly commercial takeover. The change in management led to many great puppet groups and theatres boycotting the 2049 event; and, thereafter, the festival never recovered its status.

Didier's *Les Géantes Invisibles* was one of the five shows immortalised by the film, and there is a brief interview with Didier, and Diana is also credited. The Raluy Puppet Circus, which had captivated Guido when we first saw it in Amsterdam, was featured, as was a Czech group's light-work puppets performing *The Unbearable Lightness of Being*. Most spectacular of all was the Ecuadorian firework puppet theatre which drew tens of thousands of people to the beach for two performances only. This latter came out least well on film.

Oddly, when watching the movie with Chintz a few nights ago, she enthused over the one show in five I did not see: *The Hollywood Stars and Strippers!*. The metre-high string puppets were manipulated traditionally by hand from a team of operators hidden in a lowered ceiling, but each puppet contained one or more semi-camouflaged screens which intermittently showed clips of old entertainments (What the butler saw!, Charlie Chaplin, Blue Toons) all coordinated perfectly with the puppet movements and their stories. Hilarious and exhilarating.

CHAPTER 25

IN WHICH I TALK TO A CHILDHOOD HERO

It is thanks to the Catalan, Joaquima Ferrer i Germa, the inspired director of *The Last Great Puppet Show*, that these magnificent shows have been partially preserved for so long. It is also thanks to Joaquima that I met one of my childhood heroes, the Mexican film director Pam (Pedro Antonio de Malancas) who had made the movie *Trumpet Boy*, the one that had made such an impression on me as a child.

I do not recall why he was in Barcelona, perhaps he was giving a keynote speech, or involved with one of the shows, or on holiday like me. Despite the demands of her filming schedule (although, in fact, large chunks of the movie were not actually shot during the two week festival), Joaquima hosted an illustrious party at her Sant Cugat villa some 30 kilometres from the city. She was a large lady, and larger than life, one of Catalunya's most famous socialites. When asked by interviewers how she managed to find time for all her many activities – film-making, socialising, media appearances, affairs (being 50 and large had not diminished her appetite for young men) – she usually answered with some variant of 'by eating instead of sleeping, and screwing instead of dreaming'.

We were all invited to the party because Joaquima had been working with Didier and Diana at the school filming *Les Géantes Invisibles*. We all squeezed into Didier's hired Siberian and drove out to Joaquima's villa. It proved to be a fabulous place for the children to explore, with its exhibition rooms, wild gardens and dolphin-shaped pool. And there were many interesting people. I distinctly remember feeling myself colourless, exotically inadequate. Diana was radiant, a partial theatre celebrity in her own right, dressed in a verdant green silk lounge-gown, and usually at the centre of a mini-crowd.

I didn't see Didier and Joaquima for hours, so I assumed they had disappeared to talk business; and Helene was a consummate party animal, as comfortable and relaxed with strangers of any type, as she might be in the bath. I sat down on a bench near the pool to watch the children splashing and screaming. With hardly a movement or a noise, an old man sat down by my side. He must have guessed I wasn't Spanish, for he spoke in English, but with a Latin American-type accent.

'You know the Portuguese word 'saudades'?' He didn't wait for an answer. 'These days, I am full of saudades for the time when my children were young. I watch these ones here – are they yours? – and I am jealous of their fathers. My youngest boy now is 18. Once I was a god to him, and now he knows everything more than me. Everything. I love him, I love them all, but it was best when they were young. Before then, in the past, they made me feel young, now they make me feel old.'

I pointed out Guido and his girlfriends, and asked the man how many children he had.

'Three wives, three sons and two daughters. All of them a great drain on my resources.'

We sat in silence for a few minutes until an American woman, in her 30s, her bare legs and arms pinked by the sun and/or the wine, rushed over to our bench. She had recognised the man next to me, and wanted to add his autograph to several others she had collected that afternoon. Thus, I discovered the man was none other than Pam. When he had shooed the woman away, in a kindly fashion, I let an aura of peacefulness around us, enhanced somehow by the children's play only a few metres away, return before speaking.

'But you know a good deal about youth and being young yourself. I was ten, my son's age, when I saw *Trumpet Boy*. No film before or since, spoke to me as that one did.'

'A lucky chance. A constellation of fates. A booming film industry, a producer with more money than sense, a genius writer who later killed himself with drink, a computer graphics team that caught a leading edge of technology and then, despite the film, went spectacularly bust, and a headstrong director with too much fame, too much power and a belief he might do some good.'

'A potent brew.'

'It is not that I stopped wanting to improve things, in the way my mother never stopped trying to improve me ... But, how shall I say this? You know, it is as though whatever I do takes me one step further back, never forward. My steps get bigger, more deliberate, more carefully placed; my shoes get more expensive, but I am always moving back, further back, losing sight of what it is I wanted to do, what I wanted to achieve ... what I wanted to achieve.'

At this moment, Guido came rushing over to me shouting, in Dutch, 'Daddy, Daddy, watch me do a back-flip.' We watched him back-belly-flop into the water, and Veronique stand over him saying, in French, 'not like that you silly boy', and Mireille try and push her sister into the water for being so rude to Guido.

Pam then turned to me, as if it had suddenly dawned on him that he was talking to someone in particular. He had a dark weathered, leathery face but, I thought, it was furrowed by too much thinking not weariness, too much action not age. He offered me a large hand and introduced himself, thus allowing me to explain who I was, and why I was there. And, on his enquiry, I told him about my position at the IFSD. This had the unexpected effect of prodding him out of the nostalgic backward-looking mood, if I can put it that way, into an active forward-step seeking mode.

I would be lying if I said I could recall the progress of our subsequent conversation. I like to imagine that the basic idea for United Artists International Forum was mine, but when I attempt to recall the logical progression of our conversation, this does not make any sense. It was Pam who, in the autumn of his life, was seeking fresh and worthwhile endeavours, not me; it was Pam who said he had already been thinking of offering his voluntary services to one of the UN agencies if he could dream up a suitable project; and it was Pam who belonged in the film world, bridging the gap between artists and businessmen, and who must have already discussed a hundred such ideas with a hundred colleagues.

But it was me who, very simplistically, wondered why there wasn't some way of using the power of film and other art media (theatre, novels, pop music) – which for 50 years or more had created pervasive trends and fashions – to teach people certain universal basic ideas, about health, disease, safety, environment, energy use or human rights. It was me who questioned why big name directors had not used their blockbuster films to try and counter the Pearly Way epidemic, for example. And it was me who brought up the subject of broadcast soap operas and how they had been effectively employed, in developed countries as elsewhere, to deliver social messages, and who confessed that, even in my 40s, I could recall powerful episodes of *Eastenders* dealing with immigration and sex issues.

Somewhere along the way of this conversation, which continued as we walked around the garden to fill our glasses and find the tapas table, we came up with the concept of an independent agency, altruistically funded by wealthy artists, that would exist to provide carefully thought-out and structured opinions on how films, music, painting, theatre, literature could advise human behaviour for the good.

We quickly arrived at a possible working arrangement for such an agency, whereby contributors would, in effect, hold a share of votes proportional to their contribution (with a maximum and a minimum), and this board would appoint independent thinkers, with a salary and a three year commission to consider how specific art forms could potentially deliver important messages of various types. Some organised internal procedure would lead to final opinions, which would then be published and thus be available for artists, producers, directors and writers to take up and use with confidence if they so wished. In addition, the board could be responsible for setting a general agenda for the types of opinions to be drawn up: defining which sectors should be targeted and in what form, and how detailed or general the message should or could be.

We were deep in conversation when Guido came to tell me that the others were waiting to leave. It was the night of the firework puppets on the beach, and everyone was keen not to miss them. I was disappointed to leave since Pam had become excited and was bursting with enthusiasm and ideas. He took one of my hands and cupped it in both his, and promised me our conversation would lead to progress, real progress; and that one day he would be at my door asking for funds.

For the best part of two years, he worked like a Trojan on the idea that had been conceived that afternoon in Joaquima's garden. As a highly respected elder statesmen of the film industry, he was a man who could open doors and help raise millions for charities simply by endorsing certain ventures. Where Pam led, others were sure to follow, so, when he decided to set up his own charity, there was no shortage of backers and sponsors. But Pam wanted to get the structure right. He took his time, and consulted widely, beyond the frontiers of the movie business into other art sectors. He and I engaged in an extended email dialogue, several long cam-phone conversations and cam-conferences, before he was ready to ask for IFSD money and support, something which would give the organisation, by then already called United Artists International Forum, credibility on a global scale.

Even as, or especially as, environment director, I was not able to wave a wand and support projects simply because they were my personal favourites, however insignificant the requested funding. Nevertheless, there was a channel through which mini-scale finance could be donated to – for want of a better word – speculative ideas targeted on our main policy goals. And, with my advice, Pam had prepared an excellent proposal detailing the kind of environment-related practices of interest mostly in the developing countries that could very easily be propagated in certain kinds of movies.

We leaked, to trustworthy journalists – lunch with Bobby Jespersen was always a pleasure – elements of the plan that we thought would play well in the press, and then I took the idea to the IFSD board. To my surprise, the board members loved it. I think they imagined themselves already on the invite list to Hollywood, Bollywood and Hong Kong premieres. IFSD funding did mean, though, that for five years United Artists International Forum (UAIF), as led by its chairman Pedro Antonio de Malancas, was largely tied down to the elaboration of opinions on sustainable development issues. But, since a surprising number of the UAIF opinions were taken up by screenwriters and directors, sometimes on the level of advertising product placements, and sometimes more integrally in the plot, the IFSD's seed funding clearly demonstrated the principle could be made to work.

As with most charitable international organisations, the UAIF went very quiet during the war years – though I'm running ahead of myself here. Thereafter, it slowly expanded again, in the movie world and other artistic sectors. Today, in 2099, the UAIF's status is as high as ever, and its opinions generally attract much art-world and media attention.

Finally, still remembering the party at Joaquima's, I should mention that she had a minor role to play in Guido's story. Her film captures a short scene from Didier's show in which two adults remove a large white bull-like costume from over the tops of Guido and Mireille who then move to one side. The adults demonstrate how the upper half cleverly concertinas up and down to hide/reveal the giant's head. At the same time, Guido is turning his face towards the camera. Mireille turns too, but to look at Guido; and then all of a sudden she pecks him on the cheek. An embarrassed Guido grimaces and wipes his face with the back of his hand. Years later, Diana used a large camstill of the cheek-pecking moment, and had it framed for a wedding present.

Inspired, I believe, by our love of Guido, who was as problem-free a child as one could wish for, Diana and I occasion-ally mulled over the idea of extending our family. With money for the best modern monitoring and caring techniques, determination, and a modicum of luck, Diana could surely have given birth in her late 40s. As time went on, we also considered adopting. But it was not to be.

For years we had sunk into a pattern of occasional love-making, depending largely on whether Diana could be both-ered, and whether I felt strong enough in myself to let her be bothered. How strange that sounds, I'm not sure I can explain it any better. With my own sexual needs easily fulfilled in private, I suppose, I became less and less willing to put myself in the position of being even partially responsible for arousing any desire in Diana that I might not be able to satisfy.

On domestic levels, the relationship worked well. Most of the time, I never felt any compulsion to discuss my daily working life: the endless difficulties with people, the intricate policy issues, the political emergencies, the bureaucratic nightmares. In the evenings, it was a relief to fall into the lively and cultured atmosphere of our home, where Diana's world governed.

On a social level, there was a fair deal of equality between us: I had learned that if I was not too demanding and kept my requests to a minimum, Diana would, without complaint, accompany me to important formal events. Also, with regard to our friends, who were mostly artistic types, there was rarely any tension. I could chat for hours about the future of Flemish theatre or the importance of Tamson Bunting's collages or the beauty of Gustave Le Gray's 19th century photographs. Besides, although they were largely Diana's friends, many of them were not as religious as Diana about their art, and, if they were, they usually had partners eager to talk about anything other than the theatre.

Without the sexual connection, though, there was a void between us. Occasionally, as I say, we reconnected emotionally, and this had led us two or three times to discuss raising a second child together. This happened for the last time in Barcelona towards the end of the two weeks; but, once back in Leiden, the subject was never raised again.

EXTRACTS FROM CORRESPONDENCE

Crystal to Kip Fenn

June 2043

Thanks, it was good. Made me feel lots better.

I'm with Donna now, and she's cool. Should be OK.

Looking for a job. Say hi to Guido. x

June 2043

Thanks for the emails. You shook hands with Ojoru; my Dad has met Ojoru. That shines.

Saw Mum yesterday. Shouting. Bronze has done exams and gone to Wales with churchy friends for two weeks. I don't think Mum wanted him to go, so I don't know where he got the money from. You?

No Dad, thanks for offer, I don't want handouts. I start work Monday. Screen work (scream work), data-matching. I'm trying, it's going to be OK.

How's Guido, Diana? x

July 2043

Sorry I've not been writing. I wasn't good. It's the bad things. I wrote them down in a list. And then I wrote down the good things. I can't tell you where I am, and my phone's gone. I went to sleep but Donna woke me up, and ... well I'm OK.

July 2043

Thanks Dad, for the letters and money.

But the problem's in my head. One minute it's like I'm in so much pain, and then it's the world in so much pain, and then me again. I can't stop any of it.

July 2043

Dad, I'm good, it's going to be OK. I've moved on. I'm not with Donna any more, but Kingston. He's rancid. And ace.

I said I would try and write, you see, and I'm being good.

July 2043
No Dad, I can't tell you where I am. It's good. I'm good. Kingston's kind. (NO, he's not a druggy! Rancid means cool.) He
understands about the pain. He listens.

September 2043
Sorry Dad, I'm not good. Can't come to Grandma Julie's. Give
a hug from me.

September 2043
Dear Dad, are you here tomorrow. I want to tell you some-
thing. I should be OK. I'll wait by the flower stand, outside
Paddington Station at 6:00.

September 2043
I don't want any more emails like the last one.
    It's a good thing. Don't you see. It's action, not inaction.
Kingston's gone, but I'm good.
    Don't tell Mum any of our conversation. Please.

Arturo Magalhães to Kip Fenn

January 2044
I am so grateful for the journey home. You are kind man, kind
father.
    I saw the children of the sister of my mother, and many
friends.
    I stay in Parati for Ano Novo.
    And now I am in Horace's flat. It is very cool. I am so
lucky.
    Muito obrigado.

March 2044
Thank you for your email. I am studying very hard. Imperial
College have agreed to my application, but I must pass the
English exam. I am doing an extra exam in English: molecular
biology.

At nights, I work in a pub. I like it. English drunk people are funny.

Um embraço.

April 2044

Thank you so much for the money and the e-cartoon from Diana. On my birthday night, I went to a club in the End West (foreigner joke) with friends from my English class (I am good student, top of the class), and last night Horace took me to a very fancy restaurant. He is funny, I like him. Very serious and very English and pompous and very silly. He told me when to watch the screen, and I saw him speak in the House of Commons. Important people are the same as everyone. I like it.

Um embraço for my generous father.

May 2044

Today must be a bad day for you (Crystal's birthday), so I just wanted to say hello, and tell you how grateful I am for all your help.

I am doing well in English. Yesterday I went out with Lucy. She is very sexy girl. I like her.

Um embraço, and remember me to Diana and Guido.

June 2044

Thank you for the card of Colossus. I see my brother is growing up fast. I'll come to visit you for a few days in July, if this is OK. And then I'll go with Lucy for two weeks to Scotland and the Isle of Skye. Would it be too bad to ask my father for some extra holiday money?

Did you know I have a relation (a two cousin) in San Francisco. My aunt tells me he is OK, but it is the same as a war was there. He knew a family crushed. The Americans always appear so invulnerable, don't you think, and this reminds us they are human.

Um embraço.

PS: Horace took me to see *Peter Grimes* at Covent Garden last weekend. Why are you English people so sad?

October 2044

Congratulations on your promotion. You are the right man for the job.

It is very exciting at Imperial College. So many clever people and professors. I am so happy to be here. And it is all thanks to you.

Um embraço, and one for Guido, tell him he's a dude.

PS: It is one year since you are my father.

February 2045

Apologies, I haven't written for a while, I was very happy to go home at Christmas for beach and sun, but I had a lot to catch up with when I got back.

I must tell something that happened, because I know Horace is your friend. He came round a few nights ago without calling. Usually he calls first. And I was with a girlfriend. He got very angry. I can't stay here much longer.

I'm going to find a pad with some friends, and I will apply for a student loan, to help pay. And then I will work all through the summer.

Um embraço.

February 2045

That is very kind. I am grateful. What would I do without you.

April 2045

Thank you very much for the birthday present. You are a very generous man, a generous father. I am getting accustomed to my pad-mates in Islip Street: one more Brazilian studying genetics; a very tall American girl who wants to create and then marry a bio-robot; and a Portuguese girl who loves to cook for us all and studies music theory. I like it here.

Um embraço.

Guido, Bio-fests and Al Zahir

'If Europe had stood firm and NATO had approved [the US] resolution for a nuclear strike, many Christian and Muslim lives would have been saved. The war would have ended, not in the appeasement of evil, but in victory for the forces of good. Al Zahir would still be burning in hell as I write; instead, the devil is amassing arms for a new assault on the free world. I have no doubts about this.'

Life's a Gamble by President Steve Tarbuck (2065)

CHAPTER 26

IN WHICH DIANA'S BIO-FEST TURNS INTO ANDERS DAY

For most of *Homo sapiens'* history an individual could count himself very lucky if he survived for 50 years or more. By the middle of the 21st century, though, it was possible to hope – if you were rich or had managed to secure a reasonable life-long pension – that your life was only halfway through.

When people greeted me, on my 50th birthday, with the usual medley of comments implying I had only reached the halfway stage, and that life would be as long in the future as it had been in the past, I laughed or smiled and tried to avoid a disdainful reply. Centenarians were already ten-a-penny (one of Tom's expressions I picked up in childhood) by 2050, but I could not see myself growing that old. And, even if I could have done, I would have had no desire to spend decades doing little more than managing my health and monitoring my funds. Besides, although we all tried to live and work in the belief that the world would become, with the right policies and enough effort, a better place, there was scant evidence to support such convictions.

Perhaps if I had known I would live this long, I might have stopped to take account of the mid-life moment. But I doubt it. For most of my days, I've had too many external preoccupations to waste time in self-examination. There was that uncomfortable period of cam-psychology or cam-quackery, as some called it, with Gillian; and later, after the break-up with Diana, I took a helpful course in musical psychotherapy. But even in retirement I kept fairly busy, thanks in part to Lizette, who was also responsible for the idea of writing these Reflections and thus for keeping me occupied in extreme old age, beyond my dotage.

In retrospect, I can confirm that in many significant ways my life was more than half over by 29 December 2049. The drama, joys and despairs, the achievements and disappointments, the important events and meetings of a life stand out, as it were, as if they were extraordinary buildings in a dark landscape caught by the sun. But the sunlit memories from the first 50 years of my life far outnumber those of the second 50. And, although there have been many dramas, joys, despairs, achievements, disappointments, events and meetings in my post-50 years, they came after earlier experiences and so rarely registered in the memory as firmly; thus they seem to catch less light, to glisten less.

An independent biographer might, however, put more emphasis on my later achievements – within the International Fund for Sustainable Development and during the war years – since I worked at a higher and more important level than I did when younger. Furthermore, there was nothing insignificant about my relationship with Lizette, which filled up much of the second half of my life. But, to put it another way (and to mix and match my metaphors), change and movement in one's early years create memorable landmarks while routine and habit in later years are accompanied mostly by dull visits to old monuments.

Thus, and I do wish to explain this, the chapters dealing with the latter half of my life may – although I can't be sure at this stage – be blander than those already gone by; and the Reflections to come may be more artificially selected than those I have already recorded.

For instance, to start this chapter, I am going to visit, as briefly as I can, two 50 fiestas, Diana's and my own, even though I went, sometimes on sufferance, to other parties which, in their own way, might have been more memorable. For the year 49 alone, I could write about the UN-sponsored reception in a tulip palace to celebrate Indonesia's centenary at which Diana and I were forced to lie on the ground by a protester brandishing what turned out to be a toy gun, or Peter de Roo's barge extravaganza which indirectly led Guido and I to buy our own barge. Also that year we went to the Rocard ball in Paris and Amy Mistral's *Third Man* centenary event in Amsterdam, both of which would certainly have featured in Diana's Reflections had she ever written any.

***

Diana decided years in advance that she would celebrate her 50th birthday by hosting a bio-fest.

As happens so often with cultural trends, bio-fests emerged in the alternative artistic world, and then became popular among celebrities, which in turn led everyone else to try and emulate the idea. But there were bio-fests and bio-fests. At one end of the scale, Hollywood actors would hire bio-fest contractors to manage a package deal, including netsite broadcasts, books and, occasionally, high-cost ticket entry for strangers. At the other end of the scale, A N Other would put up a couple of 20th century photos of his grandparents and play childhood camclips on the screen and call it a bio-fest. Diana's bio-fest fell somewhere in-between the two extremes. Personally, I could not help thinking such demonstrative displays of self were mostly vulgar, a dressed-up way of bragging, of swaggering. I could, though, forgive Diana and other artists this vanity, since bio-fests were often no more than another means of self-expression.

Diana used up much of her spare time over a period of months in preparation for the occasion. Guido and I became fully involved a couple of weeks before the (Easter) weekend of her birthday, in April 2047 (this was the year before our puppet festival trip to Barcelona).

All the rooms in our house, and most walls and surfaces in those rooms, were given over to some aspect of Diana's life. Our bedrooms and Diana's studio became exhibition spaces for the models and designs of her most successful shows, demonstrating her early, middle and later periods respectively. The screens in each area carried sequences from the plays themselves and from broadcast interviews with Diana about her work, while printed reviews, praising her sets, had been enlarged and posted nearby the relevant models. Various awards, certificates and trophies, some dating back to school and college and some more prestigious, were on display.

Guido had been given a fairly free hand to prepare a mini bio-fest for his own room, since Diana felt that he was an extension of herself. Nevertheless, she tried to guide him and this led to a few loud arguments which Diana, gracefully, let me adjudicate. In my office, we covered the walls with photos of Diana's friends, going back as far as her primary school, but trying to make sure there would be at least one picture of everyone who had been invited.

The bathroom was decked out with paraphernalia she had kept from *Tic-tac-toe*, the barge she'd once owned and shared with Karl. Since Karl had been such a large part of Diana's life, I was quite relieved to see his presence confined to the bathroom. The hall, dining and large lounge areas downstairs were taken up with family and domestic photos and mementoes, along with the very best of Diana's own framed photos and designs (mostly theatre related), and the most treasured art works acquired from friends, such as the Rocard puppet works. In the lounge, the big wallscreen showed a silent loop of family photos and camclips. Photo-collages and Guido-drawings of Diana, Guido and me dominated the kitchen.

The bio-fest spread across the whole weekend, with family and neighbours mostly visiting on Saturday, and friends coming on Easter Sunday. We hired a mini-marquee, with heating fan, which was easily attached to the back of the house and accessed through the lounge door. Diana had wanted to solicit friends to look after the food and clearing up, but I insisted on hiring help for both days. We put food and drink for the adults in the marquee, and for the kids in a couple of tents in the front common garden area.

Both days went smoothly – with two exceptions. On Saturday we had the garage roof crisis: Guido confidently led two girls, younger than him, across Oldwijkgaarten to the garage area, up some stepped brickwork and a wall, and onto a roof. Once there, the girls refused to follow Guido down. Tears, rescues, and recriminations followed in succession but were then soon forgotten when Guido promised to make the girls a paper jumping frog each. (While other boys had been learning to play football, Guido had nurtured an interest in origami!)

And on Sunday we had the Anders crisis. This is Diana's story more than mine, and replete with names that I will not use again, but Jay was moved by it when I told him a few days ago, as we all were at the time. To recall this accurately, I need to play the camclip someone helpfully took of the bio-fest exhibits.

The photos displayed along the hall from our front door start with Anders and Claudine van der Klein, Diana's maternal grandparents. There is one photo of them at a flower market; and another of them standing outside the Utrecht house, the same one Dominique occupied for much of her life, which is a long story in itself although it had a happy ending, inasmuch as Dominique and Diana never fell out over the inheritance.

Anders and Claudine had four daughters, of whom Neeltje (Diana's mother) was the oldest. On the bio-fest camclip I can see there are several photos of the daughters together and some of their offspring. Two of Neeltje's sisters (Diana's aunts), Betje and Kaatje, were alive at the time of the bio-fest.

And then there is one photo of Diana's paternal grandparents, Eduwart and Maartje Oostlander.

Next along the hall, I see from the camclip, are Diana's parents, Powles and Neeltje Oostlander, both of whom were long since dead. Powles had trained as an architect, become diverted by architectural history and ended up as curator of a local history museum in Utrecht. Neeltje, too, assisted Powles at the museum, but not before she had spent most her life working as a nurse fitting in different kinds of jobs around her child-rearing responsibilities.

There are two photographs of Powles's sister, Saartje (Sarah) and her English husband Anthony Nash, both with Liam their son. This is because Diana knew that Liam, her cousin, would be flying over from Bristol in England for the bio-fest. He proved to be a most interesting man. On inheriting a water pump business from his father, he had eschewed the chance of making millions by selling the manufacturing plant, and instead used the regular profits to invest in research and the development of cheap and ultra-efficient filter technologies. Whenever it was possible, he had opened up the patents for his designs and techniques through, as it happens, an IFSD-sponsored technology-transfer netzone. But this is a complete digression.

Then, in the dining area, there are the photos of Powles and Neeltje's children: the four Ds. The oldest was Demeter, known as Dimi, then aged 59. She had married young, gone to live in the north of Holland, and worked as a family doctor her whole life long. Emulating her mother and grandmother, she too had four girls (plus several grandchildren, perhaps the girls who got stuck on the roof).

Dana, in her early 50s by that time, had emigrated to New Zealand when young, married, and was running a local chain of pharmacies in Whangarei. She sent Diana a camclip of herself and her husband riding horses along a beach, which we found quite bizarre. Diana was the third daughter, and Dominique the youngest.

The bio-fest camclip shows all kinds of photos of the four Ds, with and without their parents – as toddlers, juniors, teenagers and adults, some funny, some beautiful and some enchanting. Many, but not all of these, had been sent to Diana by Dimi who kept the largest collection of family memorabilia.

All the photos were much admired during the Saturday, but it was not until the following day that the festivities were disturbed by Helene's discovery. The Rocard family had driven from Paris for a few days holiday in Leiden to coincide with the bio-fest. During the afternoon, when the kids were taking advantage of the spring sunshine, and the adults had settled into conversation cliques, she noticed, among the half dozen photos of the four Ds as babies, photos of five different children.

At first she assumed Diana had mixed them up and included a cousin or nephew with Neeltje's offspring. She called in Diana, who admitted that she could barely tell the difference between the babies' faces, but, on closer examination, agreed that one of them did look more boyish and different from the others. Dominique (who, with Waltar, was present on both days) was summoned next. She could shed no light on the matter. The three of them went to Diana's room and computer to examine the store of photos that Dimi had sent. The toddler in question had been clearly labelled, by Dimi, as Dana, but when they looked at other photos of Dana, there was no resemblance.

A camphone conversation ensued, and Dimi promised to have a closer look at the archive. While waiting for her to call back, Helene, Dominique and Diana came to find me. I was refereeing a volleyball free-for-all in the garden. They were showing me the photos and explaining the mystery when Dimi rang to say she had found one other similar printed photo, but there was no name attached. And so Diana called her aunts, Neeltje's sisters.

The youngest, Betje, who had been there on the Saturday with her son, was suffering from an early form of senile dementia and her memory was very unreliable. Kaatje, however, who was immobile but happily ensconced in a nursing home near Arnhem, was still very alert. She solved the mystery immediately, without any fuss. Before having Dimi, Neeltje had given birth to a son, but he had died from meningitis when only about 18 months old. It was a great family tragedy at the time. The boy had been called Anders.

Initially, Diana was angry because this important piece of family history had been kept secret. She forgot her guests and the bio-fest and made several more calls, to her sisters and her aunts, accusing each of them in turn of a conspiracy of silence. But Kaatje was clear that her sister, Neeltje, had made the definite decision not to talk about Anders or to remember him in any way, and so there was never any reason for her, Kaatje, to do otherwise.

And then, suddenly, Diana became suffused with guilt, not only for having, umwittingly, chosen such a doomed name for her own first child, Anders, but for not remembering or acknowledging him within the bio-fest. Diana's mood shifted from anger to despair. She broke down. We all tried to comfort her in different ways, but it was Dominique's idea to re-assemble the Anders co-op (since we were all there) that provided the necessary healing balm. Taking a photo to record the co-op took longer than expected since we could not agree on whether to smile or look sad. Eventually, serious won the day, and Diana prepared and printed the photo out on her high-spec machine. She then juggled the pictures on one of the lounge walls to make room for it. It was a cathartic experience for Diana. Thereafter she never referred to her bio-fest but only to Ander's Day.

CHAPTER 27

IN WHICH I TURN 50, AND REMEMBER OAKLEY

My own 50th birthday party, two and half years later, was also memorable for different reasons. Most years, we either got together with Peter de Roo and his family and/or others for a meal on 29 or 30 December, or subsumed a birthday celebration into some theatrical New Year's Eve party or other. But, for my 50th, Diana decided we should mark it more deliberately. I suspect she felt this was necessary, despite my protestations, because we had all put so much effort into her own bio-fest. We chose the afternoon of 1 January so our gathering would not clash with New Year's Eve (new half-century's eve), and because it was a Saturday.

In contrast to Diana's Day, this was no bio-fest, and there were no theatrics, unless you count Imam Al Zahir's New Year message, which I shall come to all too soon. But it was a very special day, simply because of who was there. Not ever before or after were so many of my friends and family all gathered together in one place.

It was the only time, for example, that all three of my children met together: Guido had just turned 11; Bronze was about to turn 22; and Arturo was already 27. Since Arturo had been back in Brazil for more than a year, and, thus, was taking no money from me at all, I offered to pay his fare and living expenses for two weeks over the Christmas holidays.

Bizarrely, the three boys had nothing in common – except me, and these staged photos that I have on my screen now. I don't believe they developed any brotherly bonds, or ever sought each other out in life. Here is Bronze, smiling but still managing to look miserable, and Arturo with a face full of mischief. They are kneeling down slightly apart, and Guido is standing on tip-toes in-between them. All their heads are at roughly the same level, making for an awkward looking picture. There is another photo, even less elegant, of all four of us. Both these photos make me feel sad. They do not remind me of the one day when we were all together, which was, as I say special, but of the fact that, on a personal level, my life has been chaotic and defective.

All our regular friends were there, including the Meijers and the de Roos, as were several neighbours and a few colleagues from the IFSD. My uncle Alan and his partner Anna Mastepanov came from St Petersburg, bless them. They stayed for several days, which allowed me more time with Alan than I'd had since I was child. He looked weary, but had lost none of his calm or wisdom. I must have spent half our time together enthusiastically seeking his views on various issues, as if I were 12 again and he 40, that had already crossed my desk as the IFSD's new environment director. I also attempted to persuade him to take on light duties as a paid advisor for my department. Whether Alan was interested or not, I never found out, since Anna firmly vetoed the idea.

My mother, against the advice of doctors, made her very last trip overseas. Bronze, dutifully, drove her. It was a strain for both of them and for me. Bronze and I had nothing to talk about. He didn't seem to trust me, and my questions only ever elicited meaningless replies. I let him lock my office for an hour so he could use the screen to join in prayer time with his church; and, later, Diana caught him preaching to Guido.

During the journey over, Julie reported to me, Bronze had revealed details about his current life, details that I would not have discovered otherwise. On leaving college with an inferior degree in sociology, he had worked for a religious marketing company. After nine months he had got bored and left. Julie, reading between his lines, thought he might have been sacked for prolonged illness, whether imagined or not. A period of unemployment followed until he was recruited by an organisation called the New Crusaders, and given a place in a hostel near Newbury. He was working as a net-recruiter, and learning Arabic. Life was 'a bliss', Bronze had told Julie.

Also from England came: Horace, already by then a cranky backbencher (Spoon's coalition government had fallen early and consequently Horace had lost his ministerial role), with his partner of several years; Miriam and Doug Turnbull, who were back together after Miriam's sorry affair with a family friend; and my old university friend Pete Sampson with a new youngish wife, Clarity, and one year old baby, Joan.

Furthermore – and this is partly for Chintz, who wanted to know the other day if there were any famous people at the party – I should mention Oakley. Although he had a Christian name, Finbar, he was universally known by his surname. Diana worked with him years earlier when Karl directed the German productions of two his plays. He was about ten years older than me, and had emerged as a formidable playwright around the time I was leaving school. While other writers were stuck in a 20th century time warp churning out self-obsessed material about their failed relationships with people or drugs or possessions, Oakley opened up a new and rich genre of theatre: the theatre of international politics. He was far from prolific, producing only one play in three or four years, but the majority of them proved to be masterpieces. Many imitators followed, but few managed to equal his ability to blend the political with the personal, and create dramas that resonated so loudly with people's concerns for their own backyard and the world beyond. Angelika Stockmann, who Diana also worked with, was one of Oakley's more successful followers.

Oakley came to live in Amsterdam in the 30s. He and I met, thanks to Diana, at a press night. Thereafter, Oakley initiated several meetings – lunches in The Hague mostly – because he wanted to research some of the mechanics and politics behind the IFSD's work. At his request for a contact in West Africa, I put him in touch with Alfred. Consequently, we are both thanked, recognisably but anonymously, in the play script for *Pilgrimage to The Hague*. This is one of his most controversial plays, and the only one to tackle religion head on. It tells the fantastical story of three African men – one Christian, one Muslim, one a believer in tribal gods – who go in search of financial salvation for their peoples. Oakley wrote it in the early 40s, round about the same time I was working on the Alfred/Ojoru mission. But that does not necessarily mean I would know why he elected to use the IFAD, the UN's agricultural aid agency, to thump home messages about corruption, inefficiency and bureaucracy!

After *Pilgrimage to The Hague* was finished and throughout the 40s, Oakley and I continued to meet once a month. This was usually at his instigation, for I rarely initiated any social contact with anyone. But I soon came to look forward to our lunches. We rarely talked about anything other than the main political issues of the day, but, whereas I dealt with the world's ills in the way a doctor deals with a patient's pain, he seemed to feel the ills himself. I guess it gave him some relief to analyse and diagnose the causes of the pain with someone in the medical profession, if that makes any sense.

Over time I came to love him for his combination of intelligence and humanity. He hated being a celebrity, nor was he the slightest bit flattered or interested in the theatre world's sycophants. He never married, and as he got older he found socialising more and more onerous. He accepted my invitation on 1 January 50 not because he wanted to, for by then he was already finding any kind of festive gathering uncomfortable, but out of friendship for me, and because I'd never made any such demands on him before.

Oakley's last play, produced in London in 2053, bombed, as they say. One cruel tabloid writer said that Oakley had finally 'vanished up his own intellectual backside'. In truth, even before the war, the middle-class public had long since grown tired of being reminded of the world's troubles, what with the FTM riots, the climate disasters and the suicide epidemic. For more than a decade, they had been flocking to farces and musicals. Oakley never wrote another play, and he himself never recovered. He returned to England in the mid-50s, bought an isolated cottage on Dartmoor, and lived as a recluse until grief – grief for mankind – drained all life out of him. I believe he may have suffered more than some of those wounded and killed in the war that he, personally, had failed to prevent.

162

I should record that I did try to contact him several times after his reclusive move to Dartmoor; and once, because he would never respond to my calls and emails, I borrowed a friend's car and drove to the cottage. It was a pretty enough house, in a charmingly wild location, but neither the gardens nor the property itself showed any signs of maintenance. I hammered on the door for several minutes before Oakley answered it. He looked the part, an anchorite with long hair and a beard down to his chest. But I was not welcome. He spoke to me as if I were an annoying nosy neighbour, saying he was busy and had no time to invite me in. Come again another year, he said, and closed the door in my face.

Because Oakley turned his back on society and culture, the middle classes, the artists, the intellectuals, the media all in their turn rejected and ignored him for the best part of 20 years. The few biographies published during his life, largely failed to reveal the man or to assess confidently his worth, which is not surprising since the authors had no access to the man or his papers.

Ironically, it was not until his death, in 2063, that his reputation as one of the most important playwrights of the century began to solidify. Chintz, who in common with most youngsters these days, studied Oakley at school, would be pleased to know that my excellent medical care, and thus my ability to be writing these Reflections, has been made possible, in part, by the royalties from *Pilgrimage to The Hague*. Oakley left clear and unambiguous instructions in his will that I should inherit all the rights for the play, and that I should use the income 'not for humanity for which I can do nothing, but for a human man, a man that was my friend'.

I have much appreciated the additional income (and Jay will benefit until the copyright runs out), but there was an unexpected bonus to the inheritance. For more than 30 years, I've had biographers of all types, whether students or heavy-weight academics, seek me out for information, and this has allowed me some slight influence over their feelings about, and opinions of, the great writer.

CHAPTER 28

IN WHICH AL ZAHIR SENDS THE WEST A MESSAGE

And so, to conclude these specific recollections of my fifty fiesta, I must unfortunately move on to Imam Al Zahir's 'New Year message for the United States, the Europe Union and their NATO allies'.

First came a call from Tommy Chowdhury – he who I had first met as a student while at LSE and who now worked for me at the IFSD – on my phone. A minute later, while I was still on the phone, Oakley darted into the lounge urging me to switch a newsfeed onto the screen. So as not to disturb the party, a group of us went upstairs to my bedroom where we watched a live broadcast from Esfehan, Iran. Most historians came to consider Al Zahir's speech that day as the starting gun for, what in the West we now call, the First Jihad War.

By this time, Al Zahir, Iran's effective leader since the late 30s, had spent more than ten years trying to unify the Islam world. Early success came through Iran's United Brothers Treaty with Iraq and Pakistan, which effectively defused the chronic friction between the two main Muslim camps. This he managed, *Encyclopaedia Universal* tells me, largely because of his status as a Hujjatul Islam ('a living proof of the reality and the veracity of the message of Islam') which allowed him to be seen as transcending the differences between the Sunni and Shia. Then he set about uniting the Arab nations in the International Islam Brotherhood for Peace (IIBP).

In response, the Christian world became increasingly two-faced. On the one hand, it kept a diplomatic smile fixed on the laudable stated aims of the IIBP. On the other, it concealed a strategic grimace at the IIBP's success and growth, especially as Arab governments turned fundamentalist and less tolerant of non-Muslim minorities or neighbouring countries, and more willing to abuse international rules, whether on issues of trading, immigration, the environment, armaments, crime or whatever. As they had always done, European and other NATO member countries gave preferential treatment to the more moderate governments within the IIBP whenever it was politically acceptable to do so.

Most of the time, however, Europe, with its many divided interests, looked to the United Nations to find compromise solutions wherever possible. An increase in development aid and the expansion of the IFSD was one of the few areas where compromises and progress had been found over the years. It is also worth recalling that, throughout the 40s, there was an unholy alliance between the US and the Russian secret services which intervened regularly to undermine the most fundamentalist Arab regimes, and to fund opposition and underground parties favourable to the West, and that these actions were consistently opposed by senior United Nations representatives and by most leaders in Western Europe.

In the late 40s, Al Zahir and the IIBP extended their ambitions and influence beyond the Middle East and North Africa. A preliminary step was Turkey, which had tried to dance with Europe so many times and been jilted once too often. Then came Indonesia. Supported, bribed and armed by the West, a secular government had held on to power for one year after the summit that agreed the Djakarta Settlement, but it had then fallen to a popular coup led by Islamic fundamentalists. Within weeks, Indonesia's new leaders signed up the country to be a full participating member of the IIBP, inclusive of mutual defence treaties. Furthermore, by the late 40s, and since Ojoru's complete retirement from politics in 2047, the countries of sub-Saharan Africa had begun to fall under the influence of Al Zahir.

There was no doubt that Imam Al Zahir's rhetoric had been hardening, albeit slowly, over the years. But he knew how to talk to Western leaders, how to deal with the Western media, and how to explain away, to the millions of Muslim followers, his apparent friendship with the West.

Up until New Year's Day 2050, whenever doubts were raised publicly about Al Zahir's long-term aims, whether by archbishops, popes or the leaders of right-wing political parties in the Western world, commentators were obliged to admit that there was no real evidence that the man was anything other than an enlightened leader of the Muslim peoples. If the IIBP was challenging the Western invented and regulated institutions this was not, in itself, reprehensible from an objective point of view. If the IIBP was legitimately encouraging and helping Islamic-run states, this may have been unpalatable for Washington, Tokyo and Brussels but why shouldn't the IIBP countries help each other, the independent commentators asked. And, if Muslim communities across Europe were gaining in strength and demanding proper representation at every administrative level, then this too was but equality at work.

Nevertheless, it was not only American nationalists and Christian zealots that feared the future, many people in Europe especially, on both the left and the right, were not blind to the direction of world events and the lessons of history.

Al Zahir picked New Year's Day because he knew it was a traditional time for Western leaders to deliver their own messages, and he chose the late afternoon to ensure coverage across Europe and the US. Here are some quotes from that famous speech.

'Islam is the guardian of human rights and nobility. Islam is the religion of justice, freedom, salvation, wisdom and knowledge. Islam is the religion of life. Islam is the religion of innovations and new ideas. Islam is the religion of civility, science and development. Islam is the religion of logic and rationalism. Islam is the religion of sacrifice and tolerance. Islam guarantees and protects ethical precepts and moral decency. Islam is the religion of unity, fraternity and world peace. . .

Those who try to depict Islam as a religion against human rights, civility and security, are launching the most ignominious lies and accusations against our religion. These tactics are intended to justify the brutalities committed against Muslim nations and peoples. . . The Eastern and Western regimes speak with untrustworthy tongues. . . In the Name of Allah, the All-beneficent, the All-merciful, we reject unity with those that would oppress us, those that would seduce our youths, steal our food, take our wives, slander our beliefs, and with those that would be rich when others are impoverished... The officials of Islamic states, be they in legislatures or executives or judiciaries, or armed forces or anyone who is working anywhere, must overcome their weaknesses. The way to ensure prosperity for our nations and peace for the world is through the Koran...

Mohammad, the Messenger, and those who are with him must remain firm against the unbelievers. Did he not say: "I have been ordered by Allah to fight with people till they bear testimony to the fact that there is no God but Allah and that Mohammed is his messenger, and that they establish prayer and pay Zakat. If they do it, their blood and their property are safe from me."...

A new horizon is opened, where from we are able to see more visibly, hear and understand better the way to eternal salvation. The blossoms of knowledge and Islamic fraternity, and divine guidance flourish and appear before our eyes... We have struggled for 20 years and still the rich in the West are unbelievers, and still they rule some of our precious lands, and still they refuse to pay their Zakat. In the name of Allah, Islam is the religion of Jihad.'

Apart from other expletives muttered under the breath of those collected in my bedroom, a collective gasp went up at the word 'Jihad': since becoming Iran's leader, Al Zahir had never been heard to utter it in public. But we had no time to comment on this, for he went on to inform the world that the IIBP would, within the next few days and 'after 100 years of conflict', be considering a request from the Kashmir libera-tionists for a final and decisive offensive against the last remaining India-held territories.

This simple statement lightly disguised two messages: within the IIBP, Pakistan had finally agreed to an independent Islamist Kashmir state, and, secondly, the IIBP nations were willing – never mind the 'request' terminology – to join

Pakistan and the guerrilla organisations fighting for Kashmir's independence. And we all knew this meant NATO – which only months previously had celebrated its centenary – would be obliged to respond in support of India.

There was no quick fix for my mood that day, as there had been for Diana's on Ander's Day. Even the Marc Ferrez print that Diana gave me as a birthday present could not lift my spirits. When the last of the guests had departed or retired, I spent a few minutes alone in my office. I was tempted to tune into the BBC for some analysis on the Al Zahir speech, but instead took the book-sized package, still partially gift-wrapped, down from a shelf. I had deliberately left it there and not prepared it for the cool storage because I knew I would want to re-examine its contents.

There were many things wrong with the (175 year) old gelatin print. The photo itself was over-exposed, the print was flawed with flecks, and the corners were bent and cracked. Diana never told me how much she paid, but it would have been over 1,000 euros. It wasn't a picture of a deserted Co-pacabana beach (I would have to wait nearly 40 more years to get my hands on one of those), but it was a Ferrez, and I had longed for one since the early days of my interest in old photographs.

This photo showed a man sitting on the ground, between a track and a creek, by a small thin-trunked tree rising up, at a crooked angle, into, and silhouetted by, a cloudy sky full of dark foreboding clouds. My eye wandered across the postcard-sized photo searching for some artistic merit, but there was none so it kept returning to the man seated on the earth. I could barely see his face, the detail being lost in the darkness of the print, though I thought he looked weighed down with thoughts. It was a magnificent possession, especially when I contemplated the fact that this fragile item had once been in Ferrez's very own hands. Yet it was a depressing picture: the black clouds, the morose man, the half-fallen tree. I carefully placed it between two acid-free transparent membranes, inside a sealable transparent bag, and then inside another sealable but opaque pouch. The whole thing then joined dozens of others in the specially-designed cool storage trays on top of one of my filing cabinets, to be removed and examined occasionally in the years to come.

Diana was already asleep when I went to bed (Julie was in my bed, and Bronze was sleeping in the lounge). I kissed her lightly, lovingly on the cheek, not wishing to disturb her, but she drifted back to consciousness. I said 'thank you' for the party and for the Ferrez; and I told her dark clouds were coming.

***

Having already delved into my photo databases to remind myself of the Ferrez, I am tempted now to access Portia and look through some of the very earliest war photographs, all dating from approximately 200 years prior to the First Jihad War: Hippolyte Bayard's haunting images of the French Revolution; Roger Fenton's gentlemanly look at the Crimean War; Felice Beato's artistic pictures taken during the Indian Mutiny and the Second China War; or Matthew Brady's documentary photos of the American Civil War (not forgetting the most famous early war photograph of all, Timothy O'Sullivan's *Harvest of Death*).

But I must resist the ongoing temptations to be diverted by history or antiquarian photographs and proceed with my own story, such as it is. I've promised myself to complete my manuscripts by the end of the year, the end of the century, and my time is running out.

I have had a rush of visitors in the last few days. Lovely Josephine came on Monday, bustling as ever with news of the Collection, her fund-raising activities, and of mutual acquaintances. She brought a large bunch of roses (flame-coloured) which, later, Chintz carefully arranged in the over-speckled vase that dominates the windowsill in this room. Then, on Wednesday, by coincidence or not, Belinda came, offering me gossip of a more mundane kind about The Josephine Collection museum and about herself. On Tuesday, Irene and Yewla, two of Jay's cousins, Lizette's nieces, came together. I like them both very much, but not together. They have visited before, on their own, and then I could cope. They're all the same, these media creatures, they seem to live in a faster, and dare I suggest shallower, river than the rest of us.

CHAPTER 29

IN WHICH THE FIRST JIHAD WAR TAKES HOLD

In early 2050, I was still coming to terms with the tasks and responsibilities of my position as environment director; and the IFSD itself was still re-establishing itself after the Djakarta Settlement decisions and the shake-up created by the new director-general.

I spent most of the day following my fifty fiesta, a Sunday, on the phone with IFSD advisers and various other colleagues, not least Alfred whose star had unfortunately fallen with Ojoru's departure from power in the late 40s. Much of that working week I sat in emergency conferences, with my staff, with the IFSD director-general, with internal and external UN committees, with the main financial donor countries and with the representatives of some very anxious recipient countries and regions.

Despite all the feverish activity, and the sketching out of dozens of horrible and not-so-horrible future scenarios, information on which to base practical decisions was hard to find initially. Before long, though, Pakistan stated publicly it would no longer claim Kashmir for its own, and was prepared to mobilise all its armed forces to fight to give the region nationhood once and for all. Several leaders of Islamic states issued statements supporting Pakistan's 'decisive move' to bring stability to the region. By April, the IIBP nations had agreed unanimously that, unless India acceded to an independent Kashmir, they would go to war 'for peace'.

During these months, I tried to focus my time and energy fairly across all my tasks, but Kashmir was in the news every day; and, almost every day, there were new elements to discuss or decide on. Luckily or not, depending on which way I look at the matter, I had Tommy Chowdhury running the Kashmir desk. We had become friendly during my final year at uni through the Government Club, but then lost touch. After a miserable period working for a multinational in Lahore, he spent time with Amnesty International before moving on to run an independent information netsite about Kashmir.

The responsibilities of a wife and children drove him to find better-paid work. Given his skills, he had no trouble getting a post with the IFSD as a project manager. In the early 40s, he was assigned to the Climate Response Division; he then moved to the Poverty Alleviation Division. Not long after my appointment as environment director, I poached him to come and work for me. He was much relieved to get back to analysis and to using his intelligence for preparing policy advice instead of sifting contractor proposals and monitoring project performances. What Tommy did not know about Kashmir – its history, politics, organisations – was not worth knowing. And, given the chronic troubles in the entire region, successful project development and implementation in the area relied heavily on detailed and local policy advice.

Already as a student, Tommy had decided to disguise his heritage so that no one knew if he came from a Muslim or Hindi background. His surname was no definitive guide, and he adamantly refused to claim a particular faith. Personally, I never observed any bias in him to one side or the other. He did not care about the territory, but only about the people whatever their nationality or religion. Because there were never any pat solutions, his private views on the political situation changed as the century wore on. He had once thought, for example, that a repartitioning of the region between Pakistan and India would be the best solution. Then he had come round to accepting the Chinese plan for a jointly-administered protectorate (though this was much opposed in Washington). Tommy believed an independent state would be the best outcome in the long run, yet he also understood the costs of getting there, and of holding independence, would be very high.

During that year, 2050, Tommy moved heaven and earth to provide me with the detailed arguments for maintaining IFSD funding and projects in the Kashmir region. It was a great asset to have someone so knowledgeable about the subject; but it took extra time to manage him and the passionate approach he took to the job.

By the spring of 2051, the matter was out of our hands. It had been decided at the highest level. The IIBP pronouncements had led to a series of emergency summits between the three major international groupings (I've checked the encyclopaedia to ensure I get this right): the G13, representing broadly the biggest and most important industrialised countries (US, Japan, Germany, France, Italy, GB, Canada, Russia, Spain, the Netherlands, Australia, Ukraine and Korea) most of whose armed forces were largely united through NATO; the I9, the Islamic nine, representing the largest and most important of the IIBP nations (Iran, Indonesia, Turkey, Saudi Arabia, Algeria, Pakistan, Egypt, Bangladesh and Morocco); and the non-aligned four (China, India, Brazil and Nigeria), which at times expanded to eight (with Mexico, Thailand, Vietnam and the Philippines).

All kinds of international deals and fixes were proposed, some in secret, some in public, but Al Zahir played his cards – the demands for Zakat from the West, and a string of territorial claims – as efficiently as a poker player with a rigged deck. He did not want to win, he wanted war. At times, it appeared the IIBP was on the verge of some compromise with the G13, but then it would become clear that Al Zahir had simply been trying to stir up conflict within the G13 and between it and the non-aligned countries, especially China.

In early 2051, one G13-I9 summit broke up in disarray, and a subsequent one was cancelled. Meanwhile, the main IIBP nations suddenly all signed non-aggression pacts with China, thereby tacitly approving the latter's claim to the Indian state of Ladakh, north of Kashmir. Immediately, orders came down from on high for all IFSD (and other UN) activities connected with Kashmir to be frozen, and all personnel in the region to be withdrawn.

Tommy was devastated. Unlike most of us, he had continued to believe that a war in the region could be avoided. Because we all hoped any conflict would be short-lived, with as few lives lost, and as little damage to the region's infrastructure, as possible, I kept him assigned to the Kashmir desk producing daily, and then weekly bulletins. But as the war moved through the usual stages, from smart bombing to peace talk attempts, from random bombing to peace talk attempts, from air battles to peace talk attempts, and to the inevitable ground and guerrilla war, so Tommy became increasingly unstable, and emotional. If my secretary stalled his calls, he would come storming into my office, his spiky black hair all disarranged, spectacles in one hand, papers in the other, with some vital piece of news which was of no relevance to our work at all.

Having persistently failed to follow my advice or that of a senior personnel officer to take holiday, he disappeared without notice. I waited a few days for him to contact me, and then I called his wife, Tamarind, a deeply serious woman who had often worked as a volunteer for one of the Dutch religious tolerance organisations. She told me Tommy had gone to Amritsar, India, to the Red Cross base there to replace an operations manager who had been killed on a mission. When I expressed anger at his failure to inform me, Tamarind defended him, saying he was a man of many divided loyalties, and that he had not wanted to let me down.

The next day I received a short email in which Tommy apologised. He explained that he had been going mad pushing paper, and doing nothing. He sounded like someone who had been let out of prison. I called the personnel department immediately and pulled rank to ensure he was given an immediate six month sabbatical (three of them on full pay). Thankfully, he had been with the IFSD long enough to allow such a leave of absence. He came back after five months, shell-shocked, far less driven, more stable, very grateful to me, and more than ready to play his part in keeping our work going in those areas of the world where we could make a difference.

Al Zahir's forces, as they were often called by the media, continued to make slow advances in Kashmir, winning territory through the attrition of men. Indian nationals were dying at ten times the rate of NATO soldiers, but it was the NATO deaths and the prospect of losing the Kashmir war that, finally, in early 2053, led the US hardline Republican President Steve Tarbuck (who had taken over the White House from the Democrat Betty Arklington in 2051) to press for the nuclear option. There was much head-banging, especially between the European leaders, before NATO made two class C nuclear strikes on military-dominated towns in Iran and Pakistan, killing a total of 21,000 civilians and military personnel. As is well documented, this action played right into Al Zahir's hands. Intelligence material had indicated the IIBP alliance would fall apart if faced with the realities of nuclear devastation and this claim had been crucial in convincing the European doves to accept the class C strikes. However, it transpired that the intelligence material was not only flawed but wrong in almost every detail.

The two nuclear bombs led the IIBP to set in motion immediately a series of devastating suicide bomb missions on Tel Aviv and – horrifyingly for those of us safe and cosy in Europe – on Constanta and Athens. It announced Turkey would be sending more armoured troops to the Kashmir front. It called to arms terrorist warriors lying low in the more hawkish European countries. It further restricted oil and gas supply to NATO members. And, worst of all, for this is what many in the world had feared, the IIBP declared the rich West had left no alternative but for an extension of the Jihad into other areas where unbelievers were suppressing the Islam message.

Three weeks after the nuclear missiles, Al Zahir pronounced that the IIBP had received (i.e. had agreed) requests for military support from the Islam Liberation Front in Mindanao, from Sudan to support the Muslim rebel movement in Chad, and from Uzbekistan and Kyrgyzstan for border disputes with Kazakhstan.

What Al Zahir pronounced usually came to pass. From halfway through 2053 the conflict between NATO and the IIBP escalated rapidly. As with the Cold War 100 years previously, open wounds and hidden sores of the conflict could be found across the world's geography. Although in Europe we were largely free of any direct experiences of the war, we quickly became accustomed to a new level of terrorist alert, to seeing and dealing with racist tensions; some countries demanded oaths of allegiance from Muslim nationals and expelled non-nationals. We also got used to a steady stream of dead youths returning home in body bags. To add to Western government difficulties, the anti-war movement flourished, and this led to some of the largest protest demonstrations seen since the First Tuesday Movement peak two decades earlier.

NATO found itself neutered by an inability to use its most destructive weapons, and the IIBP ratcheted up the pressure. Every week, there was talk of fresh attempts to solve one crisis or another, or to find a global solution, but the IIBP's demands continued to escalate, always to a level beyond that which the (largely) Christian nations were prepared to give.

For the first two or three years – this was in the period when the war was confined to Kashmir – I was able to make a reasonable contribution in my new position as environment director. Apart from Tommy, I established a good team of policy advisers and heads for the regional departments. I should mention Ninel Horeva who was never given sufficient backing from Moscow to get a top posting herself. She sat comfortably at my side, so to speak, for many years, and provided invaluable advice on Ukraine and the Russian sphere countries. And there was Chidi Naiambana, a shiningly intelligent Nigerian ex-diplomat that Alfred, through Ojoru, had managed to parachute (meaning the normal channels were not followed) into the IFSD. He was tall, although not to Alfred's standard, with thin gracile features and long fingers which he wiggled around when trying to make a point.

In addition, I redesigned the organisational structure of the whole division, so as to allow us to channel our energies efficiently into the new priorities which had been established by the Djakarta Settlement.

I did, though, spend too much time on infighting, a chronic disease of the UN, and a speciality of the IFSD which had grown so large and powerful at the expense of other international organisations.

Two times, once in the 20s and once in the 40s, the world's major management consultancies, different ones each time, had clubbed together in altruistic year-long missions to help streamline the UN system. On each occasion, the recommendations were only partially implemented due to entrenched interests and the growing political divides which led to increasing levels of distrust at all levels.

In particular, the UN's failure to reform the agricultural agency (IFAD), in the late 30s, meant it had become no more than a political tool for certain countries. The situation had resulted – partly thanks to Alfred and me, as I have recounted – in the IFSD moving into the same policy territory as the IFAD. And, like it or not, the Djakarta Settlement had turned the IFAD into little more than an advisory arm for the IFSD – and like it, the IFAD did not.

Much of the IFSD's responsibilities for sustainable agriculture and training/education for same fell under my command. The IFSD director-general and the UN Secretary General washed their hands of the whole dispute, and so it was left to me to find a way of breaking down the barriers between our two organisations. Pravit Krishnamurty, who I wrote to now and then seeking his wisdom, commented: 'Well, my friend, you know it is all reaping and sowing. Not much has changed in 10,000 years.'

I took no pride in the task, nor did I employ any special skills. I simply persevered with calm patience, and used any opportunity to expose the IFAD's intransigence and failings. In this, the journalists Bobby Jespersen and Ike Davidson, who had moved to Brussels to cover, among other things, the NATO command side of the war, proved useful. After a widely publicised but unwarranted counter-attack on me, the IFAD's chief retired early, and his replacement – who eased out several obstructive deputies without much difficulty – proved more willing to cooperate.

CHAPTER 30

IN WHICH I DISCOVER DIANA'S DECEIPT

Although Diana and I recovered some stability in our relationship, around the time of the Barcelona trip and for two or three years thereafter, my IFSD promotion and the global conflict brought with them new personal tensions. It is possible that, without the war, we might have stayed the course through to old age. I make this assessment in retrospect, and only after reading writers such as Gregory who have never been short of a theory or two to put us mere mortals in behavioural boxes. Gregory rehashed a theory on how war was responsible for leading individuals into more short-termism ('decisions driven by passion rather than consideration') but this can only partially explain, if at all, Diana's decision to leave me in 2055.

As Guido moved into his teens and no longer needed to be looked after by us or Elly, so our time and logistic problems evaporated. Nevertheless, Diana liked me to be around, to be there in the evenings and weekends to discuss ideas, to consider some new design, or to accompany her to an opening night; and she became increasingly intolerant of my absences. I too was growing old and more selfish and less tolerant, and I became less able to cope with her egotism. Moreover, for years I had never acknowledged any frustration concerning her disinterest in my work or international politics. Yet, soon after my promotion, it began to rankle seriously for the first time; and then, with the war preoccupying my working day and all my spare thoughts, this frustration took on a life of its own. Thus, despite my best intentions, I slipped back into old habits of working late at night and on Saturdays.

And on Sundays, I gravitated to spending most of the day with Guido, tinkering about on *Ginquin*. Peter do Roo had grown tired of my idle musings about buying an old boat and learning how to repair and rebuild it, so on the day of his barge extravaganza in 2049, when I was a touch glossy, he provoked me into accepting an offer for him to find us a boat. Both he and his son Rudy promised to help with advice and contacts, and Guido, who really enjoyed using his hands, was very keen on the idea. Within a few months we had acquired a small and shabby motorised skutsje, along with a mooring less than a kilometre from Peter's. It was Guido's suggestion to rename the barge after our cat, Ginquin, who had died months earlier. Initially, Diana approved of the project wholeheartedly and took part in our plans and helped with a few of the early tasks, but before long she lost interest.

The first year of owning the boat tested my resolve. Even with Peter's support, we were way out of our depth. The boat had to be dry-docked twice, the second time because I had failed to deal knowledgeably and efficiently with the professionals at the yard. Moreover, we ended up employing various tradesmen, mechanics and fitters, for example, although I had imagined we would persevere with much of the work ourselves.

In March 2053, Diana went to Berlin for three full weeks, the longest she had ever stayed away on a job at one time. Guido, at 14, was already highly responsible and could be trusted to get on with his homework and prepare his supper if I wasn't home. If he knew I was going to be late, he would sometimes go to a friend's house. We lived well in the house together, albeit in a practical way, very quietly and humbly, yet, whenever Diana was absent for more than a few days, we tired of the novelty quickly and missed her presence acutely.

As it happened, she was away when the IIBP bombers shocked the world with the retaliation suicide bomb raids on the two European cities. This led Guido to insist on a reassuring camphone conversation with me and his mother, even though she was only 500 kilometres away, while Constanta and Athens were 2,000 kilometres away on the other side of the continent.

After Guido had gone to bed, I did a very unusual thing, I went to Diana's desk. It was only later that I worked out my motives. I had seen a painting in the room where Diana was sitting during her conversation with Guido. The style was similar to a picture, painted by Karl, Diana had owned. I had first seen it hung in a cabin on *Tic-tac-toe*, the barge she had owned with Karl. It was stored somewhere in our Old-wijkgaarten house. The visual clue must have unconsciously triggered some anxiety I had kept buried for years, probably since the night we went with Peter and Livia to see the Stock-mann play in Antwerp.

With no particular motive, I flicked through a number of files in her cabinet: financial receipts, supplier account state-ments, project proposals, reviews, business letters and so on. I did feel guilty about this especially as we had always respected each other's privacy, and knowing she would be horrified if she discovered I had trawled through her papers. What I really wanted to do was to look at her emails. But, if I switched on her computer console, she would surely know someone had used it in her absence, and neither Guido nor I would have any reason to do so. It took me 24 hours to decide on the details of an elaborate excuse to use if necessary, and then I returned to her computer. Thus it was I learned she was working and staying with Karl in Berlin – and had done so before.

***

I have not seen Flora for more than a week. Chintz says she's had a relapse and the doctors are worried about her condition.

'She was flying too high, anyone could see that,' I said.

'Don't understand much, me, but I do know it's tough to get the pill menus right, every person's so different, and their metabolisms shift and change with the weather and the food and the company. And then some want more than others. It's more luck than judgement. That's what I think. But don't tell.' She has such a twinkle in her eyes.

'I'm doing well, I hope.'

'You? You'll be here forever, you're the fittest one in this place. You don't look a day over 50. What you got on the movies tonight darlin'? Anything I might enjoy?' she asked in a mock cockney accent.

'Chintz, don't you have a boyfriend to go home to? It's none of my business, but I'm worried what might happen if you hang around us dead folk too long?'

'Loving's for those needing heartache. You should know that, watching all those Movie Martyr flicks.' She turned away to check the display on a monitor, and then turned back. 'But if I had had just one sweetie same as you, a couple of years younger maybe, I might've put on the white.' Later, when her shift was over she returned and we watched a very old film called *Niagara*, with Marilyn Monroe playing a deceitful wife.

Which put me in the right sort of mood to try and record my conversation with Diana.

***

I collected her from Schiphol Airport on a Saturday afternoon, and drove home in near silence. Guido was out but had left an origami bird for Diana with the message 'welcome home' written inside the beak. I started speaking in Dutch but soon switched to English. Yet even in my mother tongue, I was unable to find adequate words or phrases to communicate the anger I felt and the sense of betrayal.

'You've been with Karl.'

'So what?'

'You've been with Karl, staying with him, and this is not the first time.'

'So what? It's not your business?'

'Not my business? You spend three weeks in Berlin, working with your ex-husband, living with your ex-husband, screwing your ex-husband, and it's none of my business?'

'Yes, it's none of your business. I'll work where I want to work, I'll stay where I want to stay, and I'll screw who I want to screw. All right, English man, are you happy.' Diana flew out of the room and up to her office, where she soon discovered my own deceitfulness. She stamped back down into the lounge to find me by the back doors staring into the garden, my fists and teeth were clenched.

'So, now you are a spy, a dirty grubby snipper,' she paused, it would have been funny at any other time, 'no, I mean snooper. That's what children – humans who have not grown up – do, they snoop in other people's belongings.' There was no protection against my shame about this, all I could do was let my rage ride on.

'And what do adults do? Lie, cheat, slip off whenever they can to fornicate behind their partner's back. Very grown-up. You know what I've been thinking about this last week, since I found out? About that big row we had six or seven years ago when you were working in Antwerp. That was about Karl wasn't it, you wanting to be with him. It's been going on since then hasn't it. Or longer. Is it longer?' And, as I was saying the words, the worst scenario was dawning on me. 'Did you ever stop seeing him, did you ever stop screwing him?' Diana dropped down into one of the lounge chairs and curled up, as she did sometimes when upset, but never before as a result of me being angry.

'Make some chocolate please,' she whispered.

So I made hot chocolate. This is the person I was, who I had always been, and who I would always be. I was not one of those Hollywood or soap opera husbands who, when discovering they have been cuckolded, unleash violence on their surroundings. No. I made hot chocolate.

By the time I came back with the drinks, Diana had dropped her defences and become meeker than I had ever known her. Although it was possible to construe her story as an attempt to blame Karl, I understood this was not her intention. She was trying to make sense of the situation for her and for me. Yes, she had worked with Karl on four plays, starting with the one in Antwerp, and each time. for two or three weeks only, she had fallen back into his arms. She had never planned to, or wanted to. Before accepting each commission she had sworn to herself not to get involved, and she had made him promise – very touching this – not to try and seduce her. But he was her first serious love, and it was as if he held a spell over her that she was powerless to resist. Once working together, and in each other's company, Karl had broken his promise and re-unleashed her passion for him; and she had been weak, unforgivably weak.

After the confession we talked for a long time. It was the most earnest, honest and loving conversation we had had for many years. Diana promised she would never work with or see Karl again. I believed in the sincerity of the promise, but I doubted whether she would be able change who she was, any more than I could change who I was.

CHAPTER 31

IN WHICH I SPEND TIME WITH HORACE AND PETER

In June that year (2053), and on the back of a series of meetings, I spent five days in England. I met up with Arturo, who was in London to speak at a commercial conference on advances in human cloning. This was the first time I had seen him in the flesh since my fifty fiesta. In only a few years, he had matured from playboy student to besuited scientist, yet was as beguiling as ever.

Given his respectable appearance I invited him to accompany me to the 500 year anniversary celebrations at my old school – once called Witley Academic. I had planned to take my mother, Julie, but she was not well enough to go. On our way there, Arturo and I talked about the latest developments in the war, his girlfriend Edna, who was shortly to become his wife, Guido, and his work. Once we arrived, and prior to the main event, Arturo was content to wander around on his own leaving me to meet up with old school buds.

Horace Merriweather found me soon enough and we circulated together enjoying the occasional exuberant cry of 'my word, it's Hip and Kip'. When Arturo suddenly appeared with a huge grin, Horace went as white as a sheet, especially when my son pressed a kiss on his cheek.

It was a great occasion with several highlights, not least the short performance by the 30s' popidol, Gold Spencer, one of Witley Academic's most famous sons, and the tumultuous applause for our old history teacher Philip Liphook.

After the main presentations, Arturo left to return to London under his own steam. Horace and I spent the early evening with others from our Witley Academic cohort at the five-star Greensand Retreat near Chiddingfold, courtesy of Jeff Zimmerman who was a member. Jeff lived nearby in a palatial mansion. He had made a good living as a corporate lawyer, but, in so doing, had become – to my mind any way – overly dependant on material possessions. As previously agreed, Horace and I drove (in Horace's sleek two-man Darkstar!) south. First to Winchester to dine at one of his favourite taverns, and then to Parsonville, where he dropped me off at Julie's before heading on to his Southampton house. We had much to discuss, not least what had become of so many of our old friends, but I wish to recall only one particular topic.

As a right-of-centre politician, albeit one closer to the centre than many, Horace was opposed in principle to taxing the rich heavily to give to the less well-off, whether at home or far away, and this had naturally led him to a chronic scepticism concerning the IFSD. When in government, as one of Spoon's lackeys, his scepticism had apparently hardened into a policy of obstruction against its operational enlargement. By this time, though, Horace had been a backbench MP for some years, and a liberal tendency had begun to show through his conservative front. Moreover, the war was affecting him deeply.

When our conversation moved round to my current preoccupations, I expected the usual teasing cynicism and challenging criticisms of our work at the IFSD. Instead Horace was full of genuine interest and questions. He even came close to explaining (if not apologising for) his past attitude. Much as I appreciated this mellowing of his politics, he knew as well as I that the IFSD had already been badly weakened by the war, and its future role looked very uncertain. Unkindly, I thought it was typical of a Tory to pretend sympathy for a wounded opponent, so long as the sympathy did nothing to help that opponent's recovery. However, his conversion, if I can put it that way, did have consequences, inasmuch as some years later, as I will recount, Horace helped to protect my position within the organisation; whether that was a good or bad thing for the IFSD is for others to judge.

I had forewarned my mother I might be late, so she had organised for a key to be left at the Parsonville reception/ security centre. I crept into the bungalow very quietly, but she heard me anyway. I spent a few minutes by her bedside, before retiring, and then stayed with her until the following afternoon. The retirement village was well serviced with doctors, nurses and carers, so long as you had the right insurance policy package, which she did. Mostly, we talked about the past and especially my teenage years when the two of us lived together in Godalming, and about Alan. I also went on at some length about Guido, his various theatrical exploits, his all-average school reports, and about our working together on *Ginquin's* renovation.

From Parsonville, I used a combination of taxibuses and trains to arrive at Chapel Chorlton in the Midlands, where Pete Sampson lived in a pretty lane-side cottage nearby an oak wood. Pete's ex-wife had held on to their previous house in Stoke-on-Trent where I'd stayed several times over the years, while Pete himself had set up a new home with Clarity and their daughter Joan. Pete had done well. As professor of modern history at Keele University he had managed to expand and improve his department bringing it onto a par with the best in the country, except for Oxford and Cambridge, 'the impregnable bastions of excellence, a work of history themselves' – Pete's own assessment. His department attracted substantial sponsorship from commercial sources, and occasionally advised Britain's foreign ministry.

Clarity, who was 15 years younger than Pete, had unknowingly followed in his footsteps, studying with Wilma Johnson at the London School of Economics. She had then gone to Keele to do a doctorate under Pete on the history of Kurdistan. Her father, a Kurdish intellectual, came to Britain during the early years of the century, married a Welsh lass in Chester, and brought up his only daughter with a good command of the Kurdish language. Pete and she had had a very brief affair while she was his student. They had come together seriously only after Clarity's father had died, when she had finally shed her fixation on all matters Kurdish, and gone to work as a lecturer in Pete's department.

In my honour, Clarity convened a dinner party on Sunday night, which is how I first came to meet Lizette, one of Clarity's friends.

During my short stay in England, I saw the Turnbulls, and caught up on their news. Years earlier Doug had taken over as head of the section, from my old boss Jude Singleton in fact, and then moved sideways to another department. Miriam took much pleasure in telling me about the progress of her daughters. Lucy had become an accomplished violin player and been taken on by the London Symphony Orchestra. Susannah had gone into publishing and married her boss in a whirlwind romance. A grandchild was already on the way. They also told me, with some concern, that my son Bronze had been in touch recently. They hadn't seen him since he was a young teenager, but he had called them wanting phone numbers for Lucy and Susannah. Both daughters had then reported back to Miriam that Bronze had attempted to recruit them to the New Crusaders.

CHAPTER 32

IN WHICH BRONZE TELLS ME OF THE NEW CRUSADERS

Bronze. I also met up with my son that visit. He had been too busy to see me until the Tuesday evening, so we met then, at a Scandinavian beanplace he suggested. He arrived half an hour late, and did not apologise. I barely recognised him. He had cut his dark hair short and sported a tidy beard. He wore a cream jacket, school blazer-like with an insignia on the top pocket, a dark polo neck sweater, and well-pressed white flannel trousers. Overall, the impression was of a holiday camp entertainer.

The New Crusader look, I learned on making enquiries, had been chosen deliberately to appear amusing and thus un-threatening, which was useful, in different ways, both at recruitment and official levels. It did not last. A point came, later that year, when the New Crusaders claimed to have established 500 churches in Great Britain and to have signed up over a quarter of a million members. When the media stopped describing the uniform as 'comical' preferring to use adjectives such as 'sinister' and 'ominous', it was discarded rapidly.

Until that evening, I had heard almost nothing about the New Crusaders. Bronze had joined the church more than three years previously, but, on the very few occasions we had met or spoken since then, he had never wanted to talk about it or much else. This time, though, he did.

After working on a volunteer basis, recruiting and training recruiters for the New Crusaders, and being paid scarcely more than pocket money, he had recently been taken on as a full-time employee. He worked under the admin department with a small team of computer experts setting up, or helping purchase, whatever systems the organisation needed. Mostly, he said, he was moving around the country providing net-working advice and expertise for newly-acquired church buildings. Each one had to be technically adapted so that the screens, member consoles and payment pouches for smart cards were all directly connected to the central networks.

Enthusiastically, Bronze explained how cleverly the whole system functioned to ensure members paid well for the privileges of membership – church attendance, nurture groups, Crusader counselling, beneficent personalised messages and so on.

What troubled me most was not Bronze's allegiance to a church. He was far from alone in needing a religious framework to give his life meaning, and god was a preferable route to salvation than the one Crystal had chosen. No, it was his allegiance to this particular church, as he was describing it, that made me uneasy. The New Crusaders claimed to be a Protestant church, loosely affiliated to the Church of England neither particularly high nor low. Its beliefs were rooted in traditional interpretations meshed with ways of dealing with modern insecurities and political realities. I paraphrase Bronze's way of putting it. In particular, the New Crusaders believed it was necessary to stand up for Christian beliefs in a very uncertain (and un-Christian) world.

The New Crusader organisation criticised other Christian churches for not taking a strong enough stand behind the one true god, and for their appeasement talks with infidel religious leaders. It called for the World Council of Christian Churches to launch New Missionary Endeavours; and, according to Bronze, it had announced a plan to send a preliminary wave of its own missionaries to countries considered on the verge of falling to the false prophet Mohammed. Bronze took my silence for approval and, having finished his salt-free lentil bake – or similar, Bronze's dietary demands changed with the weather – became exuberant and indiscreet.

'This war is brilliant.' Yes, my son actually said this. 'This war is brilliant Dad, it's opening people's eyes to what is really happening in the world.'

'And what is really happening?'

'The devil has stepped out from the shadows.'

'The devil?'

'Yes, and his henchman Al Zahir, and his troops.'

'His troops?'

'Muslims.'

'You believe Muslims are the devil's troops?'

'Don't you? What is the Jihad but a war to kill off the true God. At last now, good people, Christians everywhere can see the truth, there's no hiding the devil's intentions. The New Crusaders believe in action, not inaction.' He paused for a moment, looked round to check that we were not being observed, and then whispered a few words which I recognised as Arabic. 'It means, I am a New Crusader.'

'Why Arabic?'

'I shouldn't tell you, but my nurture mother has promised I will ...'

'Nurture mother?'

'Oh she's wonderful, an adviser, a counsellor, not every-one chooses to be part of a nurture group – but it's worth every cent. Any how, she says that if I learn to speak Arabic well enough, I could be chosen for mission work.'

'And that's what you want?'

'If it's my calling. Right now I'm needed here. There is so much to do. You'll be hearing a lot more about the New Crusaders in the near future.'

White citizens across Europe, especially in those countries with sizeable Muslim populations, flocked to the New Crusaders and its sister organisations. By and large the bulk of its members came from other Protestant denominations, but the church also drew in new adherents to the Christian faith, and it converted lazy non-denominational Christians into fervent believers. Mostly its members were attracted by the church's willingness to take a firm and definitely right-wing political stance. The bigger it got, the more legitimate it seemed, the more members it attracted, the more money it had, the more power it wielded.

By the mid-50s, with the Jihad war having spread to a dozen different arenas around the world, the New Crusader Church was claiming over ten million members in Northern Europe. It had a turnover, in Great Britain alone, of 200 million euros, all declared and above board. Its public relations department was as professional as that of any multinational business, and its spokespersons and leaders could regularly be seen and heard on the media. It was a very slick operation which exploited a real hunger for spiritual food with political substance; and it had a significant influence nationally and internationally.

Nationally, the New Crusaders campaigned for a tightly-monitored register of all aliens and first generation immigrants from Muslim countries, never mind the financial and social cost. Indeed, the New Crusaders helped stoke anti-Muslim sentiment whenever they could thereby contributing to a steady rise in violent religious clashes.

Internationally, the New Crusaders lobbied for a complete block on Western aid to Muslim nations, severe sanctions against all active IIBP members, a massive build up of NATO military forces in the war zones, using conscription if necessary, and a willingness to employ nuclear bombs to end the war quickly. Although these objectives were never met, they did sway public opinion and politicians, more in some countries than others, and thus affect, slightly but noticeably according to historians, NATO's policies.

CHAPTER 33

IN WHICH FRIENDS RALLY ROUND TO SAVE MY JOB

In the IFSD, as in most other UN agencies, the war took its toll on our ability to function. As each new front of the war evolved, so our operations in that area had to close down and retreat. Furthermore, while religion-based animosities were uncommon within the organisation itself, they often erupted in the various committees of experts, civil servants and lower level politicians, through which our policies, operations and projects were developed and approved. This hindered our effectiveness even in the areas without conflict. Over time, the IIBP nations became deliberately obstructive. In order to balance the stoppage in funds to Muslim areas, their represen- tatives constantly sought ways of stalling projects in Christian areas, South America being a favourite target.

By 2055-2056, the other IFSD directors – how can I put this? – had lost the will to fight the IFSD's cause. They went through the motions, but there was little incentive to strive against the current: the highest level UN authorities, other international groupings, and governments were all preoccu- pied with military matters, diplomacy or terrorism and civil disorder.

For some reason – perhaps my break-up with Diana, a matter I shall come to shortly – this was not the case for me. I worked longer hours than I had ever done before, and I expected my staff to do the same and ensure the ethic passed right down the line to our secretaries and office boys. Many a project could be saved by the right combination of persistence and pressure on the budget release mechanisms, for example, or the contractor insurance policies. Moreover, there was plenty of mileage in the basic quid pro quo system, it just took time and effort and cross-departmental communication (which I was very keen on).

Because there was a war under way, this did not mean, to my mind, that water desalination plants, irrigation projects, flood-prevention drainage, solar roofing, sustainable agricul- tural training programmes and so on, were no longer needed.

If anything, the reverse was true, the world needed a commitment to sustainable development more than ever. In my division, we would not let a project go until the door was slammed shut and bolted. I record this, not to brag, but to provide an explanation as to why I might have made enemies.

I should explain that all personnel at my level within the UN system were officially, in theory, appointed on merit. In practice, though, due regard was given to nationality. My own appointment at director level (as Pravit Krishnamurty's replacement in 2044) had depended not only on the director-general wanting me (thanks to Pravit's recommendation), but on there being a suitable opening for a British subject, and on a nod of approval from the British government. Someone within Britain's centre-left British administration at the time, led by Fuller, had given me this nod on the basis of affidavits from, among others, Jude Singleton and Matt Fortune MP. It was good to know one's friends. Had Pravit stepped down a year later, it is far from clear whether the subsequent right-wing Spoon-led government would have backed my promotion. Although director of the Environment Division was a bigger job in every respect than director of the Future Policy Division, officially it held the same UN rank, and thus switching from one to the other had not required so much political fuel. In any event, Spoon and the Conservatives had returned to the opposition benches by then.

Given that my appointment could be considered, loosely, a political one, it meant my removal could be effected through political manoeuvring. In 2056, the British electorate threw out the coalition of Liberal Democrats and European Socialists that had opportunistically held on to power for eight years, and the country ended up with a coalition which included the Conservative Alliance, led by the suave Paulina Worcester, the European Conservatives and the Christian Faith Party. The latter vehemently denied any connection with the New Crusaders or what it termed 'policies of the far right', one of which, incidentally, was to close down all IFSD operations in Islam-dominated countries. Nevertheless, it did manage to position itself closer to the New Crusader ideas than any other political grouping, and therefore catch most of the New Crusader votes.

In early 2057, not long after I had returned from a gruelling trip to Bangkok, Phnom Penh and Vientienne, I was suddenly faced with a plot – no other word suffices – to remove me. The first I heard of it was from Tommy, who had a good bush telegraph line to the British civil service. One of his friends had a colleague who worked as an adviser for the minister of finance. The new British government, the rumour went, was keen to see the IFSD undermined, and easing me out would help this cause. I might have been flattered at the idea of being considered so important, if I wasn't so fearful of the consequences for me and for the IFSD.

Very charitably, Tommy reaffirmed his loyalty to me, and, in effect, appointed himself my campaign manager. Both Ninel Horeva and Chidi Naiambana rallied round, and proved themselves loyal colleagues too. Within days Tommy had set up, through his operational level contacts, an information network across the world. We know, he advised me, that most of our clients appreciate your loyalty to the IFSD and your determination to keep things moving, so we need to ensure they make noises here and there in your favour. And we also know, he added, how determined Worcester and her chums are to remove you. Tommy said he would do what he could at his level, but suggested I call in favours among relevant European and American politicians. Even one or two might make the difference, he said. And, he advised me to work my British connections to the full. So, under cover of IFSD business, I went to London to meet with several friends and colleagues I hadn't seen for years. Some promised to put in a good word where possible, others saw no immediate future for the IFSD.

My most important contacts, though, were Matt Fortune and Horace Merriweather. Matt, a podgy genial family man with bushy sideburns but no hair on top, offered me his support eagerly. He suggested taking soundings with a view to forming a group of IFSD-friendly MPs.

Horace, too, positively enthused about taking up my case, which heartened me. As a Conservative, he could be more influential with this government than Matt. Moreover, Horace had made a name for himself, not so much because he had been a minister, but because of his speaking ability. His voice was much sought after by campaigners of whatever ilk; and, caring less and less about the party whips, he had supported some unlikely causes. As we spoke, he was already looking through his diary to see what parliamentary debates were forthcoming and how he might use one or other to weave in a mention of the IFSD, and to promote the idea that the work of the British environment director reflected well on the British government.

Before leaving the Commons zini bar, I called Matt in his office and asked him to come over and meet Horace since they only knew each other by sight. I wasn't sure they would get on, but my worries were in vain. Between them, in the next few days, they did a remarkable job in establishing a linkage between the plot to dislodge me and wider issues to do with the war. As a consequence, those who might not have raised a finger in my defence under normal circumstances were willing to do so as a means of opposing the excesses of the Worcester government and the right-wing Christian fanatics.

On my return, and therefore long before I could know how well Horace and Matt might do, I dined at Lake Toba a couple of times, once with Ike Davidson and once with Bobby Jespersen. Tommy and I had employed the services of the division's press team, but it was only geared up to deliver factual operational news. The most we could do with the IFSD's own facilities was beef up my profile, with quotes and photos, in the press and media packs that went out on a regular basis. But with Ike and Bobby, the situation was very different. They were able, if willing, to deliver articles that could be very influential.

Lunch with Ike was a trial. To be honest, I had never taken to the man. In the early days of my relationship with Diana, when we went on holiday together, I had found him boorish. In particular, his humour, which had endeared him to Diana, and to his wife obviously, struck me as crass and very North American. But, I suppose, because Diana's friendship with Augusta had seemed more important than my coolness towards her husband, I never allowed my feelings to show transparently.

After the disastrous holiday in East Timor, Ike and Augusta came to stay with us once in Leiden, but I excused myself from most of Diana's social arrangements on the grounds of some work crisis. I'm sure there were arguments about that, as there were about the summer trip to Canada in 2043, the one I never took with Diana and Guido. In fact, Diana returned from that holiday, her first visit to the Davidson home, less convinced of Ike's charms and with stories of his over-drinking and rude-ness, both of which had grown in parallel to his reputation as a news journalist.

A few years later, so Diana told me, Augusta kicked him out. In the early 50s, he was posted to a top job in Brussels. From there, he had called Diana and me trying to inveigle himself into our social world. But, having learned more about him from Augusta post-separation, Diana had declined to return his calls. Nevertheless, there remained a personal connection between us, which both he and I had employed to our professional advantage several times since his Brussels placement. I had personally briefed him on issues by cam-phone, and, once, we had met up for a drink when I was in Brussels.

With Ike I had to spell everything out, not because he didn't understand, but because he knew I was asking a favour and he wanted me to squirm, or that's how it felt. I had told him on the phone when arranging the meeting that any conversation would have to be 'off the record', but I did not press for him to acknowledge an understanding of this condition. Moreover, during the lunch itself, the one thing I failed to spell out was the importance of not implying that I had, in any way, been a source for the story. I saw no reason to do so, given the obvious sensitivity of my position and the fact that I had mentioned the condition on the phone. Also, it is probably true, I felt some awkwardness because of our friendship and did not want offend him.

Three days later, Ike's syndicated story appeared in several US news media. It quoted me extensively – even though Ike had not, to my knowledge, used a recorder or made many notes – with the headline 'Influential British IFSD director sacked?'. In Britain, *The Sunday Telegraph* took Ike's story, firmed it up with a few extra calls to prejudiced contacts in the coalition government, and bulked it out with old photos and, yes, spurious facts from one particular *Daily Truth* article published many, many years earlier. Ike's stories horrified me. For several days, I believed what he had written. I thought my career was over. The only good thing to have come out of that lunch was that I never had to meet with, or speak to, the man ever again.

By contrast, lunch with Bobby was easy and entertaining. I looked forward to her stories and rarely disagreed with what she wrote. On this occasion – the day after lunch with Ike – she saw the picture I painted very clearly, and understood instantly she would not be able attribute any information to me or the IFSD. Nevertheless, she was prepared to publish something helpful to me personally, on the basis of our long-standing 'fruitful relationship'. I suggested she call Horace if she wanted more on the politics, and Tommy if she needed testimonials from further afield.

A few days after the *Telegraph* article, the London *Times* published an excellent analysis piece by Bobby. It drew attention to several dubious practices by the Worcester government aimed at undermining certain UN activities by stealth – its attempts to remove me being just one of these. She also insinuated the British government was prepared to halt all payments to the IFSD if it could find a good enough reason. Bobby's article went a long way to repairing the damage Ike had caused – or I had caused indirectly by dealing with him so inexpertly – and proved very helpful to the endeavours of Horace and Matt.

Indeed, about three weeks after first hearing about the plot against me, Horace phoned to say he had been given assurances that my position was no longer under scrutiny by certain individuals in the government. In any case, he said, they said they had only be 'vaguely looking' at 'the IFSD situation'. I called Tommy to my office immediately to tell him, and to thank him profusely for all his energetic work on my behalf. He was delighted at the news and at my gratitude.

CHAPTER 34

IN WHICH DIANA LEAVES AND MY MOTHER DIES

By the time of these events in 2057, I had already been separated from Diana for nearly two years. Surprisingly, after her three week stay with Karl in Berlin during March 2053, our life together improved. Our sex life took a brief turn for the better as Diana tried to compensate for her guilt by making more of an effort again in the bedroom; and, in the summers of 2053 and 2054, we enjoyed two-week holidays at a rented villa near Grasse in the south of France with Dominique, Waltar and their youngest son Lukas. Although several years older than Guido, Lukas happily partnered him on day trips down to the coast to flirt with girls on the beaches.

During the autumn of 2054, Diana and I slipped further back into our chronic daily pattern of working long hours and rarely having much time for each other. As the war widened out from Kashmir and I became increasingly consumed by it, Diana was no more able to discuss international developments or politics or my work than she had ever been. And her betrayal with Karl lay in the background, always tempting me to make more of any disagreement or tension than I had done in the past.

In the summer of 2055, Guido went to Paris to spend six weeks with the Rocard family: two weeks with Didier working unpaid on a community show; three weeks working for good pay with the Le Monde Fantastique de Marionnettes production team; and one week on holiday with Mireille. The Saturday after Guido left for Paris, Diana called me into the lounge for a talk about 'something serious'. She began by apologising, and by telling me how determinedly she had tried to be a loyal and loving partner. But, she said, it was no longer working, and she had decided, therefore, to go back to Karl. She had been thinking about it for some months, and her decision had not been taken lightly.

When I protested, as one does, about the effect such a separation might have on Guido, she calmly asserted that he was old enough now for it not to matter too much. She had figured it all out. She would go to Berlin for the rest of the summer, then she and Karl would rent a flat in Amsterdam. Guido and I would continue to live in Oldwijkgaarten until Guido finished school the following year; then we would sell the house and share the proceeds. She wanted no income for herself, but suggested, since I earned much more than she, that I subsidise Guido until he was in full-time employment.

I was shattered on the inside, yet there was nothing for me to say. I made no scene. I certainly did not plead for her to change her mind. I recognised the situation as a done deal, and that I had been excluded from any negotiations.

Rather cowardly I thought, Diana wrote to Guido in Paris to reveal her plans to him. Immediately, he called to see how I was. He offered to come straight home, which would have been a great sacrifice, but I told him I was fine. He then called Diana who tried to clarify herself on the camphone, but she broke down in tears. Guido told me this; and, on my request, he gave me a copy of her letter. As far as I was aware, Guido had not known of Diana's lengthy liaison with Karl, and therefore the news had come as a shock. On the other hand, I think that for years he had sensed an imbalance in the relationship between his parents, and had known that I was more in love with Diana than she was with me. I believe this had led him naturally to respect her for persevering with me, but also to love me marginally more than he might have done otherwise.

I was deeply hurt in different ways by Diana's departure. There was the loss of companionship. Although we argued at times and we talked about important things less than I would have wished, Diana was great company, she was involving, and full of fun and imagination. Life without her was dull. And I missed her touch, in the sense that when we weren't being tetchy, she was physical with me, as she was with most friends. There was also the psychological damage that comes with rejection, I suppose, which I cannot define in any detail. I understood that I ought to feel resentment and/or some anger, but when such feelings did arise, they were soon ousted by anxieties about what problems might be waiting for me at the office.

Our lives evolved much as Diana had commanded, but with one exception. Diana had planned, without telling me straightaway, that she would carry on using her workroom in the Oldwijkgaarten house during the day, travelling there from Amsterdam several times a week. In theory, I had no objection to this plan. Guido and I did not need the space; it would save Diana renting a workshop; and it would mean she would be around some days when Guido returned home from school. In practice, though, I soon found it impossible to cope. Returning home from the office, sometimes early to prepare food and eat with Guido and sometimes not, there were often unexpected reminders of Diana: her odour mixed with a vanilla-ish perfume lingering in the hallway, a fresh batch of foods in the kitchen, or design pads left in the lounge.

Other times, I was disturbed because I noticed that she had taken a bundle of books from the shelves or a decorative item – replacing others to even out the space on the window-sill for example – or a practical implement from a cupboard she thought I would not need. Initially, I let these hints of Diana, these trails of her movements, pass over me as mean-ingless, but I over-estimated my ability to deal with them. I became increasingly depressed, without knowing why.

On the recommendation of Peter and Livia, who had both been very kind and supportive since Diana's departure, I put myself in the hands of a 'musical psychotherapist' – Eva Stibbe. I persevered for 20 weekly sessions, and, in that short time, was helped more than I expected. Firstly, Eva showed me how Diana's regular visits to the house might be contribut-ing to the depression. Subsequently, she gave me the where-withal to confront Diana, and, eventually, to insist she move out completely. Secondly, she introduced me to the therapeu-tic and meditative powers of classical music.

Astonishingly I had reached the age of 55 and been to no more than a dozen concerts, and those I had attended were usually part of some diplomatic function or other. I had no idea which orchestras I'd seen or what programmes they'd played. Moreover, and more to the point, I had never sat down on my own and done nothing else but listen to a symphony or concerto. Diana's tastes veered from smoochy schmaltz to smoky jazz, but mostly she listened to music because it was linked to her projects. As Guido grew up, his musical tastes matured from teeny pop to teen pop to pop, all of which, in my opinion, needed the volume turning down (and, preferably, off). I did occasionally put music on to play, but it was invariably on my return from some corner of the world where I had been given a sample of the local musical heritage. Few of these odd sounds appealed to any of us, so they were usually passed on to Guido's school or a charity shop.

In the musical therapy sessions, Eva obliged me to remain inert and to listen quietly to different pieces of music. First, she trained me rigorously to divert my thoughts away from anything to do with work, which was hard, but achievable. Then, she would let complete tracks finish, and we would discuss what I had been thinking about as they played. As the therapy progressed, she would switch the music off suddenly and insist on knowing in great detail about whatever had been going on in my head at that moment. If there was nothing, she would peer at me steadily and smile as if trying to work out whether I was lying or not, say 'good' or 'excellent', and start up the music again.

Matters linked to my own depression and Diana came up regularly for seven or eight sessions, but once I had asked Diana to move out completely from the Oldwijkgaarten house, my mind freewheeled more expansively over the past. When the music stopped, I told Eva about Bronze and Crystal, or my photographs, or about Melissa and my sexual initiation, or about my father. As the 20 sessions neared their end, I grew tired of the game, and could see it only as a self-indulgence, one I did not need to pay good money for. Instead, I spent time buying, downloading and storing on Neil high quality recordings of, among others, Bach, Mozart, Williams and Zanichelli. I also bought a Supremely Comfy set of blindfold and headphones, and became hooked, as they say, on my own personal music self-help sessions.

That winter, after Diana's move to Amsterdam and while I was still living in the Oldwijkgaarten house, my mother's health went downhill fast. She was well cared for in Parsonville, but, with no other relations nearby, I felt obliged to journey over to see her once a fortnight. I called each night on the camphone, no matter where I was, to check on her after the visiting carer had gone. Early in the year, she was hospitalised for a few weeks with a severe bladder infection. One doctor thought she might die, so I messaged Bronze, who went to visit once, and, on one of my trips, I brought Guido with me.

I contacted Alan too, who came as soon as he could from St Petersburg, without Anna who was unable to get away. By the time he arrived, Julie had recovered and been sent home in the care of a part-time nurse. Alan himself looked far from strong. He had shrunk in size, and flesh had fallen off his face leaving a bony lean visage behind the white beard. It was good to see him, albeit briefly. For some reason, I did not mention to him or my mother that I was no longer with Diana. I preferred not to give them any cause for concern on my behalf. It was a relief, therefore, when Alan declined my half-hearted invitation to return with me to Leiden for a few days. Alan stayed a week by Julie's side. He knew he was saying goodbye, for he told me as much in an email later.

My mother died during the night between Saturday and Sunday 14 May. I had left the camphone connected, as I did when I was most anxious about her. Early in the morning I watched the nurse arrive. She said 'hello' to me via the cam, before moving to the bedside to check on my mother. I saw her feel for a pulse, examine her eyes, and then tense up as she steeled herself ready to turn and face the cam again to tell me my mother was dead.

I waited to speak to the doctor, who came within half an hour, and then set off once again for England, this time by car knowing I would want to bring back some keepsakes. It did not take long to clear out the bungalow, distribute her things, bury her body, tidy up the life that was my mother. Everything works very smoothly and efficiently in Parsonville when someone dies.

I used to try and visit her memorial in the Parsonville remembrance garden once a year. Now I rely on a few photos. Here's one of my favourites again, from Monte Carlo in May 2003. Tom is sitting on the bonnet of a red racing car, I am on his lap wearing a baseball cap that says Ferrari. Julie is standing next to us laughing. She is wearing a light yellow frock, and a straw hat. She looks so pretty.

My mother died, and the world seemed to be dying with her too.

CHAPTER 35
IN WHICH PEACE IS DECLARED

The following summer we sold the Oldwijkgaarten house. Guido, who had lived his whole life there and had many friends in the neighbourhood, was saddest about this. As Diana had predicted, he elected to go to Amsterdam University, and decided to focus on drama. For a while, therefore, he moved into the large house Diana and Karl had taken together. I saw him once a fortnight on average. He either came to stay in the modern (and expensive) eco-roof apartment I had bought on Van Hogenhouckstraat in The Hague, not five minutes from the apartment I had once rented on Weissenbruchstraat, or else we would meet in Amsterdam for a meal and a film. When the weather was fine, we would take *Ginquin* out for a gentle cruise to one of the lakes or to a barge festival, or to visit other barge hobbyists we had met over the years.

My new life as a bachelor was lonely and depressing. I stayed long hours in the office, usually for no additional benefit. When at home, I watched news programmes, always dominated by war stories, thought about the next day's tasks, or listened to music. My stomach filled out a centimetre or two, my hair receded and turned a fetching shade of ash grey. If obliged to walk up several flights of stairs, I panted. Yet, despite these signs of aging, my colleague (and subordinate) Ninel Horeva made a second pass at me, some 20 years after the first. This time I had no cause to reject her. Although she too had taken on more flesh and needed dye to keep the grey out of her hair she was still an attractive woman.

Ninel had always been good company (for a Russian!). I admired the way she never took life too seriously, as though the world really was about to end, but was able to work with commitment and verve. As one of my deputies, she was responsible for overseeing policy and programmes in the whole Russia/Central Asia region, an area much caught up in the Jihad war. On leaving a reception, organised for some dignitary or other, we bumped into one another at the cloakroom collecting our coats. She proposed that since it was early, and we were both alone, we go to a nearby bar. There we drank more, and laughed a lot about how sad our respective private lives were.

It was Ninel who recalled, without any shame, her original proposition, and then asked if the timing was any better these days. I did not catch her meaning, and so she put her proposition more forthrightly, which left me flustered and speechless. But she made light of the whole situation and, faced with my hesitations, promised everything would be fine. In my defence, I was fairly glossy, and could think of no good reason to rebuff the advances.

We took a taxi to her apartment in Delft where she gave me a further drink and led me to a bedroom with a four-poster bed and scarlet drapes. I stood there gormless, stunned like a fox caught in the headlights of a lorry. Suddenly I was so sober, so horribly aware of my sexual inadequacy and psychological insecurity that I could no more have coped with any stranger's bed, let alone one adorned with satin sheets and scarlet drapes, never mind that it belonged to one of my key members of staff.

Ninel disappeared into the bathroom to shower, and returned wearing only a towel. I was sat, upright, on the bed as if in a trance. Ninel laughed, although not unkindly, pushed me over on top of the bed and proceeded to remove my clothes. And when, not many minutes of talk later, she discovered why I had become so serious, embarrassed and stiff – although not in the right place – she cackled theatrically, which made me laugh, and consequently eased the torture.

As promised, Ninel made everything fine. From a drawer in a bedside cabinet, she took out a vibrator – a bigger thing by far than, in the best circumstances, I could have created – and instructed me on how to employ it. The distraction of following strict instructions and doing so with some success helped me relax and lose myself in Ninel's sexuality.

For a few days, I worried how this night of mechanical passion would impact on our working relationship. But it didn't, not at all. So, when I received a private email from her with the one word 'Tonight?', I answered 'Yes'. Thenceforward, in this manner, we would arrange to meet, have dinner and sex about once a week. After two months, though, the emails stopped. She never told me why, and I never asked, and our working relationship carried on unperturbed, as evinced, a few months later, by her staunch support during the attempt to depose me from my job. Thereafter, occasionally, when I saw Ninel talking to colleagues I wondered if they too had experienced the four-poster bed.

By the late 50s, much of the UN system, including the IFSD, was close to collapse. As the tensions of the wars infiltrated our negotiating committees, so initiatives, projects and programmes of all kinds and at all levels were stalled or cancelled. Most large donors, such as Japan, the US and the European Union, had progressively frozen all their overseas development aid to Muslim countries and many more besides, citing the costs of war and severe economic depression. Contractors and all non-staff personnel were disengaged as soon as their projects ran out of funds or came to a standstill for some other reason. But, beyond that, a lack of administration funds began to choke the life out of us. Every few weeks I had to take decisions on which staff to make redundant. And those of us that remained were no longer working for the good of mankind, but simply to keep the IFSD functioning. My division had remained the most effective for the longest but, by 2058, there was little I, or my skeleton department, could achieve.

Retirement was not an option. I had no more wish to stop working than I had to expire. I did consider stepping down, and trying to find another role for myself, but concluded, gloomily, that I had invested too solidly and exclusively in my work for the IFSD, especially having called in so many favours to hold on to the job a year or so previously. Ironically, it might have been better for me personally to have allowed the British government to bully me out of the IFSD in exchange for something else, something different.

Moreover, I felt had been foolish to sacrifice so much of my life to the organisation and to my high position within it, meaning that, following my separation from Diana, I had very few friends and an impoverished social network. Most depressing of all, I recognised that there was no one, not even Peter de Roo, with whom I could discuss my own personal problems and situation. Thus, in my own way, I was as closed off from society as my old friend Oakley.

Regrettably, I was not able to diminish my own despondency by comparing it to the suffering of millions in war zones and immigration camps beset with disease and poverty, nor by reminding myself that further millions were losing their lives, their homes, their loved ones because of climate change catastrophes, while I continued to sleep in a dry comfortable bed, and eat good food, and wash myself in clean hot water.

Then, suddenly in March 2059, as is well known, the First Jihad War came to an abrupt end, in the sense that the IIBP and NATO stopped fighting each other, although of course the so-called 'left-over wars' carried on regardless. We had all grown so accustomed to the media telling us about 'fresh peace talks' or another G13-I9 summit or an 'intervention' by this or that peace-broker, that we had long since stopped investing any hope in them. But, in 2058, there had been a very significant escalation of the war when the IIBP's forces turned their full attention to Israel, as though they had been biding their time, and this had been their target all along. The NATO countries rallied to Israel's defence, although not very effectively. For most of the decade, they had already been sustaining financially and politically expensive campaigns in Kashmir, Central Asia and West Africa among other war zones, and their citizens were losing patience. The US, still led by President Tarbuck, tried to bully NATO towards the use of class B nuclear strikes as a last resort. Because this was acknowledged to be such a high risk strategy, it became known as Tarbuck's Gamble.

Unfortunately for Tarbuck, the Spanish government collapsed within weeks of suggesting it might support the US policy. Although there was a deep-seated fear in Spain of a new Moorish invasion, it was nowhere near as strong as the people's revulsion for weapons of mass destruction. Thereafter, the governments of most European countries, many with large Muslim populations, constant civil unrest and extraordinarily high levels of opposition to the use of nuclear or biochemical weapons, refused to back the US. Consequently, NATO found itself back-pedalling trying to hide its impotence with long declarations of threat and intent and offers of compromise. Israel, too, lost its nerve when faced with Al Zahir's threat to use every last IIBP atomic bomb in retaliation if Israel employed one single nuclear weapon.

Tarbuck's Gamble failed, and NATO members and affiliates began secret negotiations with the IIBP, China, the Philippines and other involved countries. A Peace Treaty was signed in Singapore on 25 March 2059. China took over the north Indian state of Ladakh; Kashmir was declared an independent Muslim country (but later united with Pakistan after a rigged referendum – causing yet more bloodshed when the nationalists refused to accept the decision); the whole of sub-Saharan Africa shifted noticeably towards Mecca, with several secular governments giving way to Islamic administrations and new constitutions; and the Philippines agreed to an autonomous Islam region.

According to *Encyclopaedia Universal*, the NATO group members, for their side of the deal achieved the following:

- peace, which was politically much more important to them than to the IIBP members;

- a confirmation of the primacy of the UN system, the Peace Treaty was subsequently enacted through UN declarations;

- the continued independence of Israel, although Palestine did make a significant territorial gain; and

- a limited increase of development aid by rich nations to poor nations up to 2% (i.e. not the 2.5% Zakat demanded by the IIBP). Although, the IIBP had demanded a bias towards Muslim countries in the distribution of this aid, it knew this would never win acceptance in the UN and so gave way during the elaboration of the complex donor/recipient formulae that underpinned the funding of the agencies, such as the IFSD.

Furthermore on the NATO side, Russia was appeased by the agreements that Uzbekistan and Kyrgyzstan signed with Kazakhstan.

It took a while for the UN declarations to be concluded, but once they were, I began restoring my division's staff levels, restarting projects and programmes, and negotiating new arrangements. I expected personnel changes at the highest level, but I didn't care to think about my own future. I'd done enough of that in the last year or two. I kept my head down and paid no attention to UN gossip.

In early autumn, Tommy came into my office one day to ask if I'd heard a rumour that I was being considered as a possible replacement for the director-general, who we all knew was on the way out. I told Tommy not to listen to tittle-tattle. Instead, we discussed how quickly he could get a team to Srinigar to help the new government plan its aid programme tenders.

When the phone rang, my secretary, MarySue, told me to hold for the private secretary of the British foreign minister, within the recently-elected centre-left government led by Charlie Venables. Tommy moved to leave me alone, but I gestured for him to stay.

Would I, the lady asked, allow my name to go forward for the director-general post. I muted the phone for an instant and told Tommy 'not tittle-tattle'. He gave me a thumbs up sign.

Months later, after a horse-trading international summit and various high-level meetings within the United Nations system, a basket of new agency chiefs were decided, not least my own appointment as executive head, director-general, of the IFSD.

PART THREE APPENDIX
EXTRACTS FROM CORRESPONDENCE

Diana Oostlander to Kip Fenn

(freely translated from the Dutch original)

December 2049

It is no hard thing to be 50!!!

Can I suggest my English man that you get up on your feet, turn around, and clamber up that tree (you see it has been placed at a slant to make it easy for you). If you climb high enough, perhaps you will be able to see faraway, beyond the hills that block any normal view, towards those views of a wild and empty Copacabana Beach. Views that are, frankly, beyond my bank account and, no doubt, that of the IFSD too.

It's a small flawed thing; a small flawed token of my love.

Happy birthday. xxx

Diana Oostlander to Guido Oostlander-Fenn

(freely translated from the Dutch original)

July 2055

I have bad news. I should have told you in person but it has been a difficult time for me, and I thought it might be easier for both of us if I were to try and write to you first. I am leaving your father, so that I can return to live with Karl. We will rent a flat together in Amsterdam, and, during your last year at school, I hope you will be a constant visitor at the weekends. Perhaps, then, you will want to go to Amsterdam University and you could live with Karl and me. But that is for the future.

This is a hard thing for me to explain, and I want you to be clear that this is nothing to do with your father (or, of course, you), it is to do with me, my needs, my desires, but most of all my weaknesses. I can be a very selfish person, and for this I am very sorry.

It is possible that I have never stopped loving Karl. He was my very first love. He is a theatre director, a gifted one. We worked and lived together for many years. He was/is not an

211

easy man, and he hurt me many times. But, we are both older, and I am certain now that we want the same thing.

This war is a terrible thing, and may get much worse. I do not know how to explain this properly, but I feel as though Karl and I have a common purpose in the way we are, and especially in our work. Now, I am going to Berlin for the rest of the summer, and we will prepare a show for the protest festival in September.

You must have sensed that I have no connection with your father in this way. He is a good man, a great man perhaps in his work, but I cannot share in this greatness, and I know he finds that difficult. He has grown distant recently, and I hope my move away will not distress him too much. But, in any case, I can rely on you to be a friend to him. You and he have established such a good connection in these last few years.

But I will be coming to Oldwijkgaarten often, to work in my studio many days during the week. We shall see each other all the time as before.

Let's talk on the phone when you've received this.

Give my love to Helene, Didier and the girls.

Very much love.

List of characters

This is a full list of characters appearing in one or more of the trilogy volumes (excluding those referred to only once) by surname (where mentioned in the text) or, otherwise, by first name. For national leaders, dates for their period or periods of office have been noted (as listed in *Encyclopaedia Universal*, 2098 edition).

A

Abd al-Jabbaar, David (son of Sami and Iona) – VOL 3
Abd al-Jabbaar, Iona (wife of Sami Abd al-Jabbaar's) – VOL 3
Abd al-Jabbaar, Sami (Kip's neighbour) – VOL 3
Acklow, Rosemary (therapist) – VOL 1
Ajose, Alfred (Kip's friend) – VOL 1, 2, 3
Ajose, Fayola (Alfred's wife) – VOL 2, 3
Ajose, Fela (son of Alfred and Fayola) – VOL 2, 3
Akilina (Anna Mastepanov's cousin) – VOL 3
Almond (half-brother of Yewla) – VOL 3
Al Zahir (Muslim leader) – VOL 2, 3
Amado, Jorge (Brazilian author) – VOL 1, 2, 3
Anders (stillborn child of Diana and Kip) – VOL 2
Andrasta (Mercurio Sanderson's friend) – VOL 3
Angela (daughter of Alicia Gonçalves) – VOL 3
Antonia de Malancas, Pedro (aka Pam, Mexican director) – VOL 1, 2, 3
Arklington, Betty (US president: 2047-51) – VOL 2, 3
Armstrong, Neil (US astronaut) – VOL 1, 2, 3
Asquith, Jill (Alan Hapgood's friend) – VOL 1
Asser, Eduard Isaad (Dutch photographer) – VOL 1, 2

B

Bayard, Hippolyte (French photographer) – VOL 2, 3
Beale, Martin (teacher) – VOL 1
Beato, Felice (British photographer) – VOL 2
Belinda (administrator) – VOL 2, 3
Bergmann, Zoe (German historian and author) – VOL 3
Brin (Jay Sanderson's friend) – VOL 3
Bronwen (Lionel Wilcox's secretary) – VOL 1

Buffer, John (volleyball coach) – VOL 1, 2
Bunting, Tamson (British artist) – VOL 1, 2

C
Carter (Caxton's go-between) – VOL 1
Caxton, William (née Shuttleworth, Ronald, politician/entrepreneur) – VOL 1, 2, 3
Chambi, Martin (Peruvian photographer) – VOL 2, 3
Chaplin, Charlie (US film actor/director) – VOL 1, 2
Chintz (nurse) – VOL 1, 2, 3
Choolee (prostitute) – VOL 1
Chowdhury, Tommy (IFSD official) – VOL 2
Corazon, Neco (Brazilian president: 2030-40) – VOL 1, 2, 3
Costa, Luigi (Italian prime minister:2043-47, 2049-52, 2055-59) – VOL 3
Courret brothers (Peruvian photographers) – VOL 2, 3
Cowerbridge, Arnold (museum director) – VOL 3
Czyzewski, Walenty (Polish prime minister: 2020-28) – VOL 1

D
Davidson, Augusta (Diana Oostlander's friend) – VOL 2
Davidson, Ike (journalist) – VOL 2
Delors, Jacques (European Commission president: 1985-1995) – VOL 1, 3
Delvreux, Kolin (Anglo-Dutch poet) – VOL 3
de Roo, Arnout (son of Rudy) – VOL 1, 3
de Roo, Livia (Peter's wife) – VOL 1, 2, 3
de Roo, Peter (Kip's friend) – VOL 1, 2, 3
de Roo, Rudy (son of Peter and Livia) – VOL 1, 2, 3
de Roo, Ulla (daughter of Livia and Peter) – VOL 2, 3
Derwent, Julia (US author) – VOL 1
Donna (Crystal Fenn's friend) – VOL 2
Duck, Alexander (British civil servant) – VOL 1
Dufkova, Giselle (museum director) – VOL 3
Dumas, Alexander (French author) – VOL 3
Durring, Lindsay (school pupil) – VOL 3

E
Elly (childminder) – VOL 2
Engelhard, Karl (Diana Oostlander's friend) – VOL 2, 3

F
Fenn, Barry (Tom's father) – VOL 2, 3
Fenn, Crystal (daughter of Gillian and Kip) – VOL 1, 2, 3

Fenn, Evvie (Tom's mother) – VOL 1, 2
Fenn, Gillian (née Tilson, Kip's wife) – VOL 1, 2, 3
Fenn, Julie (née Hapgood, Kip's mother) – VOL 1, 2, 3
Fenn, Tom (Kip's father) – VOL 1, 2, 3
Ferrer i Germa, Joaquima (Catalan film maker) – VOL 2
Ferrera Magalhães, Conceição (Kip's friend) – VOL 1, 2, 3
Ferrez, Marc (Brazilian photographer) – VOL 1, 2, 3
Fortune, Matt (British politician) – VOL 2, 3
Fragrance (Tom Fenn's second wife) – VOL 2, 3
Fuller, Garth (British prime minister: 2037-45) – VOL 1, 2

G
Gabriella (bus passenger) – VOL 1, 3
Gagarin, Yuri (Russian astronaut) – VOL 1, 2
Garibaldi, Giuseppi (Italian military leader) – VOL 3
Gemma (Alfred Ajose's girlfriend) – VOL 1, 2
Gonçalves, Alicia (née Magalhães, daughter of Arturo) – VOL 2, 3
Gonçalves, João (Alicia's husband) – VOL 3
Gregory, Crispin (British historian) – VOL 1, 2, 3

H
Hapgood, Alan (Kip's uncle) – VOL 1, 2, 3
Hapgood, Eileen (Julie Fenn's mother) – VOL 1, 3
Hapgood, Oswald (Julie Fenn's father) – VOL 1
Harris, Chuck (US author) – VOL 3
Hilde (Wood Junior's secretary) – VOL 1
Hitler (German dictator: 1933-45) – VOL 1, 3
Hoop, Vi (Canadian singer) – VOL 1, 2
Horeva, Ninel (IFSD official) – VOL 2, 3

I
Imogen (Rob's friend) – VOL 2
Inti (son of Guido Oostlander-Fenn and Mireille) – VOL 3

J
Jackmann-Ives, Rhoda (Lizette Sanderson's friend) – VOL 3
Jensen, Sydney (British materials science professor) – VOL 3
Jespersen, Bobby (journalist) – VOL 2, 3
Jessop, William (doctor) – VOL 1, 2
Johns, Unwin (British poet) – VOL 1, 3

Johnson, Wilma (British history professor) – VOL 1, 2
Jones, Adam (UK prime minister: 2022-32) – VOL 1, 2

K

Kallström, Ingrid (Swedish environmental campaigner) – VOL 1
Karel (son of Tamara) – VOL 3
Kingston (Crystal Fenn's friend) – VOL 3
Kiselev, Boris (IFSD official) – VOL 2
Koper, Melanie (Phil Rumble's wife) – VOL 1
Krishnamurty, Pravit (IFSD official) – VOL 2, 3

L

Lambert, Aaron (British film director) – VOL 2
Le Gray, Gustave (French photographer) – VOL 2, 3
Liphook, Philip (aka Flip, teacher) – VOL 1, 2, 3
Lipman, Rupert (doctor) – VOL 1, 3
Lobo, Se (Brazilian journalist) – VOL 3
Lock, Josephine (née Shuttleworth, daughter of William Caxton) – VOL 2, 3
Lola (net madam) – VOL 1, 2
Lomax, Lorraine (technical director) – VOL 3
Luz (Arturo Magalhães's friend) – VOL 3
Lyndquist, John (UK prime minister: 2032-37) – VOL 1, 2

M

Madan, Triti (Indian international politics professor) – VOL 1, 2, 3
Magalhães, Arturo Fenn (son of Kip and Conceição) – VOL 1, 2, 3
Magalhães, Edna (Arturo's first wife) – VOL 2, 3
Magalhães, Eliane (née Silva, Juliano's wife) – VOL 2
Magalhães, Fatima (Arturo's second wife) – VOL 2, 3
Magalhães, Ignacio (son of Arturo and Fatima) – VOL 2, 3
Magalhães, Juliano (son of Arturo and Fatima) – VOL 2, 3
Magalhães, Tina (daughter of Fatima and Arturo) – VOL 2, 3
Magalhães Silva, Maria (daughter of Eliane and Juliano) – VOL 2, 3
Mallow, Vincent (aka Mush, British actor) – VOL 1, 3
Marcella (Olive Norrington's partner) – VOL 3
Maria (Pope: 2052-74) – VOL 3
MarySue (secretary) – VOL 2, 3
Mastepanov, Anna (Alan Hapgood's partner) – VOL 2, 3
May (Mercurio Sanderson's friend) – VOL 3
McFeather, Andrew (US president: 2017-21) – VOL 1
Meijer, Dominique (née Oostlander, Diana's sister) – VOL 2, 3

Meijer, Jurian (son of Waltar and Dominique) – VOL 2, 3
Meijer, Lukas (son of Waltar and Dominique) – VOL 2, 3
Meijer, Waltar (Dominique's husband) – VOL 2, 3
Melissa (Kip's girlfriend) – VOL 1, 2, 3
Merriweather, Horace (Kip's friend) – VOL 1, 2, 3
Merriweather Tim (Horace's brother) – VOL 1, 2, 3
Mistral, Amy (British film/theatre director) – VOL 2, 3
Monique (Alan Hapgood's girlfriend) – VOL 1, 2, 3
Monroe, Marilyn (US film actress) – VOL 1
Montechristo, Felix Rico (Ecuadorian entrepreneur) – VOL 3
Movie Martyr (US film director) – VOL 1, 2

N
Naiambana, Chidi (IFSD official) – VOL 2, 3
Nash, Liam (Diana Oostlander's cousin) – VOL 2, 3
Nolan brothers (US astronauts) – VOL 1, 2
Norrington, Olive (Lizette Sanderson's colleague) – VOL 3

O
Oakley, Finbar (British playwright) – VOL 1, 2, 3
Ojoru (Nigerian president: 2027-35, 2037-47) – VOL 1, 2, 3
Olivier, Jean-Michele (REACH official) – VOL 3
Oosterhuis, Pieter (Dutch photographer) – VOL 1
Oostlander, Anders (Diana's brother) – VOL 2
Oostlander, Dana (Diana's sister) – VOL 2
Oostlander, Demeter (aka Dimi, Diana's sister) – VOL 2, 3
Oostlander, Diana (Kip's partner) – VOL 1, 2, 3
Oostlander, Neeltje (née van der Klein, Diana's mother) – VOL 2
Oostlander, Powles (Diana's father) – VOL 2
Oostlander-Fenn, Guido Tom (son of Kip and Diana) – VOL 1, 2, 3

P
Pacciotti (Italian film director) – VOL 1, 3
Paride Bernabo, Hector Julio (aka Caybe, Brazilian artist) – VOL 1, 3
Pattison, Flora (Kip's friend) – VOL 1, 2, 3
Pedrosa, Maria (Brazilian actress) – VOL 3
Popsicle (Kip's girlfriend) – VOL 1, 3
Pouille, Henri (photograph curator) – VOL 3

Q
Quant, Lucretia (British author) – VOL 1, 3

Quasim (Angela's partner) – VOL 3

Thomas, Rike (British civil servant) – VOL 2
Tilson, Bronze (son of Kip and Gillian) – VOL 1, 2, 3
Tilson, Constance (Gillian's mother) – VOL 1
Tilson, John (Gillian's grandfather) – VOL 1
Tindle (British politician) – VOL 1, 3
Tuohy, Clint (Lizette Sanderson's husband) – VOL 3
Turnbull, Doug (Kip's friend) – VOL 2, 3
Turnbull, Lucy (daughter of Miriam and Doug) – VOL 2, 3
Turnbull, Miriam (Doug's wife) – VOL 2, 3
Turnbull, Susannah (daughter of Miriam and Doug) – VOL 2, 3

V
van der Klein, Anders (Diana's grandfather) – VOL 2
van der Klein, Betje (Diana's aunt) – VOL 2
van der Klein, Kaatje (Diana's aunt) – VOL 2
Vaughn, Leo (photograph curator) – VOL 3
Vetch, Brian (British political adviser) – VOL 1, 2
Vidrio (Crystal Fenn's boyfriend) – VOL 2, 3
Villalonga, Eduardo (IFSD official) – VOL 3
Voll, Max (Argentinian billionaire) – VOL 3

W
Wells, Vince (Jay Sanderson's partner) – VOL 1, 2, 3
Wilcox, Lionel (aka Firey, British politician) – VOL 1, 2
Williams, Cos (media producer) – VOL 3
Wood Junior, Sterling (oil executive) – VOL 1
Worcester, Paulina (British prime minister: 2056-59) – VOL 2
Worthington, Pearl (teenager) – VOL 1, 2
Worthington, Xanthe (Pearl's mother) – VOL 2

X
Xiangjun, Liu (IFSD official) – VOL 3

Y
Yewla (daughter of May and Mercurio) – VOL 2, 3
Yvonne (Gillian Fenn's friend) – VOL 1

Z
Zanichelli (Italian composer) – VOL 2, 3
Zimmerman, Jeff (Kip's friend) – VOL 1, 2, 3

FAMILY RELATIONSHIPS

BACKGROUND

Evvie+Barry Fenn   Eileen (+Oswald Hapgood)   Percival

Tom Fenn+Julie   Alan (+Anna Mastepanov)

Neil (aka Kip) Fenn

PARTNERS AND CHILDREN

CONCEIÇÃO

Kip Fenn+Conceição Magalhães

Arturo Magalhães (+Edna)   + Fatima

|(cloned)

Alicia (+João Gonçalves)   Tina   Juliano (+Eliane)   Ignacio

Angela+Quasim   Maria

Renato

GILLIAN

John Tilson

Constance Tilson

Kip Fenn+Gillian

Crystal Fenn   *Bronze Tilson*

DIANA

Claudine+Anders van der Klein   Maartje+Eduwart Oostlander

Betje   Kaatje   Neeltje +   Powles   Saartje +Anthony Nash

Kip Fenn+Diana Demeter   Dana   Dominique+Waltar Meijer   Liam

Guido Oostlander-Fenn+Mireille Rocard   Jurian Lukas

Inti

LIZETTE

Wendy+Mervyn Sanderson

Kip Fenn+Lizette (+Clint Tuohy) Samuel (+Lynn) Mercurio+May +Andrasta

Jay Sanderson Saul   Irene   Mahonia   Yewla   Esos

www.ingramcontent.com/pod-product-compliance
Lightning Source LLC
Chambersburg PA
CBHW060211180626
46813CB00007B/2786